'A ROLLERCOASTER OF SUSPENSE AND SURPRISE ...'
Guardian

'FUNNY, THOUGHTFUL ... WISE AND LIVELY...
ANOTHER COUP FROM COWELL'
The Sunday Times

'HIGHLY RECOMMENDED ... A GREAT NEW WORLD'
The New York Times

'THE DETAIL OF COWELL'S WORLD IS A DELIGHT ...
THIS ONE WILL RUN AND RUN'
Observer

'COWELL IS MOVING TOWARDS NATIONAL TREASURE'
Big Issue

'A FUNNY, CLEVER ADVENTURE'
Sunday Express

'THIS IS A TRIUMPHANT RETURN FOR COWELL'
The Telegraph

This book is dedicated to darling MAISIE with so much love

'HOW TO GET INTO THIS BOOK. Knock the Knocker on the Door . . . Then, if you are very quiet, you will hear a teeny tiny voice say . . . "Take down the key." . . . Put the Key in the Keyhole, which it fits exactly, unlock the door and WALK IN.'
English Fairy Tales, Joseph Jacobs, *1890*

HODDER CHILDREN'S BOOKS

First published in Great Britain in 2019 by Hodder and Stoughton

1 3 5 7 9 10 8 6 4 2

A CIP catalogue record for this book is available from the British Library.

HBK ISBN 978 1 444 94144 9
PBK ISBN 978 1 444 94147 0

Printed and bound in Great Britain by Clays Ltd, Elcograf S.p.A.

The paper and board used in this book are made from wood from responsible sources.

Hodder Children's Books
An imprint of
Hachette Children's Group
Part of Hodder and Stoughton
Carmelite House
50 Victoria Embankment
London EC4Y 0DZ

An Hachette UK Company
www.hachette.co.uk

www.hachettechildrens.co.uk

The
Wizards
of
Once
Knock Three Times
written and illustrated by
CRESSIDA COWELL
Hodder Children's Books

The girl, Wish, is a Warrior...
BUT underneath her eyepatch
she has an EXRAORDINARILY
POWERFUL Magic Eye.

The boy, Xar, is a WiZard...
and he means well, but he has
a Witchstain on his hand,
that is trying to control him.

Sea road to Giants' Last Stand
OG
GIANTS' FOOTSTEPS
sea road
Cliffs of Eternity
The Sweet Track
SLODGER TERRITORIES (THE OOZE)
GIGANTICA
WITCH MOUNTAINS
Breedling Fort
Beware of the Breedlings
WIZARD
Pook's Hill
Lake of
THE ISLE OF THE NUCKALAVEE

CONQUERED WARRIOR TERRITORIES

This way to the Warrior Capital

host Mountains

WARRIOR EMPIRE

The Sweet Track

Iron Warrior Fort

The QUEENDOM OF SYCHORAX

THE BADWOODS

Sinister littl Clearing

LD WOODS

Wizard Fort

Ragged River

ENCANZO's KINGDOM

the Lost

Mmm...
How
absolutely
fascintresting
...

Note by Cressida Cowell Lost Language EXPERT

A long time ago, a young girl exploring the back of a cave somewhere in the British Isles discovered these papers, known as the 'Wizard books', hidden behind a large stone. Nobody has ever been able to read them, for they were written so very far away in the distant past that they used a vocabulary and a script that has never been seen before.

I have spent many happy years translating the papers of Hiccup the Viking from Old Norse into English. So I was excited to accept this even greater challenge, for these Wizard books were written in such a dark age that the language they used has been completely lost to us over the years.

After many years of study I have finally cracked the code of this lost language. And in doing so, I have uncovered something TRULY extraordinary.

Believe the unbelievable.

Every fairy story you have ever read has its basis in some truth.

It was not only dragons living in the distant darkness. Dragons were only a very, very small part of it.

THIS was a time of MAGIC

Once
there
were
Wildwoods . . .

Prologue

Once there were wildwoods.

The Wizards had lived in the wildwoods for as long as anyone could remember, and they were intending to live there forever, along with all the other Magic things.

Until the Warriors came. The Warriors invaded from across the seas, and although they had no Magic, they brought a new weapon that they called IRON . . . *and iron was the only thing that Magic would not work on.*

From that moment on, Wizards and Warriors were fighting each other to the death in the wildwoods.

Until one day . . .

A young Warrior queen called SYCHORAX fell in love with a young Wizard king called ENCANZO. Wizards and Warriors should NEVER fall in love. So Sychorax had taken the Spell of Love Denied to make her love die. And the love had died indeed . . . and Sychorax had married a Warrior, like she was supposed to.

And Encanzo had married a Wizard, just as a Wizard should.

So the danger of a curse ought to have been avoided.

But . . .

Thirteen years ago, Sychorax had a daughter whose name was WISH.

And Wish had a terrible secret. The lingering true love kiss of the Wizard Encanzo had made Queen Sychorax's daughter Magic. And for the first time in human history, *Wish had a Magic-that-works-on-iron.*

And thirteen years ago, Encanzo had a son whose name was XAR.

And Xar had a terrible secret. Xar stole some Magic from a Witch, *and the stain of the Witch Magic was beginning to control him.*

This is the story of how Xar and Wish met, and how they made friends even though they had been brought up to hate each other like poison.

Wish and Xar have run away from their parents, searching for the ingredients for a spell to get rid of Witches. They are outcasts, hunted by Wizards and Warriors alike, and by something far, far worse.

WITCHES.

WITCHES MUST NEVER GET HOLD OF MAGIC-THAT-WORKS-ON-IRON . . .

But . . .

Twice, Wish and Xar have escaped the talons of the Witches. TWICE, they have cheated death.

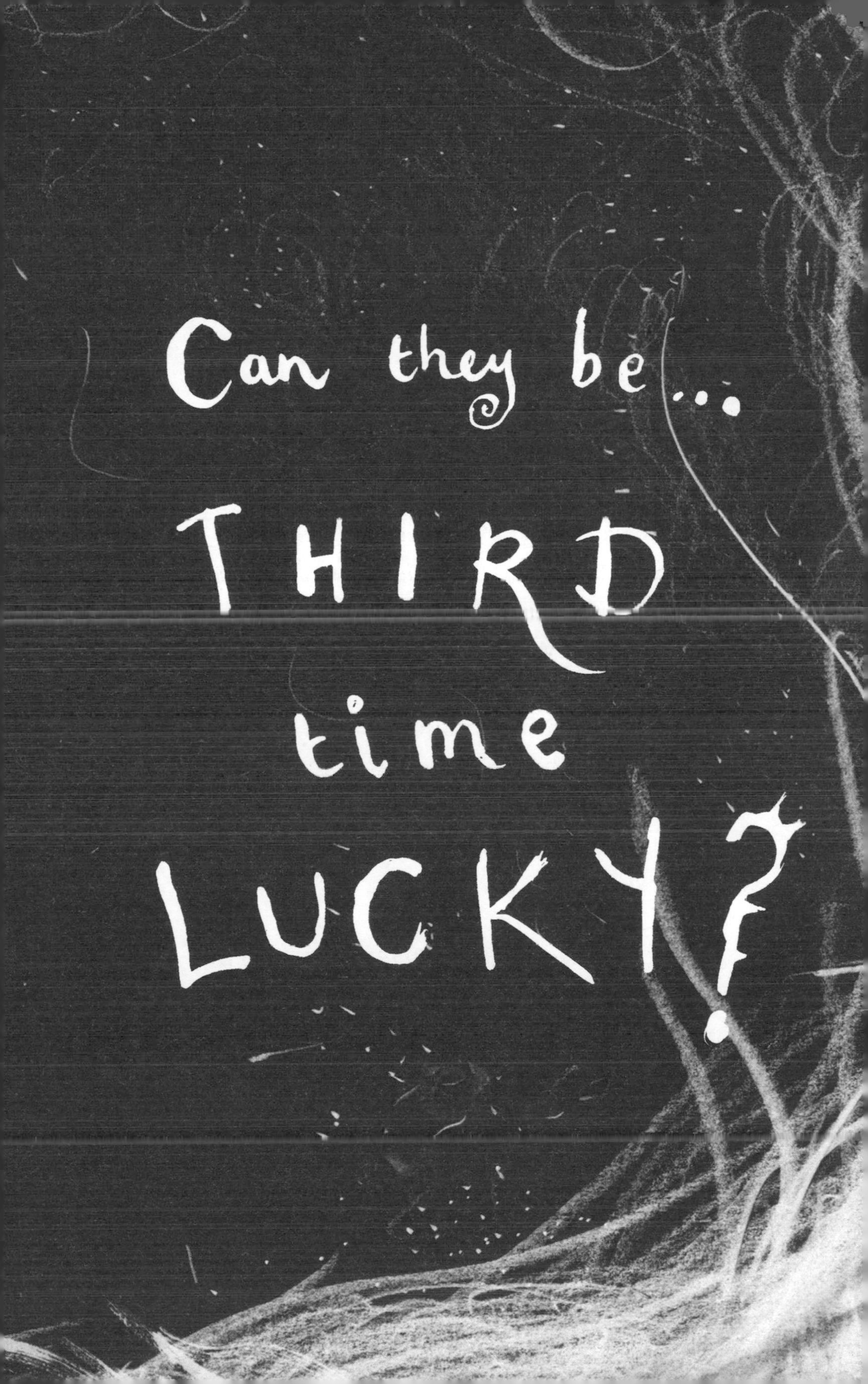
Can they be...
THIRD
time
LUCKY?

I am a character
in this story
Who sees everything,
Knows everything.
I will not tell you
who I am.
HAVE you GUESSED yet?

Part One

Forest on Fire

1. Betrayal

Three thousand years ago, at the end of the era that would later be known as the Bronze Age, the whole of the British Isles were covered in wildwoods.

Good things lived in the wildwoods, animals and Magic creatures and humans who minded their own business, but bad things lived there at that time too, some very bad things.

Two of these bad things were flying above the forest even now. The bad things were presently invisible, but if human eyes could have seen them they would have noticed that they had soft black wings like the wings of crows, and fingers that ended in talons like a bird of prey, and noses a little like a beak. In fact, they were WITCHES, not good Witches, but very *bad* Witches indeed, and they were flying high, just below the clouds, and as they flew they were watching something down below.

Xar, Wish and Bodkin

The *something* was a door, but instead of being where a door really ought to be, vertically opening and shutting between rooms that are safely on the ground in an orderly kind of way, this particular door was flying through the air, flat on its front like a carpet, just above the treetops.

It was the little moving speck of the flying door that had first attracted the Witches' attention as they flew, with lazy wingbeats in the strong currents of air high above the trees, on their way back to their nests in the Lachrymose Mountains. But it wasn't the door *itself* that was now holding their scrutiny.

There were three children lying on their stomachs on top of the flying door.

The invisible Witches looked down at the children.

And the children looked down over the edge of the flying door, looking for something in the forest.

The Witches were hungry, so hungry that long dribbles of black saliva were dripping from their lips. They hadn't seen anything so delicious as these children in weeks, no, perhaps years (and that will give you an idea why people didn't really *like* Witches, either in the Bronze Age, or any other age that the Witches happened to turn up in).

But something was making those Witches pause before swooping on the tasty, unaware little morsels below and fastening their claws into them.

'Thaw si ti gniod tou ereh?' whined Breakneck, waggling her nose from side to side. 'Yhw si ydobon gnitcetorp ti? Od uoy kniht ti dluoc eb a part?'*

Ripgrizzle was pausing too, although the smell of the blood of the human children (which to a Witch is as delicious as that of a cake baking in the oven) was wafting up to him and making him drool like a dog. He was desperate to snatch the treats from under Breakneck's waggling nose and fly back to his nest to feed on the tender darlings all by himself.

But he too was cautious. Before the return of the Witches to the wildwoods, the air would have been full of flying things – birds and sprites and cockatrices, dragons, piskies, all manner of glorious Magical creatures. But now, this early in the morning, which was too close to the night hours of the Witching-time, the forest was as quiet as death, and the Warrior humans kept their

* Witches speak the same language as we do, but each individual word is back to front. This means 'What is it doing out here? Why is nobody protecting it? Do you think it could be a trap?'

babies locked up safe in their castles, and the Wizard humans kept their babies safe in their treehouse forts. So what were *these* human babies doing then, flying, cool as you like, on the back of a Magical flying door, miles and miles away from any human habitation? Perhaps Breakneck was right. Maybe it was a trap.

The children were talking to one another, and one of them was singing rather shakily, with false bravery: '*NO FEAR!* That's the Warriors' marching song! *NO FEAR!* We sing it as we march along!'

Ripgrizzle's gigantic ears curled up at the edges, swivelling and tilting towards the child in order to catch the sound. The eye in the middle of his forehead opened up sleepily. The two Witches flew, unseen, lower, lower, to listen to the children's conversation.

The first young person was a Wizard boy called Xar (his name was pronounced 'Zar' – I don't know why, spelling is *weird*). The Witches did not know it, but Xar was the son of Encanzo, King of Wizards, and Xar had a very dangerous secret, which was that he had stolen some Magic from a Witch and was having trouble controlling it. The Witch-Magic was hidden below a glove in a cut on his right hand, but the Witches could smell it nonetheless, and the smell confused them.

The second was a Warrior princess called Wish, daughter of Sychorax, Queen of the Warriors, and Wish, too, had a very dangerous secret, which was that beneath her eyepatch she had a Magic eye, and Warriors were not supposed to have any Magic at all.

The third was a Warrior boy called Bodkin. Bodkin was Wish's Assistant Bodyguard, and he was finding this position really rather testing because he didn't like fighting very much, he had an unfortunate tendency to fall asleep in situations of physical danger, and trying to control the uncontrollable little princess was an impossible task because she seemed to have absolutely no idea what rules were at all. Bodkin was the one singing that song, rather unconvincingly.

No fear!!

sang Bodkin, Wish's Assistant Bodyguard

The three children were looking rather more ragged and sad than they had been two weeks earlier when they had run away from Wish's and Xar's parents. They had started out joyously, in the way that these journeys often begin. Running away had seemed like it would be an exciting adventure, but now they were hungry and tired and frightened, for they knew they were being hunted by the Warriors and the Wizards and the Witches, and that they must never be caught. If the *Warriors* caught them, Sychorax would lock up Wish in iron Warrior fort where the Witches could not get hold of her. If the *Wizards* caught them, Encanzo would lock up Xar in the prison of Gormincrag where his Witchstain could be treated. And if the *Witches* caught them . . . well that was such a scary idea our heroes were trying their hardest not to think about it.

So for the past two days they had been looking for the house of the sister of Caliburn, Xar's talking raven, where they hoped to be able to hide.

'I KNOW my sister lives somewhere around here,' said Caliburn for the umpteenth time. 'She moved here a while ago, back when I was still a human . . .'

Caliburn was actually a Wizard who had lived many lifetimes, and in the previous one he had indeed been a human. And he hadn't been just *any* old human, either, he had been the great Wizard Pentaglion. Unfortunately Caliburn had come down in the world and returned to the wildwoods in this

Caliburn, Xar's talking raven

present lifetime in the form of a bird. (A rather untidy bird, for Caliburn was continually losing his feathers in his anxiety at the impossible task of trying to keep Xar out of trouble.)

'I know that my sister has one of the ingredients we need for the spell to get rid of Witches, the tears of the Drood, and maybe we can persuade her to give it to us,' said Caliburn. 'And she'll give us a bed for the night, and a good meal, and she'll protect us for a while . . .'

None of them were feeling very strong at all, and the idea of a bed for a night and a good meal was even more attractive than the idea that Caliburn's sister might give them one of the ingredients they needed for their quest. In fact, it brought tears to Bodkin's eyes.

'What does your sister's house look like, Caliburn?' asked Bodkin.

Caliburn looked a little shifty. 'Oh, you know, just like any other old human habitation. I haven't been there in years. I'll know it when I see it.'

'Your sister must have a very big house,' said Wish doubtfully. 'Look how many of us there are! Are you quite sure she'll want to have all of us to stay?'

Caliburn gave an airy wave of his wing. 'Oh, my sister has loads of room! Of course she'll have us all to stay . . .'

'Even though we're a bit, well . . . ODD?' said Wish,

wistfully. 'I can't believe that your sister won't mind about us being Wizards and Warriors working together, Caliburn – everyone else hates that. And some people even might say we were sort of . . . *cursed*.'

Wish *was* a little odd-looking – a funny little scrawny girl with hair so quivering with Magic that it vibrated and lifted with static electricity every time she moved. She had a pale little face that looked as if the tide had washed over it and taken away all the sharp bits, and a kind but determined expression.

That determination of hers was being severely tested. Her armour was dented, she hadn't eaten in three days, and her face and hands and legs were deeply scratched from a terrible battle they had a week ago when they were ambushed by wyverns (a type of dragon very common in the Bronze Age).

With all her heart Wish wanted to believe that Caliburn had a sister who would

Wish WAS a little odd-looking . . .

welcome them, even though they were outlaws, disobeying the laws of the wildwood universe . . . but deep down she had a hollow feeling that this was very unlikely.

'Let's face it, Caliburn,' said Wish, trying to be practical and not mind too much, 'we don't really fit in anywhere. No one is going to want us.'

'My sister isn't as prejudiced as everyone else,' said Caliburn. 'There are kind people in the world. You just have to find them.'

'You're quite sure your sister hasn't died and come back as a raven too, and the reason we can't find her house is that she's now living in some sort of NEST?' said Bodkin suspiciously.

'No, no,' said Caliburn. And then, less certainly,

'Probably not . . .'

Bodkin didn't quite know how to say this without hurting Caliburn's feelings, but they had been searching for Caliburn's sister's house for quite a while now without finding any sign of it. 'Are you quite sure that you've got this right, Caliburn?' said Bodkin. 'You've only just remembered that you HAVE a sister.'

'Living many lifetimes is difficult,' said Caliburn, rather flustered. 'It takes a while to remember what happened in the previous ones. But now my memory has been jogged I know I have a sister and she's down in that forest somewhere . . .'

'Well, I think we should give up looking for your sister and march right into that Drood stronghold on the Lake of the Lost, and just take their tears from them,' said Xar, who was not a patient person.

'You don't understand!' said Caliburn. 'The Droods are unrelenting, unforgiving and the greatest Wizards in the wildwoods, and they really don't like having their tears taken! They'll kill us if they catch us . . . Much easier for my sister just to GIVE them to us . . .'

And then Wish spotted something that wasn't the welcoming fires of Caliburn's sister's house, but something much more sinister.

'Some people are following us down there in the forest,' whispered Wish, putting up her eyepatch a smidgeon because she could see better through her

Magic eye. Sure enough, down in the tangle of green woods below them, way in the distance, there were the little flickering lights of many, many torches coming through the trees in their direction.

'Do you think it could be your sister, Caliburn?' Xar whispered hopefully, his tummy giving the most gigantic rumble. Only Xar could mistake the ominous torches of what was clearly a hunting party for a welcoming greeting from Caliburn's sister. But then, Xar was an optimistic sort of person, who hoped for the best at all times.

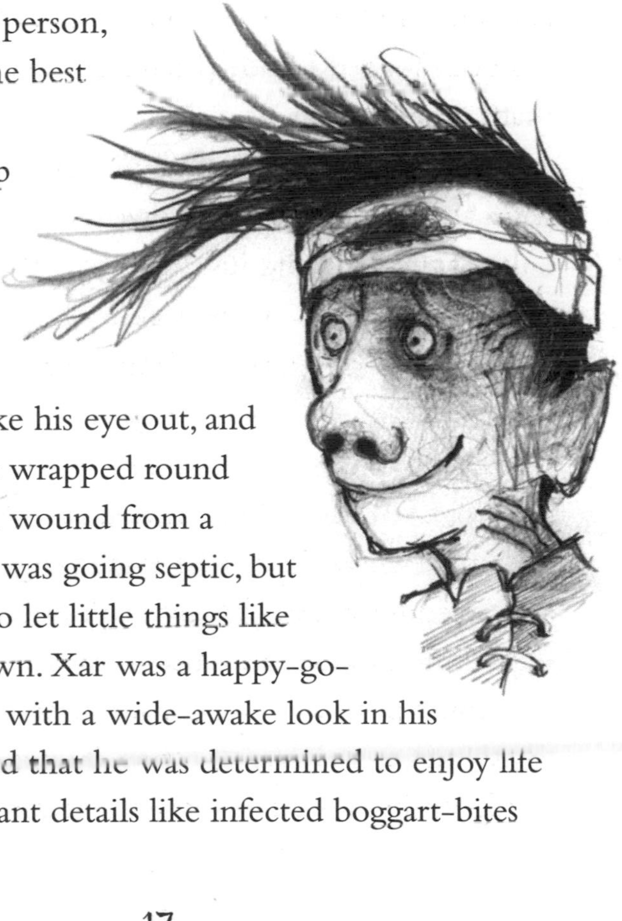

He had a deep cut over his right temple from where a wyvern had earlier tried to take his eye out, and an old bit of shirt wrapped round his leg covering a wound from a boggart-bite that was going septic, but he wasn't going to let little things like these get him down. Xar was a happy-go-lucky sort of boy, with a wide-awake look in his eyes that suggested that he was determined to enjoy life despite unimportant details like infected boggart-bites and wyvern injuries.

As Xar was also a boy of considerable charm and charisma, he had a lot of companions, and flying with the door were six of his sprites and three hairy fairies. These tiny little insect-y creatures, so paper-thin you could see their hearts, were buzzing around in a state of such alarm that blue electric sparks were coming out of their ears.

'Beware . . .' they hissed. 'Beware beware beware . . .'

'No, it's definitely not my sister,' said Caliburn, shading a wing over one of his eyes and squinting so he could see better. 'They're banging war drums. My sister wouldn't bang war drums, unless she's changed a very good deal in the last twenty years.'

'Don't worry, sprites,' said Xar soothingly, for although Xar often led his companions into difficulty, he did take his responsibilities as the leader of his band very seriously. 'I'll look after you . . .'

'Of coursse you will, Masster!' squeaked Squeezjoos, one of the smallest and most enthusiastic of the hairy fairies. 'You iss the most brilliantastic leader in the whole world ever and you woulds never leads us into any trouble!'

'But I don't understand it . . .' said Wish,

bewildered. 'Nobody knows which way we went – the sprites have dimmed their lights, we're flying so close to the tops of the trees that nobody can see us from below, so how can they be following us?'

'Maybe they picked up the scent of Crusher and the snowcats,' Bodkin suggested.

Xar had other companions too and they were down on the ground. A giant called Crusher, three beautiful snowcats, some wolves, a bear, and a werewolf called Lonesome were following on foot, way below on the forest floor.

'Impossible!' Xar whispered back. 'I'm unbeatable at running away and so are my companions! We're completely untrackable . . .'

As well as being just a *trifle* conceited, Xar was indeed very good at running away. He was the most disobedient boy in the Wizard kingdom, always getting into trouble for doing things like:

you woulds never leads us into any trouble . . .

Getting his sprites to charm his older brother Looter's spelling staffs so that every time Looter tried to use them, they spanked him on the bottom . . . Painting spots on the Magic mirror in the main hall so everyone who looked in it thought they were coming down with something infectious . . . Pouring Animation Potion on the trousers of Ranter, his least favourite teacher, so whenever Ranter tried to put them on, the trousers skipped out of reach.

As a result, Xar had spent his entire short life running away from the wrath of his father, his teachers, and the other Wizards, so he had become something of a running away *expert*.

'Maybe someone'ssss betrayed us,' hissed Tiffinstorm, one of Xar's larger sprites, eyes narrowing jealously. 'Probably that werewolf. Never trust a werewolf who you met in a prison. That's good advice, kids.'

'Don't you dare accuse the werewolf just because he's a werewolf!' said Xar fierily.

Wish agreed with Xar.

'Nobody's betrayed us,' said Wish, soothingly, 'we're on the same side, now, Tiffinstorm. We're all outlaws together, remember?

'But who is chasing us down there in the forest?' worried Wish.

Caliburn began to list their enemies. 'Well, it could be the Droods . . . or Xar's father . . . or Wish's mother . . .

And what about the Witchsmeller? *He* hates you . . . Or the Warrior emperor? He'll want to get rid of Magic-that-works-on-iron at all costs . . .'

Squeezjoos bared his little teeth and squeaked, '*I'sll* gets them for you, Master! I'sll bites great chunks out of their iron bottoms! I'sll makes their noses drip for a week and ties knots in their sandwiches! I'sll makes holes in theys socks so theys keep puttings theys big toes throughs it in a REALLY ANNOYING way! I'sll put itching powder in theys knickers and I'sll leave little fluffballs in theys tummy buttons and theys will NEVERS KNOW where the fluff is coming from!'

As Squeezjoos was not a great deal bigger than a dormouse, and the threat of fluff-in-the-tummy-button was not exactly life-threatening, none of this was likely to be terribly worrying to a Drood or a heavily armed iron Warrior, but Xar thanked him solemnly and said, 'Yes of course you can, Squeezjoos, just as soon as I give the order.'

The one enemy that Caliburn did not mention was *Witches*. Which, given that there were two very large Witches hovering right above their heads at that very moment, was a tiny bit ironic. There was even rather a large clue that Witches were closer than they might realise. Around Xar's waist, attached to his belt, hung two Witch feathers, and when Witches were close these Witch feathers burned green with a strange unnatural light. They were burning green *now*, my goodness they were, greener than emerald, brighter than starlight, but Xar and Wish and Bodkin had not noticed, so intent were they on staring down at what was going on in the forest below them.

The only person who HAD noticed the glowing of the Witch feathers was The Baby. The Baby was the smallest hairy fairy of all, and he was going wild with agitation.

But The Baby was still in his egg, and he could only say one word: 'Goo!'

And nobody listens to babies, even when they have something very important to say.

So although The Baby rolled around urgently in his egg, bumping into people and shouting 'Goo! Goo! Goo!' at the top of his Baby voice, none of the other sprites would listen and Xar just batted him away, saying, 'Not now, Baby, we can't play now.'

The Witches, sharpening their talons and hovering not more than ten feet above the door, grinned at each other – nasty grins, for Witches have nasty senses of humour. How amusing! These children were so busy worrying about the danger from *below*, they were completely ignoring the much more serious danger threatening them from *above*.

And they were running away from their parents!

That would explain why they were out at night, so far away from their Tribes and their kinsmen . . . it wasn't a trap at all . . .

The Witches prepared to swoop.

But then the Witches stiffened as something poked out of the back of Wish's waistcoat, swivelling, as if sniffing the air, and then hopping up on to the top of Wish's head to peer over the edge of the door with the others.

The something was a spoon, and it happened to be alive.

The Enchanted Spoon was followed by a key, and a fork and a number of little Enchanted Pins.

None of this was odd to the Witches. Enchanted objects were perfectly normal back in those days.

But these enchanted objects weren't normal at all, they were very odd indeed . . .

These enchanted objects . . .

. . . *were made of iron.*

The Witches' eyes blazed red and visible for one horrified moment.

'It'sssss herrrr . . .' hissed the Witches.

'It'ssss HERRRRRR . . .' The Witches growled like dogs. 'The girl with the Magic eye who has *Magic-that-works-on-iron* . . .'

In an unusual coincidence, Wish, peering

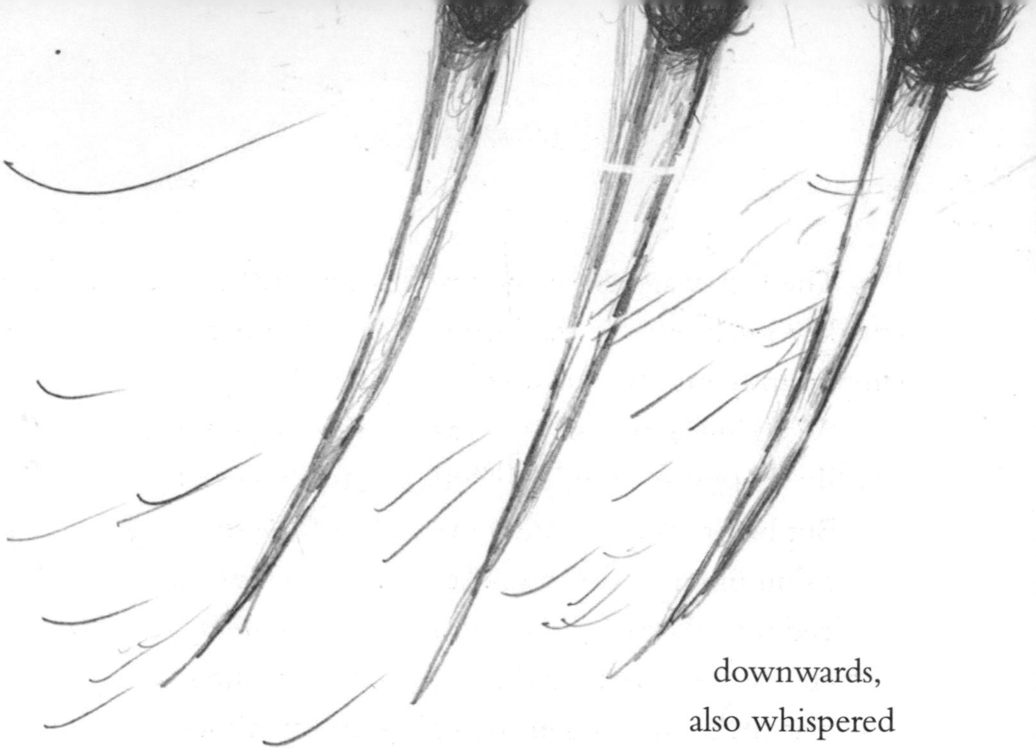

downwards,
also whispered
under her breath at the very
same time as the Witches: 'It's *HER* . . .'

'It's her . . . it's her . . . it's HER . . .!'

'It's my mother!' cried Wish. 'That's who's following us! Okay, nobody panic . . . Stay calm . . . Key! Could you hop into the keyhole for me?'

When Wish wanted to fly the door as quickly as possible she needed the key to be in the keyhole so that she could steer the door at speed.

'Of course,' boasted the key in a creaky little voice. 'You see, spoon? The fork is a mere food carrier, a pathetic little potato piercer . . . but *I* have a very important role.'

The key and the fork were both in love with the Enchanted Spoon, so the key never lost an opportunity to show off.

The fork waggled its prongs furiously at the key, and the key stuck out its little iron chest and hopped self-importantly into the keyhole.

'We'll just very quietly sneak away . . .' said Wish. 'Softly, everyone . . . make as little noise as you can . . .'

But before Wish could move the key and send the door skimming silently away across the treetops, she noticed something very odd was up with Squeezjoos.

He had been getting thoroughly over-excited, doing somersaults in the air, squeaking dire threats about making holes in people's socks, and protecting Xar, and accidentally biting his own tail, and at the sighting of

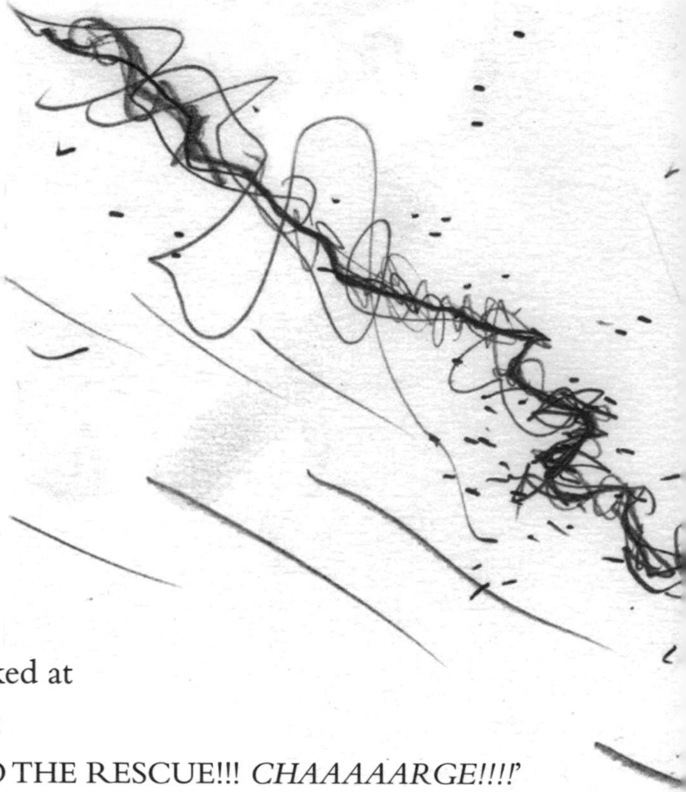

Wish's mother he seemed to completely lose it. His little bumbly body shot fizzily with sparks, his spotty eyes lit up a luminous bright green, and he shrieked at the top of his voice:

'SOOJZEEKS TO THE RESCUE!!! *CHAAAAARGE!!!!*'

And the little sprite threw himself in a mad zooming dive downwards in a lunatic one-hairy-fairy attack on Queen Sychorax's entire advancing army.

'What . . . is . . . he . . . *doing???????*' gasped Xar.

And just as the goggle-eyed children on the back of the door were taking in this *first* incomprehensible disaster, a *second one* sprang up, bright, fierce, flaming, in front of their very eyes.

'My mother!' cried Wish. *'She's setting the forest alight!'*

SOOjeeks to the RESCUE!!
C-H-A-A-A-R-GE!!

Ariel

Bumbleboozle

Squeezjoos

The Baby

Hinkypunk

Xar's Sprites
Mustardthought
Tiffinstorm
Timeloss
the Once Sprite

2. The Trees are Screaming

Meanwhile, down on the ground, Crusher the giant, and Xar's snowcats, Kingcat, Nighteye and Forestheart, his werewolf, Lonesome, his bear and his wolves were making their way swiftly and quietly through the wildwoods. Wolves and giants are quite common, but I wish you could have seen the snowcats. Beautiful creatures they were, larger than lions, fur as deep as powder snow, padding through the ancient forest, whiskers twitching. Like the children on the flying door, they were looking skinnier and hungrier and a lot more bedraggled than they had been two weeks earlier. The snowcats had deep wounds from the talons of wyverns on their faces, the bear had torn his ear, and Lonesome was limping.

None would have known that they had passed that way, for as Xar said, they were untrackable, untraceable. Even giants know how to tread lightly on the world, so although Crusher was nearly as tall as the tallest of the trees around him, he did not make a footprint on the undergrowth below as he walked through the holloways, planting his great walking staff gently in the ground and humming happily to himself. Crusher was a Longstepper

High-Walker giant, and these giants are BIG, so they tend to have BIG thoughts. Wandering gets their giant brains working, so as Crusher walked, his head was smoking with inspiration, and he was thinking in time to each giant gentle step:

'I wonder if you could say that trees have brains? They certainly learn . . . and just because they learn in their roots, is that enough to say that they do not have brains like humans and giants do?'

And then he stopped suddenly. He put his ear to the nearest tree.

His face, with wandering lines like an ancient map, normally gently interested in the world about him, assumed a very concerned and grim expression indeed.

Slowly he bent down to his animal companions.

'Now, I do not want you to panic, creatures of the forest,' said Crusher. 'But the trees are screaming.'

There are people who think that just because trees do not have mouths, they cannot talk. Those people are wrong, and they are often the kind of people who think that other people have to be exactly like themselves to count as people at all. Trees speak to each other just as you and I do, but you have to have the right ears for listening. They send out messages on sound waves that

"Do not worry, dear trees..." said Crusher

giant ears can hear, scent chemicals that giant noses can smell, and just because our tiny little human ears and noses are too small to hear or smell or detect them, this does not mean that those messages are not there.

As Crusher said, the trees were screaming.

And the message they were screaming, with the crackling of their roots and every electrical and chemical signal they could muster, was: 'FIRE! FIRE! FIRE! FIRE!'

It was very generous of the trees to scream that message, really. For it was not a message that their fellow trees could respond to. Trees live life in the slow lane. So although they can move their leaves in the direction of sunlight, and they can grow their roots in the direction of water, this all happens very slowly, and what they cannot do, in the face of the immediate, instant, quick destruction that is FIRE, is wrench up their mud-clogged roots from the ground they are growing in and run as fast as they can for their lives.

But the animals can. And maybe the trees are more intelligent than we are, and know that their species' lives are eventually dependent on the other species around them.

So the snowcats' ears pricked up, the werewolf's nose was set a-sniffing, sniff, sniff, sniff: they caught the smell, the sound of the messages the trees were screaming, before even the first whiff of burning wood, the first howl of a distant terrified fox.

And they panicked.

Snorting, howling, wild with fear, the animals and the Magic creatures ran as fast as they could, uncaring of the brambles that ripped, the branches that spiked, joining a deluge of other fleeing animals – hedgehogs, wolves, bears, deer, birds, insects, hobs, goblins, all careering madly through the forest to get away from the age-old enemy, fire.

The sprites and the birds and all things with wings were the lucky ones.

Crusher had to follow more slowly, for giants, like trees, do not move quickly, and tears were trickling down his wrinkled face as he moved through the forest, touching each precious ancient tree in sympathy as he walked.

The fire caught from tree to tree, faster than fairies, faster than Witches. Trees that had been growing for hundreds, sometimes thousands of years, burned bright and were destroyed in an instant. The roar of the flames as the wind carried the bright, destructive inferno faster, swifter, higher, bigger, brighter, bolder, quick as thought and more terrible than could be imagined.

Up above, the children on the door responded instantly.

Wish grabbed the Enchanted Key and pointed DOWN.

'We have to save Squeezjoos and Crusher and the animals!' shouted Xar, and with a great screech, the door shot downwards towards the burning forest, the sprites bravely following behind it, in a wild screeching trail of humming sprite dust, even though every sprite instinct was telling them to fly away.

It was unbelievably fortunate that the door and the sprites and the raven chose that blink of a second to plunge downwards.

For at precisely the moment that they swooped, the Witches attacked.

SSSSSCCCCRRIIIIIITCH!!!!!!!!!

There was a tearing noise, as if the air itself was being ripped apart.

Just in case YOU have never been dive-bombed by a Witch, I will explain what happens. When Witches are invisible, they can do no harm. Their hands just pass right through you, like the hands of ghosts. So as Breakneck and Ripgrizzle screeched downward, they were turning themselves visible as they plunged. First two screaming heads appeared, liquefying at the edges into spitting sparks and foul vapour, and then the two Witches blasted down on Wish and Xar and Bodkin on their Enchanted Door like a couple of infinitely evil peregrine falcons.

When Witches attack, they assault all your senses at the same time. Their stink is unbearable, the most nauseating bad egg and rotten corpse smell you can possibly imagine, and they release it in a cloud of venom. Their scream is like the death agony of five hundred foxes, and it buries itself in your brain and reverberates around your head till you feel like you might go crazy.

Ripgrizzle had two fish-like eyes buried so deep on either side of his axe-sharp nose you could not see into the pitiless depths of them – not that you would want to.

The mouth, dripping that revolting black saliva from the fangs. A body like a human mixed with a panther, talons long as swords, and black feathery wings.

Breakneck was no prettier.

The Witches swooped, but they were a blink or two too late, for the children on their door had that very second gone into a dive downwards to help their friends, so the Witches' talons closed only on empty air, and they let out screeches of infuriated disappointment.

The sprites and the children and Caliburn the raven FINALLY looked over their shoulders and realised they were being attacked.

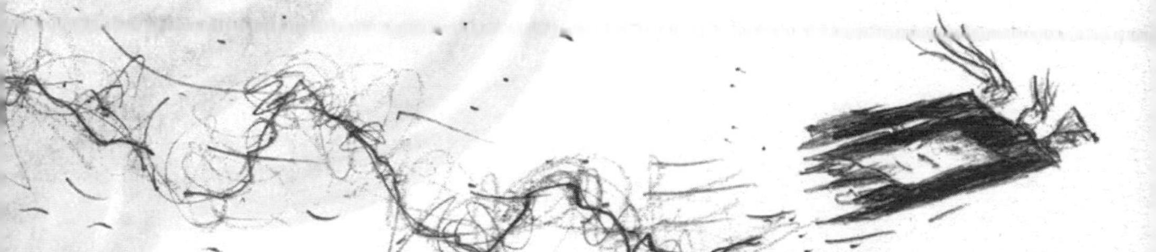

Pandemonium ensued, as the rescuing-Squeezjoos-and-Crusher-and-the-animals mission turned abruptly into a desperate-flight-from-the-attacking-Witches mission.

'AIEEEEEEEEEEEEE!!!!' screamed the Witches.

'Goo!' cried The Baby, which in Baby-language means: 'I've been *trying* to tell you this for ages, but nobody listens to babies, *oh* no . . .'

'FLYYYYYYYYYYY!!!!!' yelled Xar, shooting arrows at the Witches as Wish desperately hauled the key back and forth in wild swivelling motions so that the door slalomed this way and that in crazy swirls to evade the mind-boggling horror of the pursuing Witches, while still following the little tiny spark of the charging Squeezjoos, who was continuing to shriek, 'SOOJZEEKS TO THE RESCUE! *CHAAAAAAARGE!!!!'* at the top of his voice.

'Don't worry, princess!' said Bodkin, trying to draw Wish's Enchanted Sword*, but unable to get it out of the scabbard, so he had to pull out his bow and arrows instead. '*I'll* save you!'

But Bodkin had a bit of a disadvantage as a bodyguard. He had a medical condition that caused him to fall asleep in conditions of extreme danger.

He had barely said these last brave words before he collapsed, snoring loudly, and began to slide downwards on the door.

Snore, snore.

'Bodkin! Wake up!' yelled Wish, and Xar had to give up shooting arrows at the Witches, while he and Wish took hold of Bodkin by both arms to prevent him from slipping off the door entirely.

* The Enchanted Sword was a special Witch-killing sword

Bodkin woke up with a start, mumbling, 'Who? What? Where?'

'Forest in Drood Territory . . .' panted the little princess. 'Being chased by the Witches . . . Squeezjoos attacking my mother's forces entirely on his own . . .'

'Oh! Yes!' said Bodkin, scrambling back on to the Enchanted Door. '*We can do this!* My iron arrows will work much better on Witches than Xar's bone ones!' Bodkin put away the Enchanted Sword, and instead fitted an arrow into his bow, took careful aim, and then fell asleep again, shooting himself in the foot and falling heavily on Wish. This jogged her hand, and the key that was controlling the steering shot out of the keyhole so violently that the door went into abrupt reverse, travelling backwards with such speed that it nearly shot into the open jaws of the pursuing Witches.

What with one thing and another, the young outlaws weren't really working together in the most brilliant fashion . . .

The key had got entangled in Wish's hair, so the fork came to the rescue, leaping into the keyhole, using its prongs as a key substitute. Wish took hold of the fork and got control of the door again, narrowly avoiding the swiping talons of the Witches.

The upside-down fork looked up smugly at the furious key, and that look meant: '*Look at me, spoon, look at me!!* . . . us forks can be important too!'

'Forks are mere *food carriers*, they're not qualified to operate keyholes!' squeaked the key. 'Come out of there right now or this flight will end in disaster!'

'SQUEEZJOOS! COME BACK!' roared Xar.

REEEEOOOOOOW! The flying door swooped and swirled and dodged through the treetops, shaving off leaves and nearly unseating its riders, who were hanging on for dear life. Bodkin reawoke, and this time didn't even attempt to shoot anything, shaking the arrow out of his foot and concentrating on not falling off the door.

Wish was trying not to lose sight of Squeezjoos, who was flying at full speed over the burning trees towards the approaching torches and flares of the Warriors. Goodness knows how the little hairy fairy thought he was going to attack an entire Warrior army all on his own, but that appeared to be his plan.

Down below on the forest floor, Queen Sychorax and her iron Warriors were at full gallop as they raced through the trees on horseback.

Queen Sychorax didn't look a bit like Wish.

It was most out of character for Queen Sychorax to have a daughter so unlike herself, but even great queens cannot *entirely* control what their offspring are going to look like.

Queen Sychorax was dressed for war, with an iron

breastplate, iron helmet, and so many weapons she looked like a statue to some alien god of war. She was also loaded with jewels, furs, and clothes of the finest materials the early Iron Age could supply, for Queen Sychorax felt that if she was going to be forced to travel into the wilderness of the godforsaken forest in pursuit of a disobedient daughter, she should jolly well do it in *style*, for mistletoe's sake.

She was in a bit of a mood.

'Witches,' breathed Queen Sychorax, looking upwards from the back of her galloping horse. 'I knew it! I KNEW they'd be after her! *SHOOT DOWN THE WITCHES!*'

ZING! ZING! ZING!

Arrows shot upwards from the forest floor, narrowly missing both the door and the Witches.

'Your mother's shooting at us!' said Bodkin in amazement. 'As if we haven't got enough problems . . .'

'She's not shooting at *us*, she's shooting at the Witches,' said Wish, grim with determination as she flew that door – really rather *well*, actually, considering that she was having to use a fork in the keyhole instead of a key, if anybody had had the time or been in the mood to appreciate her growing door-flying skills – at astonishing speed just above the smoke and the chaos of the burning forest.

Arrows rained upwards, narrowly missing their targets.

'Oh for goodness' sake!' snapped Queen Sychorax to her Warriors. 'Can't you even hit a couple of great gawping Witches at close distance?'

She sighed.

'I don't know, if you want something doing, you have to do it yourself . . . ' Queen Sychorax pulled up her horse, got out her bow and arrow, and took careful aim.

REOOOOW!

Wish made another desperate turn of the door through the billowing smoke, but this time it was just a smidgeon too late, and one of Ripgrizzle's talons got hold of the door, and sent it revolving in circles, shooting into the talons of Breakneck. Breakneck got a good hold of the spinning door, kept it steady, and Ripgrizzle gave an evil grin as he prepared to swoop.

They couldn't get away now.

But one final ZING! from below, and Ripgrizzle's grin of gloating triumph turned to an expression of acute surprise.

And then Ripgrizzle fell from the air, dead as a stone, with one of Queen Sychorax's arrows in his heart.

BOOM! He landed on the forest floor, Warriors scattering in all directions from the ensuing Witch crater and a whole load of billowing green smoke.

With a whine of horror and fright, Breakneck let go

of the Enchanted Door and fled for her life in a whirr of black feathers.

Sychorax's arrow also stopped the charging Squeezjoos.

On the arrow's path to Ripgrizzle, it had skimmed so close to Squeezjoos that it had removed the tip of one of Squeezjoos's antennae, giving the little hairy fairy such a shock that he stopped mid-charge. He blinked twice and the green faded from his little spotty eyes, as if he was just waking up from a sleep, like Bodkin, and—

'Where am I?' squeaked Squeezjoos, giving a violent start as he took in Sychorax's Warrior army gathered in horrifying masses below him.

'Save meeeeeeeeeeeeee!' He panicked, and turned around, flying as fast as his little humming wings could carry him back to what he thought was the safety of Wish and Xar and Bodkin on the back of the door, and hiding himself in Wish's hair beside the spoon and the key.

'Good shot, Queen Sychorax!' said Bodkin in relief, looking down over the side of the door and trying to see Wish's mother through the smoke of the Witch's landing way below. 'Yes, you were right, she was shooting at the Witches. Thank goodness she's such a good shot . . .'

Xar hated Queen Sychorax, but even *he* was impressed. 'Maybe she's not as bad as I thou— Hang on a second! What is she doing?'

Sychorax had got back on her horse. 'Now shoot down the door,' she ordered her deputy. 'I'm presuming you can at least hit something as large as *that*?'

'But your Majesty!' spluttered the deputy. 'Your own daughter is on the back of that door!'

'My own daughter,' spat Queen Sychorax, grinding her pretty little teeth, 'has more than one life.* And if she didn't want her door shot down, she shouldn't have got born with this Magic-that-works-on-iron in that abnormal and eccentric fashion. SHOOT DOWN THE DOOR!'

* LONG story.

Arrows rained upwards once more.

'Put the door in reverse!' yelled Xar. 'I take it back, she IS as bad as I thought!'

'But what on earth is Queen Sychorax doing? Why is she shooting at us?' said Bodkin, thoroughly bewildered. 'Has she gone totally mad?'

'Well, she's never been exactly a HUGGY sort of mother,' said Wish. 'But I'm sure there's some sort of perfectly reasonable explanation . . .'

And they were about to get that explanation.

BAM!

A direct hit on the Enchanted Door by a carefully aimed spear pierced the Magic that was delicately holding the jigsaw pieces of the door together.

'Keep it together, Wish!' shouted Caliburn. 'Think of the door as a complete door!'

But Wish was not yet sufficiently in control of her Magic powers when taken by surprise like this. The door shattered into a thousand pieces, and the three children plummeted towards the ground.

3. Queen Sychorax is not a Huggy Sort of Mother

They were extremely fortunate that their door was shot down right above Crusher and the running animals.

'LOOK OUT, ABOVE!' cried Crusher, coming to a crashing halt as bits of door rained down. The animals, mad with terror though they were at the following fire, came to a trembling halt, for they loved their humans, and they ran back to see if they could help.

Xar and Bodkin fell into the branches of a tree, and Wish was saved by all six sprites catching bits of her clothes and breaking her fall before she finally fell into the cupped palms of Crusher.

Little Squeezjoos nearly came to an untimely end. He fell out of Wish's hair, and was too late to duck a flying fragment of the shattered door that hit him momentarily unconscious, and he would have fallen down into the blazing undergrowth if Xar had not risked his life by reaching out way too far from the tree and saving him.

Crusher then gently extracted Xar and Bodkin from the tree and put them and Wish on the ground, telling them to climb aboard the snowcats who would carry them quicker than the giant could run.

'RUN SWIFT,' said the giant.

Bodkin and Wish and Xar leapt aboard the snowcats. 'FLY!' cried Xar, and with great, terrified bounds, their soft fur blackened and raised in petrified quills, Kingcat, Nighteye, Forestheart and the wolves and the bear leapt through the dark dusty rain that was now falling, bits of soft grey ash, and ROOOOARR! The hot roar of the fire pursued them, mixed with the noise of the Warrior hunt, the scream of the dogs, the screech of the Warrior horns, the iron sound of the beating hooves as they pounded through the burning forest.

That was the sound of the new Iron Age, that Warrior hunt.

The forest was being burnt down, so that the Warriors could build their forts and their fields and their new modern world. For the Warriors argued that the modern way was the right way, surely? Time cannot run backwards, could it? That would be nonsense, and Warriors do not believe in nonsense. The forest had to come down so the Warriors could move humanity forward in a civilised and forward-looking manner. The giants had to leave because they took up way too much room. The sprites had to die because their habitats were needed to make all the THINGS that Warriors need. It was regrettable, but there it was. It was all in the name of progress.

So all over the wildwoods, these hunts were being carried out, with the mad barking of dogs and the shrill crying of horns, and Warriors on horseback hunting down the giants, or the shining elves, or the long-haired ogres, or the lumpen boggarts.

This time it was slightly different of course, for Queen Sychorax was hunting down her own daughter.

There she was, right at the front of the stampeding Warrior force, for Queen Sychorax always had to be the fastest, ram-rod straight on the back of her hunting horse, crying out orders, entirely oblivious to the roar of the fire behind her.

They caught up with Crusher first.

Even with his great giant strides, he moved slower than the snowcats because he kept on stopping to reassure the trees. Calm in the chaos, he laid his giant hands on oak, on elm, on ash, on alder, on blackthorn, on beech, on hawthorn, hazel, holly, on lime and maple, on yew and poplar and willow, all the dear, soon-to-be-torchlight trees, saying, 'Do not be afraid, dear trees. The forest will grow again, I promise. I will cherish your descendants . . . This too will pass . . .'

BAAAAAM! The Warrior hunt was upon him.

Queen Sychorax launched her spear first. Crusher looked down with a bemused expression, picking it out of his leg as if it were an irritating thorn or needle. The Warriors surrounded the giant, confusing him with the

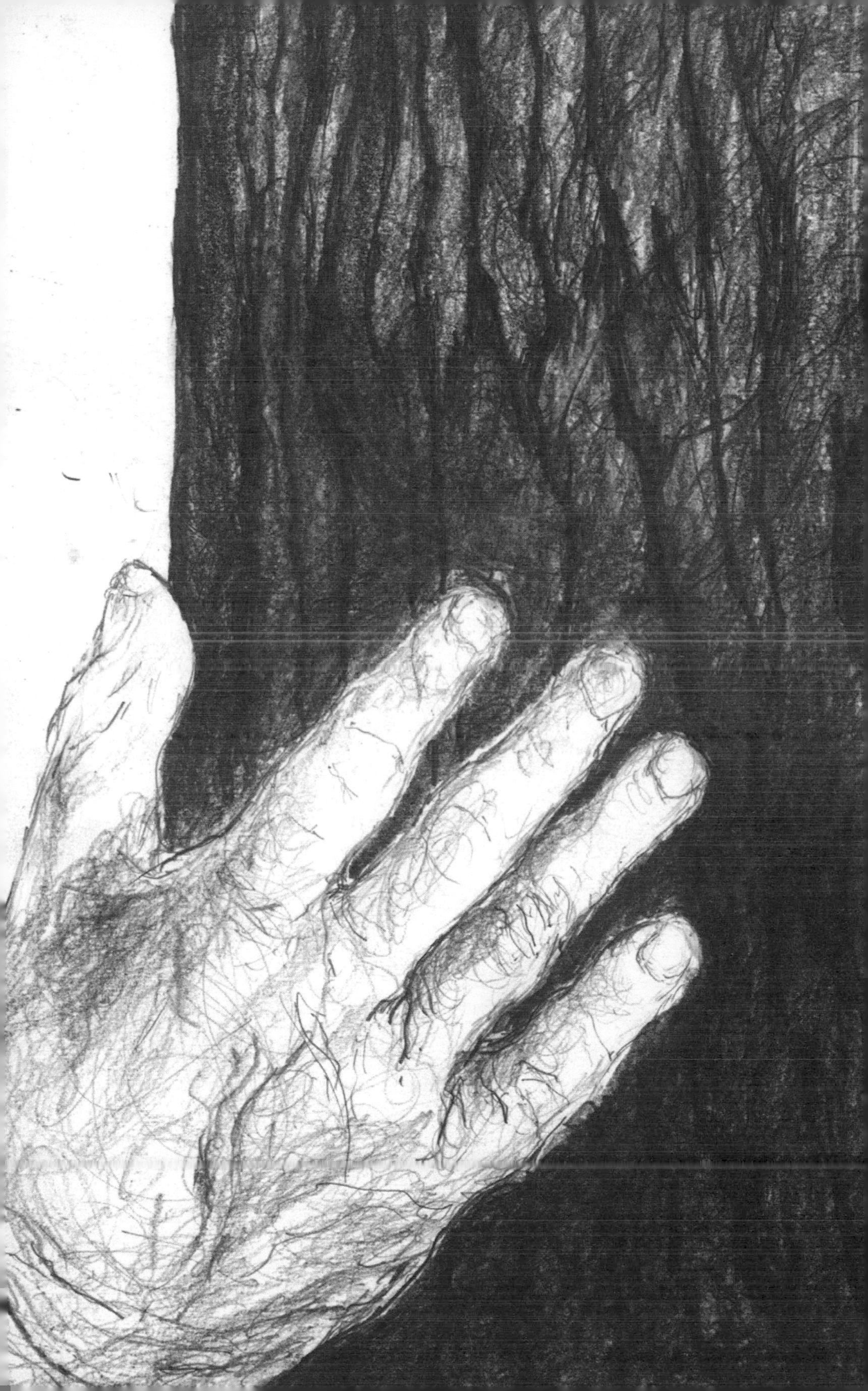

clamour of their horns, for giants have very sensitive hearing, and the loudness and the pitch befuddled his ears so much that he lost his balance and fell to the ground as suddenly as a great oak struck by lightning.

The Warriors scattered in all directions as he dropped, and then regathered again around the fallen giant, winding strands of his hair and the edges of his clothes around their weapons and then driving those weapons into the ground so that when he opened his eyes, blinking, he was stuck to the earth by a pincushion of spears, axes and arrows.

One of the Warriors then rode her horse right up the chest of the giant, rearing it up into the air and punching up her spear in a victory salute, shouting, 'GOT HIM, YOUR MAJESTY!'

'Very good,' cried Sychorax. 'Stern-and-True Justice! Vengeance! Tenacity! Unrelenting! Drama! Unforgiving!'

These were the names of Wish's six elder stepsisters, tall, good-looking, blonde young women with bulging biceps and golden torcs around their necks, heavily armed with spears and axes and every kind of helpful weapon. 'Hunt down your sister and the other two!' ordered Queen Sychorax, adding, 'Be careful not to hurt her, mind . . .'

Wish's stepsisters nodded, and with great whooping cries, they kicked their heels on the leopard-spotted flanks of their hunting horses, and galloped off after the retreating snowcats.

The stepsisters were excellent Warriors, strong of arm, fast of throw, with any softness of heart well drilled out of them, so they very quickly ran down the snowcats. They brought down the sprites with sprite nets so exquisitely thrown that it brought tears to the eyes of their teacher, Madam Dreadlock, who was galloping on a sturdy horse beside them, crying with pride at the brilliance with which her pupils knocked Wish and Bodkin and Xar off their snowcats in single blows around the midriff, and then entwined them in iron nets.

'Call off your beastly animals!' snarled Stern-and-True Justice. 'Or I will KILL your disgusting sprites!'

'She means it,' said Wish, who knew her eldest stepsister well. Justice was perfectly capable of killing a sprite in cold blood. Wish herself had automatically curled up into a defensive little ball like a hedgehog.

Wish's Enchanted Pins, Spoon, Fork and Key were all attacking the stepsisters, the pins pushing themselves into any soft fleshy bits they could find, but Wish called them off, shouting, 'Enchanted things! Snowcats! Wolves! Bear! Keep your distance . . .'

Reluctantly, the iron enchanted objects backed away, but not before Justice grabbed the Enchanted Spoon and all of Xar's animals dropped to the ground, growling.

Xar started to curse the sisters but Justice stopped him with a gentle tap of her mace that knocked him out. And then the pleasant young Warrior women dragged the three children in the nets behind them, back to where Queen Sychorax was waiting with her Warriors beside the fallen giant. The victorious stepsisters gave poor little Wish some good healthy whacks with their mace and spear-sticks along the way, just to punish her for getting them all out on this horrible journey into the middle of nowhere.

Queen Sychorax's Warriors were getting a little restive, looking over their shoulders somewhat anxiously at the howl of the fiery furnace getting louder and louder, hoping that the mother-and-daughter chat wasn't going to go on too long, for mistletoe's sake. But Queen Sychorax herself was sitting bolt upright on her horse, apparently unaware of the advancing danger.

Her stepdaughters dragged the three nets in front of her.

'Here she is, the weird little rat,' said Stern-and-True Justice, 'looking even more odd and weak than ever. She really is a dreadful, dirty little beast. Do you want us to kick her for you some more, Mother?'

'Not now, Justice,' said Queen Sychorax, getting off her horse and opening up the net containing Wish with the end of her sceptre.

Wish uncurled herself and stood up.

Queen Sychorax took off her helmet and her face underneath the helmet was rather colder and sterner than the helmet itself. As I said before, Queen Sychorax was in a bit of a mood.

'You broke your promise,' said Queen Sychorax grimly, with that awful edge of disappointment in her golden pear drop of a voice. 'You said you would return with me to iron Warrior fort, and instead you ran away.'

'I told you, Mother, Xar and Bodkin and I are searching for the ingredients for a spell to get rid of Witches,' said Wish, very white. 'And what are you doing setting fire to the forest? I think you should calm down and stop over-reacting.'

'Calm down?' raged Queen Sychorax. 'Over-reacting?'

'Look, Wish!' said Sychorax. She got hold of Wish's shoulder, turned her round and pointed her finger at a huge mushrooming cloud that was rising above the trees where the dead Witch had landed. The cloud was at least a hundred feet wide, a nasty sulphurous green, and pulsating with a poison that made the Spell of Love Denied look like lemonade.

'That crater with the dead Witch in it will still be poisonous in another twenty years,' said Sychorax. 'These are *Witches*, not mischievous little curse sprites. There is no such thing as a spell to defeat them – that is pure fantasy and wish-fulfillment on your part. Return to the iron Warrior castle, behind my wall, and I will keep you safe . . .'

Sychorax's tone had changed and become coaxing, pleasant.

'. . . and Dreadlock here, your beloved teacher, will teach you how to be a proper Warrior, won't you, Dreadlock? And then you'll forget about all this silly Magic business . . .'

Madam Dreadlock, sitting like a judgemental walrus on horseback beside Wish's older stepsisters, bowed obediently but shot Wish a look of the purest dislike. Wish was the most unsatisfactory pupil she had ever taught, with absolutely not the foggiest idea of whether the angles of the hypotenuse added up to x or y, and she couldn't do spelling HOWEVER loudly Madam Dreadlock shouted at her.*

* Editor's note: Wish was dyslexic. Of course, they didn't CALL it dyslexia back in the Bronze Age, but she was, and teachers like Madam Dreadlock weren't very understanding about this to say the least.

YOU have disgraced
your Warrior Tribe AGAIN!!

'Your trigonometry homework was due last Tuesday,' barked Madam Dreadlock automatically. 'And I need the door of my Punishment Cupboard* returned in tip-top mint condition—'

'Yes, not now, Dreadlock,' said Queen Sychorax hurriedly. 'I'm sure you can make allowances under the circumstances . . .'

But Wish had had quite enough experience of Madam Dreadlock and her mother's iron Warrior fort. She backed away from her mother.

'No,' said Wish defiantly. 'Xar and I are going to show you how Wizards and Warriors CAN work together to fight the Witches!'

'HA! HA! HA!' Wish's stepsisters laughed so hard at this that they nearly fell over.

Queen Sychorax's eyes hardened into stones.

'*Now* she's in for it,' said Drama, Wish's sixth stepsister, with satisfaction.

'YOU, a leader?' spat Queen Sychorax in a voice like an adder strike. 'A worm with the *flu* would make a better leader than you! I have met *jellyfish* with greater leadership potential! Look at what trouble you've already led your wicked and foolish companions into! Covered in wounds, even weaker than you normally are, you haven't eaten for days, you have NO FRIENDS and

* The door the children had been travelling on was originally the door to Madam Dreadlock's Punishment Cupboard and it would now need rather a lot of work to return to tip-top mint condition.

nowhere to hide . . . and I only just saved you from falling into the talons of the Witches! You call this *leadership*?'

Wish flinched. Every single poison arrow of a word her mother said was something Wish had already been worrying was true. But Queen Sychorax hadn't finished yet.

'Consorting with Wizards and werewolves and other low lifes! Riding beasts! Performing Magic! I cannot believe that my *own daughter* is so miserably unworthy compared to my stepdaughters!' said Queen Sychorax.

The stepsisters giggled smugly.

'YOU, Wish,' finished Queen Sychorax, with magnificent scorn, 'are an embarrassment and a traitor and a disgrace to your tribe!'

Six months ago a speech like this would have crushed Wish. But that was before she met Xar, and Xar had given her courage, and she found that she was no longer afraid of a mother who set fire to forests and imprisoned her beloved vegetarian giant with spears, and called her horrible names.

'I am not an embarrassment or a traitor or a disgrace to my tribe,' said Wish coldly. 'Release my giant, release my friends Xar and Bodkin, my sprites, my animals, my enchanted objects, and stop the fire!'

Queen Sychorax stared in astonishment. But she

recovered quickly.

'It is a great deal easier to *start* a fire, than stop it,' said Queen Sychorax.

She reached out and grabbed Wish's arms so that she could not put up her eyepatch.

'You are coming back home whether you like it or not!' said Queen Sychorax grimly. 'This so-called spell of yours to get rid of Witches isn't a proper spell. You have to understand that your best hope of survival is to be locked up safe forever. You need to face real life and grow up sharpish!

'*And to help you do that, when we get back home I will put your evil bandit friends in the deepest darkest dungeon I can find, and I will melt down that ridiculous Enchanted Spoon of yours, and turn him into hairpins!*'

Now Queen Sychorax probably didn't *mean* that – she had just lost her temper – but with that last, bitterly snapped out comment I think you can safely say that the mother-and-daughter negotiations pretty much broke down for the moment.

'Oh dear oh dear oh dear . . .' moaned Caliburn, for with Wish's arms imprisoned so firmly by the grim hands of Queen Sychorax, there was absolutely nothing Wish could do – she couldn't reach her eyepatch to use the Magic eye . . .

Xar was out like a light, Crusher was entirely

incapacitated, the sprites and Bodkin were all tangled up in iron-clad nets, Justice was looking delightedly at the Enchanted Spoon hoping that she was going to be able to melt it *personally*, the snowcats, wolves and bear were too scared of something happening to Wish or the sprites to move, fire was now reaching the edges of the clearing and was heating up the bottoms of the Warriors at the back of the crowd so fiercely that only the most iron-strict of Warrior training was preventing them from leaping from their saddles shouting YARROOOOO or something similar . . .

Yes, I think you could definitely say that this was a *crisis*, and we're only at the end of CHAPTER THREE, for mistletoe's sake.

And quite a lot had happened *already* – what with the Witch attack, and the capture by Warriors, it had been a very busy half an hour, what with one thing and another. You have to feel for poor Caliburn in this situation. He was the oldest creature in that clearing by far, and this really wasn't good for his old bird heart.

'What's going to happen now????' panicked Caliburn. 'I mean, I'm only a bird. I could peck someone, but I'm not sure it would help . . .'

4. Exit, Rescued By a Bear

ROOOOOOOOOOAW!

Into this scene in which Queen Sychorax appeared to have regained control of the situation – apart from the FIRE of course, for as Queen Sychorax said herself, fires are easier to *start* than they are to stop, and once started they are difficult to keep in check – there leapt a gigantic brown bear.

The bear was unimaginably enormous, three times the size of a normal bear. Its ragged fur, upraised either in fury or fright, made it seem even bigger than it actually was.

It leapt into the clearing, reared on to its hind legs, and beat its gigantic chest with its enormous paws. On its entrance, Warriors scattered in all directions in shock. Behind the bear came the thunder and shaking of colossal feet pounding into the ground like mini earthquakes, and one, two, three, four, five Thunderdell giants stormed into the clearing, followed by a little owl with spotted brown wings.

Whatever Caliburn or anyone else was expecting to happen next, they weren't expecting *this*.

Queen Sychorax was so surprised she relaxed her iron grip on Wish's arms.

Wish leapt away from Queen Sychorax and hauled up the edge of her eyepatch with shaking hands.

One of the many advantages of having a Magic eye is that you can make things happen extremely quickly. Wish had been taught by Caliburn how to make iron things move just by looking at them.

So she looked across at Crusher and then at Bodkin, Xar and the sprites, and . . .

PING! PING! PING! PING! PING! The spears, daggers, axes and maces that were pinning the edges of Crusher's clothes and his hair to the ground rocketed into the air, releasing him. The iron nets entangling the sprites and Bodkin and Xar fell open.

Then Wish looked across at Justice holding the Enchanted Spoon tight in her hands and . . . the spoon plunged forward with extraordinary strength towards Wish. For some strange reason, Justice's hands were now magnetically attached to it, as if by supernatural glue. Justice was dragged, still holding on to the spoon, off her horse and did a swallow dive into the mud of the forest floor with phenomenal velocity. And boing! Boing! Boing! As the Enchanted Spoon jumped towards its beloved Wish with an attraction that was really quite touching to see, boing, boing, boing, Justice was dragged behind it, her nose and tummy and entire front being slammed into the mud at each bounce. The fork jabbed into her bottom to make her let go, and the key rammed her knuckles, and although it was all rather undignified, I'm afraid I'm not a bit sorry for her.

ROOOOOOOOOOAAW! The bear continued to roar on its hind legs.

The noise woke Xar, who came to, sitting upright abruptly. Bodkin had already scrambled out of the net entangling him and got to his feet.

REOOOOOOOOOAW!! The bear crashed back to the ground on all four legs.

'Get on my back,' said the bear to Wish. And the bear slumped right down on the forest floor on its tummy so that they could climb on to it.

'Quick, quick!' snapped the bear. 'We haven't got much time!'

'Bears can't talk,' said Wish stupidly, because that was the first thing that came into her head.

'I'm not really a bear,' said the bear.

'Of course not,' said Wish. 'How silly of me.'

'But I *am* a friend,' said the bear.

Now, even in a situation as grim and disastrous as this one, I am not recommending that you climb on the back of a bear who is a *total stranger*.

But Caliburn swooped downwards, shrieking, 'The bear is my sister! She's definitely my sister! I'd recognise her anywhere!'

Six months ago, Wish would have found this extremely disconcerting.

But after spending some considerable time in the world of Magic, the idea of Caliburn having a bear for a sister suddenly seemed reasonably normal.

So, shaking with nerves, Wish hauled herself on to the back of the bear, taking hold of her long brown fur as she climbed it like a hillock. The bear generously barely even flinched even though Wish must have been pulling her hair, and Xar and Bodkin climbed up behind her.

'Hold tight,' said the bear, getting to her feet.

'Don't forget the door!' Caliburn reminded Wish.

'Oh! Yes! Quite right – we can't leave the door behind!' said Wish. She turned round, lifted up her eyepatch a smidgeon and focussed on the fragments of the door lying all about the clearing in thousands of tiny little pieces, and they rose, whizzing and humming into the air, delighted that they hadn't been forgotten. There wasn't time to put all the fragments back in the right places, so they just jammed together any old how, forming a very eccentric impression of a door.

And then the bear charged straight at the most fiery part of the forest.

'What is the bear doing? It's going to burn us all to death!' shouted Bodkin, terrified.

'Stay close to the bear, sprites!' said Caliburn, landing on Bodkin's shoulder and gripping so tight with his claws that Bodkin cried out. The sprites landed on the bear and the bear ran right through the flames and they did not burn. 'Illusions . . .' explained the owl, crouched down on the bear's back just in front of Wish. 'Some of these flames are illusions.' Behind the bear ran the snowcats, wolves, and Xar's much smaller, more-normal-sized bear, followed by the Thunderdell giants, who tore up the burning trees on either side and threw them down behind them, and the flames leapt up and the Warriors could not follow.

Queen Sychorax was left, mouth open, unable to stop them. One second the children were there, and in her power. The next they were gone.

5. The Tunnel of Fire

The bear ran through the fire, followed by the Thunderdell giants.

One of the bear's eyes was gleaming with a bright white star of light, and this starlight seemed to be able to see which of the flames were real and which were illusions.

Wish's heart was beating so hard she thought it might jump right out of her chest. *What are we doing, trusting this bear that we've only just met, and where is she taking us?* But somehow she knew she *could* trust this bear, that this was a bear who was on her side, and she held on to the bear's long shaggy fur with all of her might, and although the brown fur might be gleaming just a little spookily with a blue supernatural light, there was a solidity and power in the bear's body beneath her that was comfortingly real as it powered through the forest.

For a couple of terrifying minutes they ran through the inferno, the bear knowing the path to take.

The heat was so strong that the top of Bodkin's helmet started to melt. Fire, fire all around.

And then they were out of the fire and into the quiet forest.

At least we're out of the flames . . . thought Wish slightly hysterically to herself, trying to stay on TOP of the bear, because she wasn't very good at riding things without falling off.

The bear kept running, the Thunderdell giants and Crusher and the now-set-alight door following behind them, the wolves in a crazy pack all around, the snowcats with hair all-on-end with fright.

'This is the place,' said the bear, stopping a moment. The Thunderdell giants halted and with great heaves they pulled up the nearest trees by the roots. Then they turned and carefully put the trees down some distance away, whispering words of thanks to the trees as they did so.

'Oh! The poor trees!' said Wish. 'What are they doing?'

'They're creating a firebreak,' said Caliburn. 'If there's a gap in the forest, the fire won't be able to cross it.'

The Thunderdell giants were joined by more Thunderdells, and more and more and more, and the giants worked together to pull up the trees and make a gap in the forest that the fire could not cross.

Meanwhile Crusher knelt by the fallen trees, laying his hands on them and reassuring them that their sacrifice will have been worth it.

'Man-made fires are never a good idea,' said Crusher, 'but the forest will return, trust me, dear trees . . .'

'As long as that dreadful Sychorax woman doesn't try and plant her fields here,' sniffed the bear disapprovingly.

'Sprite-who-looks-like-a-bright-blue-twig, can you help me?' said the bear to Ariel.

'My name isss Ariel,' hissed Ariel.

'Nice name,' said the bear. 'Sprite-whose-name-is-Ariel, can you carry a flame of the fire for me?'

'Of coursssse,' said Ariel, flying down to a flaming twig lying on the forest floor, and putting a little bit of it in the fire-box he carried around his waist. (Warriors carried tinder-boxes, but Wizards and sprites carried fire-boxes, which had little flames like lighted candles, kept alight by the power of Magic in a tiny box.)

'I'm a fire-collector,' explained the bear, looking over her shoulder at Wish, and Wish thought, *Aren't all fires exactly the same?* But she nodded, as if fire-collecting was a perfectly normal hobby, like collecting books or jewels or money or different coloured spell-bags.

Then the bear looked up at the sky and lightning

flashed from her starlight eye, and there were gigantic rolls of thunder and the lightning criss-crossed and zig-zagged across the sky, and the clouds opened, and the rain poured down on the forest fire. The flaming Enchanted Door following them was instantly quenched by the water with a damp protesting hiss.

'Weather spelling . . . ' said Xar, impressed, for controlling the weather was very advanced Magic indeed, and even his own father, the great King Wizard Encanzo, had trouble with it.

'The rain and the firebreak will stop the fire from spreading,' said the bear.

They left the Thunderdell giants tending to the firebreak and making sure the fire did not leap across it.

The bear and the animals and Crusher ran on, leaving the fire behind, and the rain ran into Wish's eyes so that she could barely see. Eventually the animals came to a part of the forest where the ancient yews had grown so gnarled and bulging over the last three thousand years or so that they seemed to have faces, and their roots had twisted and turned into things that looked like feet, and the sprites had their wands out, for when you are in the presence of the Old Magic it makes you feel just . . . a little bit . . . *uneasy*.

A mist had descended, and the night was full of noises, of will-o'-the-wisps whooping out of nowhere and coo-ing '*Come this way*' in a spooky kind of way, and although even a five-year-old knows not to follow a will-o'-the-wisp however longingly they may coo (wisps are harmless, until you follow them, and then they can lead you to Very Dangerous Things indeed) it is still a little unnerving.

'Oh dear, I think we may be lost!' said the bear, not sounding unhappy at all, but if anything, really rather delighted. The strange blue light that had lit up the bear's fur as they ran through the fire, and had made it seem like she was from another world, had dimmed, along with the white light of her eye, and she was now just an ordinary (if unfeasibly large) wet brown bear. 'Does anyone know the way?'

'You're supposed to be taking US somewhere!' Bodkin pointed out. 'Caliburn said you had some sort of house?'

'We're definitely somewhere near the Lake of the Lost,' said Caliburn with a shiver.

'Oh good,' said the bear, 'because as it happens, I'm looking for a large mound which is currently situated somewhere near the Lake of the Lost. A mound with a great chalk horse drawn on the side of it . . . I think it's a horse, or it could be a dragon, I'm never quite sure. Keep your eyes peeled, everyone.'

On they searched, through territory where the trees

seemed to be getting older and older, until eventually they came upon the large mound the bear had described, or rather the mound seemed to come upon *them*, for it rose suddenly and enormously out of the mist like a gigantic creature creeping up on them.

The mound was as round as a wheel and as big as a hill. It was far too large to be man-made, but also far too perfectly circular to be a natural formation, so it was a contradiction of itself even at first sight. A colossal leaping animal was drawn on one side of it, just to their right, made out of paths of chalk

Pook's Hill

in the grass. They were
too close up to see whether
or not the tremendous chalk picture
looked more like a horse or a dragon.

By now everyone was as
thoroughly drenched as if they had
been swimming in the ocean. Wish was

wet through and starting to shiver, and dying to get to anywhere that might offer some warmth and food and protection from the rain.

'What is this? We can't shelter here. It seems to be just a hill without any trees on it!' objected Xar.

'That's why we go INSIDE the hill,' said the bear. 'The main entrance is around the other side, but we can get in here too. I just have to remember the password to let us in . . .'

But the bear had unfortunately forgotten the password that would let them into the hill. She tried all sorts of words: 'Magic . . . Tuesday . . . Arctic . . . tangerine . . . honeydew . . .' Loads and loads of lovely words, but none of them seemed to be the right ones.

'I don't know WHY they keep on changing the password!' said the bear irritably.

'You're the one who *sets* the password!' the little owl reminded her.

'Well I don't know why I keep on changing it!' said the bear. 'But how silly of me! We can use the door . . . whose door is this?'

They had all forgotten about the Enchanted Door that was following them, but they now turned round and took a good look at it.

The door was looking thoroughly dejected. It was burnt through, still steaming and bursting into the odd flame, and jumbled up in all the wrong places.

'It's mine,' admitted Wish.

'You're not a very considerate door owner,' said the little owl severely. 'This door needs some serious love and attention. But still . . . use the door to let us in.'

'But I don't know how to do that,' said Wish.

'What on earth are you carrying a door around with you for then?' asked the owl, fixing Wish with its beady eye.

'We've been flying on the back of it,' said Wish, and even to her own ears this sounded a little ridiculous.

The owl tut-tutted like anything.

'*Rugs* are for flying on, *carpets* are for flying on, *doors* are for opening and shutting . . .' snapped the owl. 'Who is in charge of the education of this child?'

'I am,' admitted Caliburn. 'But I haven't had very long to teach her, and—'

'Well, *I* think,' said the bear thoughtfully, 'that a flying door is a wonderfully *creative* idea. What is your name, wonderful child?'

Wish wasn't feeling very wonderful, all dripping wet sitting on the back of the bear, but nonetheless she replied shyly, 'Wish.'

WATCH me, Spoon! Watch me deal with this unlocking emergency!

'You see, a wonderful name for a wonderful child,' said the bear encouragingly. 'What you should do now, Wish, is THINK the door on to the side of the mound. Imagine it is happening with the whole of your mind . . .'

'Maybe put your eyepatch up just a smidgeon,' Caliburn whispered in her ear.

Wish put her eyepatch up a smidgeon and imagined the door fitting on to the side of the mound, and the door obligingly shuffled across to the hill and shrugged itself dejectedly into the side of it, dripping with water.

'Brilliant!' said the bear admiringly.

'It's not brilliant, it's very basic telekinesis,' humphed the grumpy little owl. 'I presume you have a key?'

'She does indeed!' whooped the key, hopping delightedly out of Wish's hair and down to the ground, and plugging itself into the keyhole.

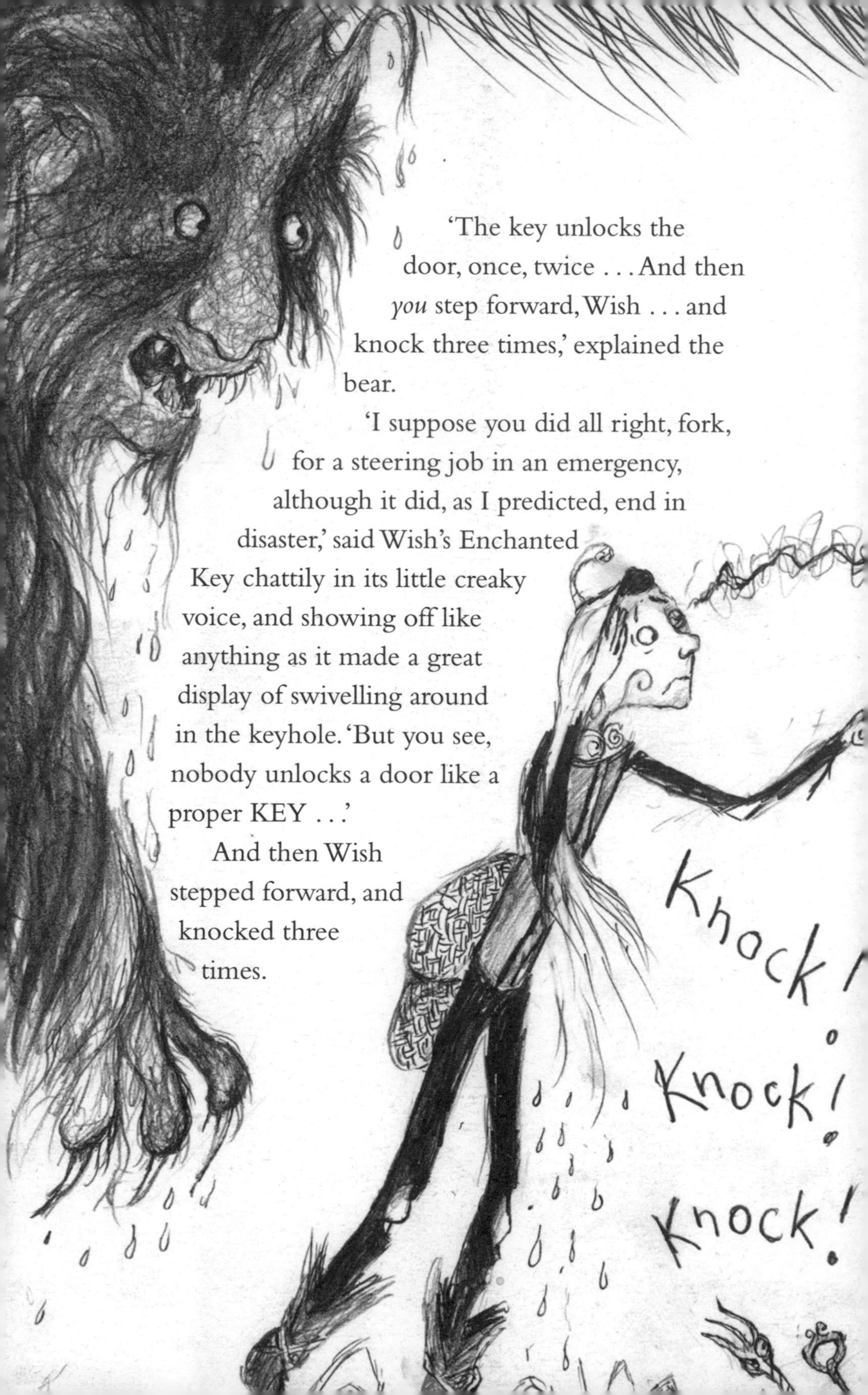

'The key unlocks the door, once, twice . . . And then *you* step forward, Wish . . . and knock three times,' explained the bear.

'I suppose you did all right, fork, for a steering job in an emergency, although it did, as I predicted, end in disaster,' said Wish's Enchanted Key chattily in its little creaky voice, and showing off like anything as it made a great display of swivelling around in the keyhole. 'But you see, nobody unlocks a door like a proper KEY . . .'

And then Wish stepped forward, and knocked three times.

Knock!

Knock!

Knock!

THE
PUNISHMENT
CUPBOARD
Magic
is
BANNED

WELCOME
to
the Learning Place
for
SPECTACULARLY
Gifted
Wizards

RAT!

TAT!

TAT!

And slowly, slowly, the poor battered door opened –

C-R-E-A-K!

– to reveal, behind it, wonder of wonders, a great open hall – or was it a gigantic corridor? To the left and right of them it carried on without stopping, until it curved away, and you could not see the end of it.

The hall was lit with candles and there was a much larger open door on the other side. Through that door they could hear a faint whispering of welcoming sprites and in the distance the sound of chattering voices, the howl of wolves and the clunk of giants' boots, all warm and cosy and homey as anything.

'That's impossible!' breathed Bodkin with an open mouth. 'That was a hill . . . a solid hillside! How can the door make a doorway suddenly appear into some kind of *hall*?'

The door felt like it had always been there, cut into the mound. One side, the rain, the forest. Step over the threshold and on the other side, the warmth of the hall.

'I'm so confused,' said Bodkin. 'Is this a house, or is this a hill? Where are we?'

'Humph,' said the little owl. 'Have you never seen Magic performed before, child?'

The hall appeared to be made out of gigantic stones, all fitting together perfectly, and any cracks between them made watertight with burnt soil. Wish had seen buildings similar in places of worship, or passage tombs, but nothing of this extraordinary size before. Many of the stones were covered in deep patterns cut into the rock – diamond shapes, swirls and, more interestingly, suns drawn in many different types of ways, crescent moons, whole moons, slivers of moons, and long wavy lines that looked like winding rivers but which Wish knew were in fact calendars, ways of telling the time. Wish's heart lifted with excitement. Wherever they were must be a very important place indeed.

They all stepped over the threshold and into the hall. (When I say ALL, of course I mean the children, Caliburn, the sprites, Lonesome and the wolves and the snowcats – the bear and Crusher were too big to fit through the door.)

'Make the door bigger so that we can all come through,' the little owl ordered Wish.

'I really can't do that,' said Wish. 'I've learnt about telekinesis, but I haven't done making things bigger.'

'Tut tut!' said the owl. 'Here's a child who really needs to work on her positive thinking. Just because you've never done something before doesn't mean it can't be done. All you have to do is—'

But the owl didn't need to explain.

On the other side of the door the bear had *finally* remembered the password.

'Oh! Don't worry! I've remembered the password now!' said the bear. 'It's my mother's maiden name! ARDEN!!!'

As soon as the bear spoke the word ARDEN there was a loud

BOOOOOM!

And the entire side of the hill exploded, leaving an enormous gap for Crusher and the bear to get through.

Coughing and spluttering, Crusher and the bear stepped through into the hall beside the children, both of them so covered with chalk dust that they looked like they had been caught out in a sudden snowstorm.

'There!' said the bear with satisfaction, showering them all with chalk dust as she gave herself a good old shake. 'I knew I'd remember the password in the end! But we mustn't get distracted . . . We need to get you to the study area as soon as we can before the house piskies detect us!'

'Pisssskiesssss???' hissed the sprites in horror. 'There are *piskies* in this house? We's HATE piskies.' They drew all their weapons and hissed with fury, because sprites do indeed absolutely *loathe* piskies for reasons that everyone has forgotten because they go way back in fairy lore, but the hatred still shines as bright as if whatever-the-original-crime-was had happened only yesterday.

'Yes, of course there are piskies,' snapped the owl. 'All the best houses are infested with piskies. They're a pain in the neck, but put away your weapons, sprites! I will have no fighting in our house, and the first one who casts a spell will be thrown out into the rain.'

Grumbling, the sprites put their sharpened thorns and bows and arrows away.

'Remember,' said the owl, 'we may have rescued you, but YOU ARE NOT STAYING HERE. This is just an overnight visit and I think that it would be best if we kept it a secret between ourselves, and piskies absolutely cannot keep a secret, so everyone needs to be as quiet as possible until we reach the safety of the study. Close the door, Wish! And bring it with us!'

Wish closed the door with her mind and – Cre-e-

e-eak! – the door closed, shutting out the view into the raining forest. And when the door detached itself from the inside wall of the hill, there was nothing to say that a door had ever been there.

'*How are you doing that?*' said Bodkin, and even Xar was impressed.

Meanwhile the bear said the password backwards: 'NEDRA!' and the entire side of the hill jammed itself back into the gap with another BOOOOOM! that made the whole mound shake and covered them all in yet another shower of chalk dust.

'*Messy*,' said the owl reprovingly.

'Sorry,' said the bear apologetically, wiping her nose with her paw and getting it all chalky.

'Come along! Come along!' said the owl, spitting chalk dust out of its beak and shooing the dripping party through the hall, and they tiptoed across the flagstones, leaving great puddles of watery footsteps. 'As quiet as you can . . .'

It was too late. The sound of the bear's entrance had already attracted the piskies' attention. There was a hissssss of excitement and a glowing band of bright warm piskies burst into the hall just as they were crossing it . . .

'*Piskies!*' hissed Xar's sprites in horror.

Now, piskies look quite a lot like sprites, but woe

betide you if you confuse the two, for they get very offended if you do. They are a bit like hairy fairies who have never grown up, but furrier and fuzzier, with weird exploding hairstyles that the sprites think they only grow that way to show off. They tend to be brown when they are inside, but as soon as they are outside they can turn any colour they want, for piskies are chameleons. They are very small and a lot of them were riding on the backs of wasps, which they keep as pets.

'Hello! Hello! Hello! Welcome, welcome, welcome!' The piskies beamed, buzzing around the visitors in great warm swarms. 'What have we here? New people?'

'Nothing to see here, piskies!' said the little owl. 'Nobody's staying! Just some hospital cases that we rescued from the fire. They're not staying long because there's an awful lot of them. They'll just be here for ONE DAY while we treat their door and feed them up. Don't tell anyone, piskies! SHOO!'

'We won't tell we won't tell . . .' buzzed the piskies. 'One bear one giant three drowned humans three wolves three snowcats eight USELESS sprites . . . one peregrine falcon and a Baby . . . all very WET . . . But we won't tell we won't tell . . . we won't tell NO ONE, will we, piskies?' replied the piskies, delighted to get a reaction from the sprites, who were hissing with annoyance.

'NONO*NO*!' sang the piskies, answering themselves

as some of their party buzzed off to tell everyone. 'We won't tell we won't tell, your secret's safe with US . . .'

The owl shooed them all through the hall, and instead of the door on the other side leading into another room, it led into a courtyard which was more like an enormous clearing where many, many trees were growing. The clearing was too large to see the other side, and it was ringed with the grassy hill, which on the inside appeared to be supported by more sacred rocks, carved again with spirals and diamonds and waves.

'Wow,' said Wish admiringly, looking up at the sky. 'How does that work? The mound looks like a normal hill on the outside, but inside it has a hollow centre.'

'Magical spaces work very differently from normal spaces,' said Caliburn.

They certainly did.

What appeared to be a normal-sized hillside on the outside was a far bigger space on the inside. This clearing was HUGE, and smoke coming out of all the trees from firesides deep underground meant that many, many chambers and great halls for all the habitations must be hollowed out in the tree roots. It was just as Wish and Bodkin had seen once before when they visited Xar's

Wizard fort on the edge of the Badwoods. There were the shadowy shapes of giants in the distance among the trees, the lights of sprites, and the outlines of crowds of chattering Wizards.

'Keep in the shadows!' ordered the little owl. 'We're nearly there! No one needs to know we're here . . .'

Tell that to the piskies, gathering in greater and greater numbers, who had now organised an entire flying band of musical instruments to follow them as well (for piskies love music and dancing) – fiddles and drums and flute-type thingummies playing themselves to a tune that went something like this:

'It's sweet to go travelling . . . in lakes and forests and on foam . . . butits*so*muchsweeter . . . yesits*so*muchsweeter . . . tocomeHOME!'

'Nobody's HOME!' said the owl. 'This is just a flying visit, FOR ONE NIGHT ONLY . . . *THESE PEOPLE ARE NOT BEING ADMITTED PERMANENTLY!*'

'Here they are!' sang the fiddles.

'LOOK OVER HERE!' boomed the drums.

'Welcome, welcome, secret visitors!' trilled the flute-type thingummies . . .

'Onebearonegiantthreedrownedhumans . . . threewolvesthreesnowcats . . . NINEuselesssprites*one*peregrinefalconandaBaby . . . *WELCOME ALL!*' sang the piskies.

'Oh for goodness' sake,' said the owl.

'You're HOME, you're HOME, welcome to your HOME!' sang everyone all together at full blast. 'Your Magical, marv-e-llous, magnifi-cent . . . new HO-O-O-OME!!!!'

'For absolutely the last time!' spluttered the owl. 'This is NOT THESE PEOPLE'S NEW HOME! There's absolutely loads of them, we haven't got room and so whoever they are, they're just passing through.'

'I told you your sister wouldn't want us,' whispered Wish sadly to Caliburn. 'It's just like I said . . . we're a bit odd, and we don't really fit in anywhere . . .'

'No, no,' Caliburn whispered back, 'I'm sure she wants us really . . . It's just that this owl of hers needs a little time to get used to us.'

'Thank goodness!' said the bear in relief. 'We've reached my study! Or as some people call it, the Lair of the Bear.'

The Lair of the Bear, or the study, was a great oak liberally festooned with countless balls of mistletoe. They managed to get there with Xar's sprites only getting into *one* wrestling match with the piskies, and Squeezjoos only biting off *one* shoe of a piskie who was trying to pick Xar's pocket, and it was in the nick of time, for the utter commotion was beginning to draw the attention of the other inhabitants of the hillside.

'Now . . . what was the password again?' the bear wondered to herself, coming to a gentle lumbering halt and accidentally sitting on a snowcat, who let out a protesting howl. 'Sorry . . .' said the bear, hurriedly getting to her feet.

'ARDEN! The password is ARDEN!' shrieked the little owl.

And as the owl spoke, the roots of the oak rustled and moved to reveal a hollow space. The roots took in the size of the various bears and snowcats, and moved wider, wider, revealing an enormous hollow that led on to a gigantic winding staircase down into the Lair of the Bear,

'Down into the tree!' ordered the little owl, all of a fluster, sending a couple of piskies scattering away with one urgent sweep of its claw, and everyone apart from Crusher went down the winding staircase. 'Wait here,' the owl said to Crusher, 'and inform anyone who asks that We Are Not to be Disturbed and It is None of Their Business . . .'

'NEDRA!' snapped the owl, and the tree roots shuffled and closed, and the little party were now in the Lair of the Bear.

This way to the Lair of the Bear →

6. In the Lair of the Bear

The Lair of the Bear was exceptionally messy. There was a fire in the centre of it and there were books everywhere, on bookcases that were higgledy-piggledy and wandered all over the place with the tree roots. Then there were birds perching on the books, and the visitors had to be careful not to step on the droppings, and not to knock over smaller fires with little cauldrons on them everywhere you looked.

Even as they came in, one of the cauldrons was boiling over. Great violet-coloured smoke bubbles came out of it and landed on some papers on the floor, that promptly burst into the flames. The bear broke into a gentle run and extinguished the flames by sitting on them. Hsss.

'Whoops,' said the bear guiltily. 'I forgot I left that on.'

'Wow!' said Wish, looking around the room. The birds whirled into the air, trilling and clucking and twittering, then flew off to fetch blankets, holding them by the edges in their beaks, and draping them round the shivering children, and the wolves and the snowcats. 'What a wonderful room! And thank you so much for saving us in the forest back there. I cannot tell you how grateful we are . . .'

'Hmmm,' said the bear. 'One of them has manners,

at least. That's a start.'

Getting to her feet, the bear continued. 'Before we go any further, can I just say, brother, what a joy it is to see you again! What an unexpected, accidental, magnificent DELIGHT!'

The bear hugged the raven.

And the bear and the raven began to dance, which was very sweet really, and although it was fine for the raven to dance in the air, the bear was too big for all the mess in the room. As she whirled around in galumphing circles, her bottom knocked over piles of books and her nose knocked over cauldrons, and snowcats had to scatter out of the way, and everyone had to pick everything up as it fell over.

'Will someone please tell me what is going on?' asked Bodkin, speaking for everyone. 'Where are we? And why is your sister a bear?'

Caliburn the raven landed on the bear's head.

'This bear is not only my sister, she is my twin,' said Caliburn proudly. 'Meet Perdita.'

There was a big silence.

'Okay . . .' said Bodkin, looking to Xar for guidance. 'This is weird.'

'Don't look at me,' said Xar, shrugging his shoulders. 'I'm a Wizard, but even for the Wizarding world, this is weird.'

Wish blinked. She looked from the bear to the bird. 'For twins, you really are not very alike,' said Wish eventually.

'Yes, I think I did mention that I wasn't really a bear, didn't I?' explained the bear. 'It's just a transformation. You see? Watch while I transform back again. Transformation is one of my favourites of the Wizarding skills.'

And in front of Wish's eyes, the bear transformed. It was a spectacular moment.

One moment the bear was a great, magnificent bear-like beast. The next, the outline of the bear melted and shrivelled and became, smaller, smaller . . . until it turned into a small, very untidy-looking woman of goodness-knows-WHAT-age, rather eccentrically dressed, but with very smiley eyes.

'You're still not very alike,' said Bodkin, looking from one to the other and shaking his head. 'One of you is small and black and feathery. And the other one is a human. Not much of a family resemblance, I'd say . . .'

'*You* transform back into a human now, brother,' urged Perdita, looking up at Caliburn, who was still sitting on her head.

The raven tipped his head down and looked sadly into her eyes. 'Unfortunately, I can't,' said Caliburn. 'At the moment this is a sort of temporarily permanent transformation, for this lifetime, at least.'

'Oh, I'm so sorry,' said Perdita.

'It could have been worse,' said Caliburn gloomily.

'I could have been a cockroach.'

Perdita (Caliburn's sister)

'That is so true,' said Perdita. 'It is always important to look on the bright side . . . And, brother, even in bird form, it's so wonderful to see you again!' Perdita held out her arms and danced, as Caliburn took flight and fluttered in and out of them.

'Oh sister, me too!' said Caliburn joyfully.

'The question is, though,' said Perdita, stopping dancing and coming to a halt again. 'Who on earth are all these people and animals and Magical creatures travelling with you?'

'Well, the humans are Xar, Bodkin, and Wish,' explained Caliburn. 'The sprites are Tiffinstorm, Timeloss, Mustardthought, Hinkypunk, Ariel, Bumbleboozle, Squeezjoos, Once-sprite, The Baby. The snowcats are Nighteye, Kingcat, Forestheart. Lonesome is the werewolf. And then there're the wolves, peregrine falcon, bears who don't like to be named because they prefer to be wild—'

'Most understandable,' said Perdita, nodding her head.

'And finally,' finished Caliburn, 'last but of course not least, the giant upstairs is Crusher.'

'This little owl here is Hoola . . .' said Perdita. Hoola, now perched on Perdita's shoulder, gave them a stiff little bow and ruffled her feathers at them. 'And it's marvellous to meet you all . . . Any friends of my brother's are friends of mine . . . but what, for mistletoe's sake, are you doing in this sacred part of the forest? And why were you being chased by that appalling Queen Sychorax, who has clearly now taken total leave of her senses

Hoola the huffy little owl

by setting fire to our beautiful wildwoods?'

'Ah yes,' said Caliburn, looking very shifty indeed. 'We have a few little problems that we were hoping you were going to help us with, Perdita . . . You remember the tears of the Drood that you gave me twenty years ago? I was hoping you might give me a few more . . .'

'Whaaaatttt??' cried Perdita. And then she looked wildly around the room, leaned forward and hissed. 'Sssshhhhhhhhhhh! What if the piskies were to hear? We're right next door to the Lake of the Lost here. If the Droods were ever to find out that I had got hold of any of their tears I would not only be out of my job but they would absolutely KILL me! They're awfully touchy about their tears.'

'Yes, I know,' said Caliburn, gloomily. 'The Droods found out I'd been using their tears in a spell when I was the Wizard Pentaglion, and that's why they turned me into a raven.'

'The Droods found out you had their tears?' gasped Perdita. 'Oh my goodness, brother, you really *are* lucky that you didn't end up as a cockroach!'

'So if you DO happen to have any more of the Droods' tears, Perdita, somewhere in this study of yours,' said Caliburn in a wheedling sort of voice, 'you'd be much better off giving them to US . . . We can take them off your hands . . .'

'I may still have a few left – I need them for some of my trickier spelling – but I absolutely can't put a dangerous ingredient like Droods' tears into your hands again,' sniffed Perdita. 'I'm already regretting giving them to you *once* . . . I'm certainly not going to make the same mistake *twice*.'

'I thought you might say that,' said Caliburn, sadly. 'And what about the scales of a Nuckalavee? Do you happen to have any of those?'

'*The scales of a Nuckalavee????*' gasped Perdita, even more horrified than she had been when Caliburn talked about Droods' tears. 'No, I don't have any scales of a Nuckalavee, brother! Worse and worse . . . Nuckalavee scales are deeply powerful Magic and only a MAD PERSON would go on a quest to get the scales of a Nuckalavee! It's almost certain death . . . What on earth have you got yourselves into? Why do you need these terrible ingredients anyway?'

'We're trying to make a spell to get rid of Witches,' explained Caliburn.

'There is *no* spell strong enough to get rid of Witches,' said Perdita.

'We think we've found one,' said Caliburn. 'If you can't *give* the Droods' tears to us, will you let us stay here and train ourselves up so we can go on a quest to get them ourselves?'

'Hang on a second,' said Xar suspiciously. 'What do you mean, "train us up"? What is this place, anyway?'

'This is Pook's Hill, the Learning Place for Spectacularly Gifted Wizards,' said Perdita.

'A learning place is just a fancy name for a *school*!!!!' said Xar in horror. He punched the air in panic. 'I've been tricked! Let me out of here! I HATE SCHOOLS! THEY SHOULD BE BANNED! *DOWN WITH SCHOOLS*!!!!!'

'Don't worry,' said Hoola firmly. 'We will let you out of Pook's Hill with pleasure. There's no question of you staying. I am in charge of admissions, and you do not fill any of the admission criteria. You are *not* spectacularly gifted Wizards. The Wish-girl had trouble with anything more complicated than the most basic of telekinesis. And the Xar-boy looks completely out of control.'

'Yes but we're not really a learning place *only* for spectacularly gifted Wizards, are we, Hoola?' said Perdita persuasively. 'You just keep calling it that.'

'It means we get sent more children,' explained Hoola. 'Every parent seems to think they have a spectacularly gifted offspring, even though it's completely obvious that not *everyone's* offspring can be spectacularly gifted.'

'ALL children are spectacularly gifted and learning should be for everyone!' said Perdita enthusiastically.

'But the second boy is an actual *Warrior*!' objected Hoola. 'You have to draw the line somewhere!'

'The boy's ancestors are not the boy's fault,' said Perdita. 'And he will have gifts – we just have to find them. I love a challenge . . .'

'I'm so glad you said that,' said Caliburn, for he had been wondering how he was going to introduce the *exact* nature of Xar and Wish's spectacular gifts. 'Because the girl and the boy here are more gifted than they may look. Underneath her eyepatch, Wish, for instance, has a Magic eye . . .'

Even Hoola was impressed by that, and let out a HOOO! of admiration. Magic eyes were very rare indeed. Only one or two Wizards every generation have a Magic eye.

'I can't take my eyepatch off,' explained Wish, 'because the eye goes a bit crazy when I do.'

'Don't worry,' said Perdita. 'I can see through eyepatches.'

Perdita knelt down in front of Wish. Wish tried to look at the kindly face in front of her, even though it made her eyes water to do so.

Powerful Wizards are always hard to look at, and Perdita was a good deal more powerful than most. So her face was constantly changing, the outline blurring and moving and hazing, like smoke coming off the sea, and sometimes it looked like she had a lot of wrinkles wandering over her face like the lines on an old map, and sometimes it looked like she was only a little older than Wish herself.

Only Perdita's eyes stayed steady, so Wish concentrated on those, and it was a moment before Wish realised that the eyes that twinkled at her were ever so slightly different colours . . . and as Wish carried on staring at the left eye, little spots began to appear on it, like raindrops landing on a lake, and slowly the eye changed to a colour that Wish had never seen before, apart from in her own eye when she was looking in a mirror . . .

'Oh!' said Wish in delight. '*You* have a Magic eye too! But I would never have even noticed if you hadn't pointed it out to me . . .'

'That's because it's under control,' said Perdita, and swiftly the eye changed colour again, back to something more ordinary.

And then Perdita stiffened. All the joyful kind delight at recognising one of her own kind went out of her face in a blink.

And it was because the Enchanted Spoon had hopped up out of Wish's hair to say hello.

Now that they weren't in the hurry and scurry of running away, Perdita could get a good look at that spoon and, up close, it was quite clear that it was made of iron.

Perdita turned absolutely white. And then she straightened, and for one second she stood before them as a bear again, roaring, before turning once more into a human. A very grim-looking human. Even her eyes had stopped twinkling.

'She has Magic-that-works-on-iron . . .' whispered Perdita.

Turning to Caliburn she said, 'Oh brother, what is going on here, and brother, what have you done?'

7. Are They IN the Learning Place for Spectacularly Gifted Wizards or Are They NOT?

Caliburn had to give quite a *long* explanation about what was going on, about Sychorax and Encanzo being in love once long ago, and the Spell of Love Denied and everything – I won't go into it all again, because you, dear reader, know it already.

Perdita was furious. 'You mean that's what you wanted my Droods' tears for???'

'Yes, but I'd looked into the future, you see, and I saw that a curse would fall on the wildwoods and disaster and calamity would follow if I didn't stop the love from happening . . .' explained Caliburn.

'The curse fell on the wildwoods anyway!' stormed Perdita. 'And I think what we have here is disaster and calamity in spades. When will you ever learn, Caliburn, to be very, very careful about looking into the future? It can so easily end in tears, and you can't change it anyway!'

'I know, I know,' said Caliburn, hanging his head. 'I really have learnt my lesson this time . . .'

However, Caliburn ended, rather craftily he felt, with: '. . . but the children's ancestors are not the children's fault, and you have to admit the girl's enchanted objects are *charming* . . .'

Realising that it was its moment, the Enchanted Spoon gave a happy little somersault on Wish's head, and the fork and the key came hopping out enthusiastically, followed by the pins, and they put on a lively little gymnastic display, trying to look cute in order to win over Perdita. The little owl, Hoola, put a wing to her forehead and groaned.

'They're delightful, you see!' said Caliburn. 'Very well-intentioned little enchanted objects . . . reflecting the character of the girl . . .'

'*But they're made out of iron*!' objected Perdita. '*Everyone's* going to be after that kind of Magic! The emperor of Warriors, Sychorax, the Droods and, oh my goodness . . . the KINGWITCH . . .'

'And . . . *hang on a second*.' Hoola's head swivelled round three hundred and sixty degrees, in that disconcerting way that owls are so fond of, to get a good look at Xar. 'We've heard about the *girl*'s disastrous, dangerous gift . . . what's wrong with the *boy*?'

'I beg your pardon?' said Caliburn innocently.

'You heard,' said Hoola. 'What's wrong with *him*? You said he had some sort of gift too . . .'

'The boy just had this *teeny* accident with a Witchstain . . .' said Caliburn, and again, he went into a long, complicated explanation about what had happened, trying to play it all down, but ending with,

'He is, admittedly, finding it a little difficult to control . . .'

'That's not true!' objected Xar. 'I have it perfectly under control!'

Xar took his glove off to show Perdita how brilliantly he could control the Witchstain, and a green bolt of lightning shot randomly off it and incinerated her chair. Hurriedly, Xar put his glove back on again.

There was a horrified silence.

'Maybe not *perfectly*,' admitted Xar.

'The spell that gets rid of Witches will get rid of Xar's Witchstain as well, though,' explained Wish.

'If it really is a true spell,' said Hoola. 'It could be just make-believe . . . Wish wants so much to find a cure for Witches that she has made up this spell of yours.'

'However the spell was written with MY feather,' said Caliburn. 'So it might be a memory of a spell written by MYSELF in a former life, when I was the great Wizard Pentaglion.'

Perdita was impressed. 'Yes,' admitted Perdita, 'that does mean the spell is worth a closer look.'

'Spelling Book!' commanded Wish, putting up her eyepatch a little. The Spelling Book jumped out of Wish's pocket and eagerly turned its own pages to the spell to get rid of Witches.

Perdita snapped her fingers. The desk that she had sent flying with her bottom when she was a bear was currently upended, the top against one of the walls, legs stretched out stiffly in the air. The little wooden desk legs softened and waggled as the desk struggled to turn itself upright. With a final heave the desk tipped itself the right way up, all four legs landing on the floor, and then it scuttled sideways like a crab towards Perdita, coming to a halt in front of her. Everyone had to duck as papers, feather pens, books and boxes flew through the air and landed higgledy-piggledy all over the desk. A chair scuttled into place just in time to catch Perdita as she sat down.

Perdita knocked once, twice, thrice on the top of one of the boxes sitting on the desk. The box opened, and five pairs of eyeglasses waved their legs in the air and grappled with each other in a tangled and untidy mess.

'Oh!' exclaimed Wish in delight, 'living spectacles!'

The spoon, the key, the fork and the pins hopped

forward curiously, unsure of what to make of these new enchanted cousins. None of them had ever met anyone else who had enchanted objects before, so this was a fresh and fascinating experience.

The spectacles were horrified at this attention, firmly snapping down the lid of their box.

'They're a bit shy,' warned Perdita, and in response to a quiet word from Wish, the spoon and its companions retreated back into Wish's pockets and hair so as not to alarm the eyeglasses further.

Slo-o-owly the box opened and the eyeglasses blinked through the crack of the lid, like the huge bug eyes of jungle creatures that had just woken up.

Blink, blink.

Wish held her breath with the effort of trying not to laugh.

Gra-a-adually the eyeglasses climbed over the edge of the box like cautious spiders. Haltingly, they stalked gently forward on their long unsteady limbs, still clearly a bit sleepy, and circled in front of Perdita with tentative daddy-long-legs strides so that she could choose one of them to look through.

'Choose the one with the limp,' whispered Wish. She had already decided that her favourite was a pair of glasses that had clearly been through a difficult time, and had one smashed glass and a stem that had been broken and mended again several times.

'Yes, I love that pair,' said Perdita, 'but this time I think I'll go for . . . the rose-coloured ones.'

'Oh nooooooooo . . .' said Hoola, furiously putting her wings in front of her eyes. 'Mistress! Not the ROSE-COLOURED ones! When will you ever learn?'

But the four other pairs of spectacles scrambled back into the box, clearly delighted to be able to go back to sleep, and the pair with the pink glass and twig-like stems stalked up Perdita's untidy clothes on to her face and settled themselves on her nose.

'Let me see now . . .' said Perdita, adjusting them more firmly and opening up the Spelling Book.

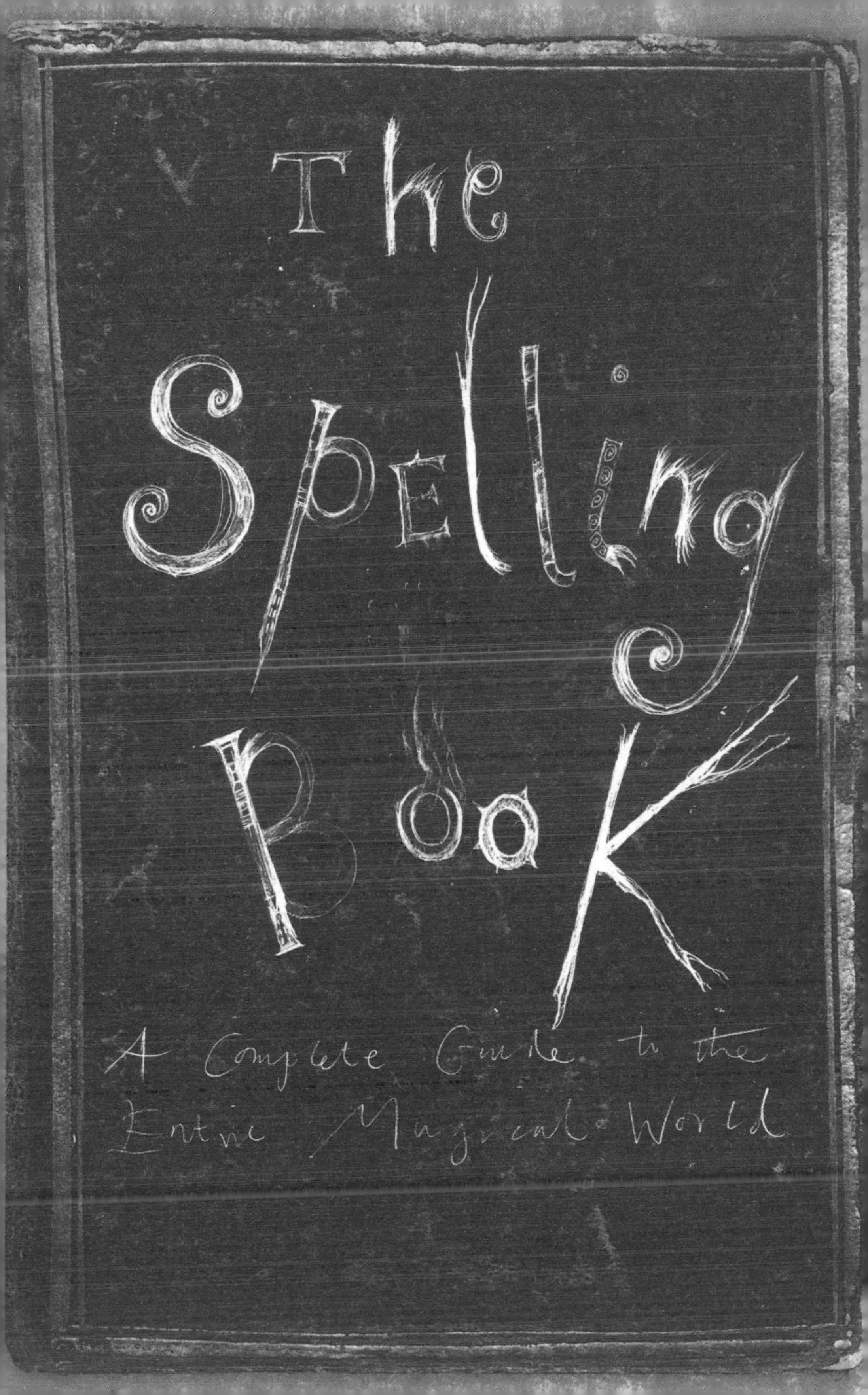
The Spelling Book
A Complete Guide to the
Entire Magical World

THE SPELLING BOOK

Invisibility

Wish making
her own hand
invisible with her
Magic eye

Invisibility is a Magical power to be used with caution, because if you stay invisible too long, it can start to affect your mind in dangerous and unpredictable ways. Here, Wish is using her Magic eye to turn her own hand invisible.

page 4,310,690

Fire-Collecting

For Perdita, fire represents a source of light and wisdom. The fire that she burns in the grate at Pook's hill, (or in her own fire-box, if she has to travel), is part of a fire that has been burning for many, many years, back into deep and distant time, and therefore she must never let it go out.

The Spelling Book

Dragons

Dragons had long ago retreated to the freezing cold of the northern polar regions, but ever since the end of the Ice Age, they had been moving south, and many dragons were now making their homes in the jungles of the wildwoods.

Page 2,130,134

The Spelling Book

Fluffbuttles

Fluffbuttles have a slight problem with CAMOUFLAGE...

Fluffbuttles are creatures whose innocence and lack of defence methods puts them in peril in the dangerous wildwoods. This is not helped by the fact that they have a large and distinctive target mark on the end of their fluffy tails. Werefoxes are their main predators.

happy little Fluffbuttles bouncing through the grasses

A Spell to Get Rid of WITCHES

Ingredients:

1. Giant's Last Breath from Castle Death.
2. Feathers from a Witch
3. Tears from a Frozen Queen.
4. Scales of the Nuckalavee
5. Tears of the Drood from the Lake of the Lost.

'Yes, this is clearly one of our real Wizard spells and it's an exceptionally powerful lovespell.'

'I knew it!' said Caliburn in delight.

'There are five ingredients,' continued Perdita, 'and the number five is very important in Wizard beliefs because there are five elements: air, fire, water, earth and aether. There are five seasons: spring, summer, autumn, winter and eternity. And there are five directions: north, south, west, east and centre.'

'Why would a lovespell work to get rid of Witches?' asked Xar.

'Because Witches are the opposite of love, so love may be the only thing that will work against them,' said Perdita. 'The five ingredients here are all the ingredients you need for a long and lasting love. Giant's Last Breath is forgiveness. Feathers from a Witch is desire. Tears from a Frozen Queen is tenderness. Scales of a Nuckalavee is courage. And Tears of the Drood from the Lake of the Lost is endurance.'

'The good news is that we already have the first three ingredients . . .' said Caliburn.

'And the bad news,' said Hoola, determined to look on the gloomy side, 'is that the last two ingredients are impossible to get.'

'But you can help us, Perdita, because you're the best . . .' Caliburn reminded her, landing on her shoulder and nibbling on her ear.

It appeared that Perdita had a tiny flaw.

'No, mistress, no! Don't fall for it!' begged Hoola. 'Don't let your brother sweet-talk you again!'

But a small smile had already appeared on Perdita's face, and her eyes behind the rose-coloured glasses began to twinkle. 'I AM the best,' admitted Perdita.

'You're the best! You're the best! You're just the most marvellous, magnificent best!' said Caliburn. 'And see how you love an impossible quest!'

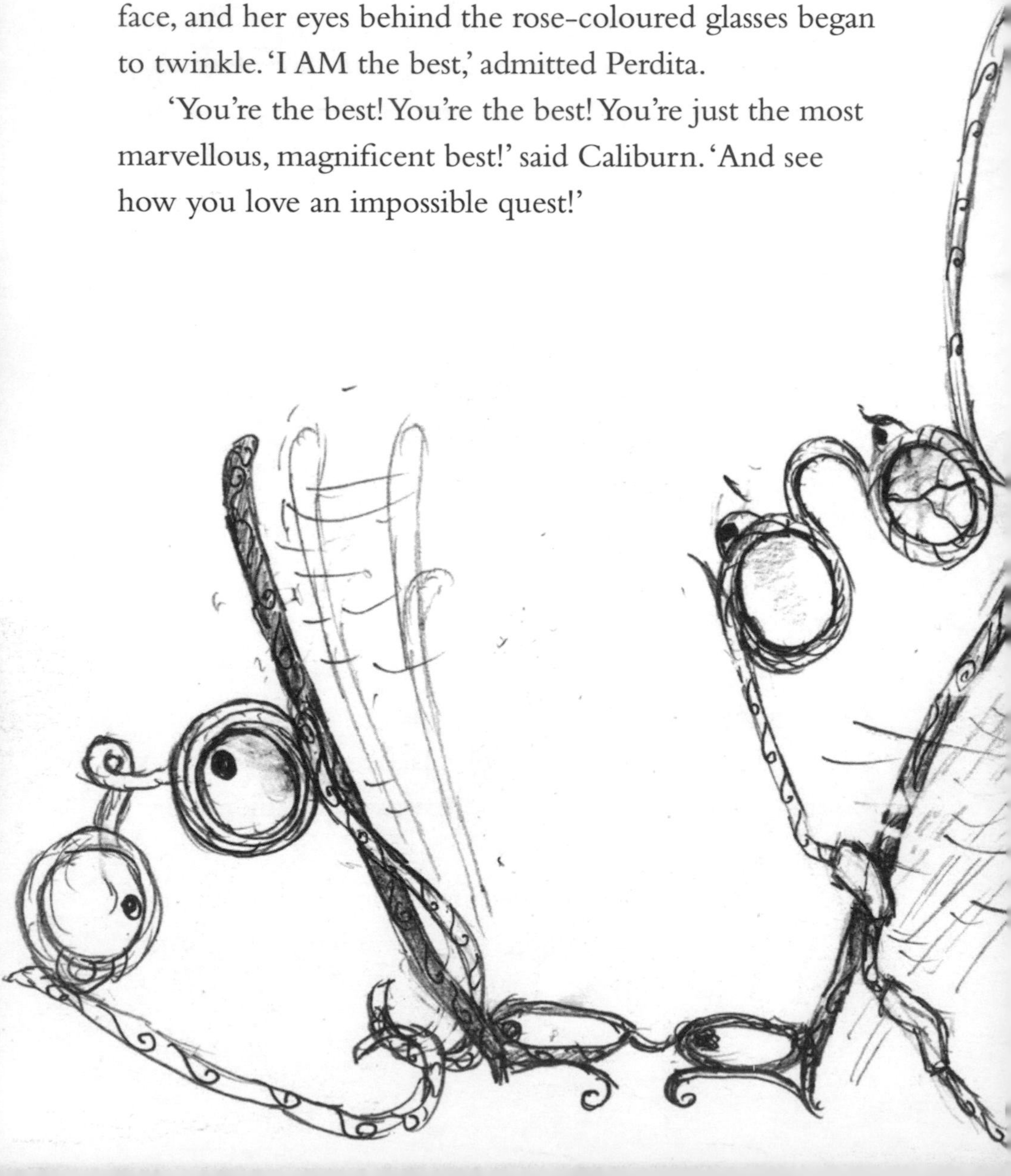

The human and the raven began to sing together, some old tune that they both knew from childhood.

And Perdita's glasses rushed to join in the dancing.

And Perdita's glasses
RUSHED to join
in the dancing

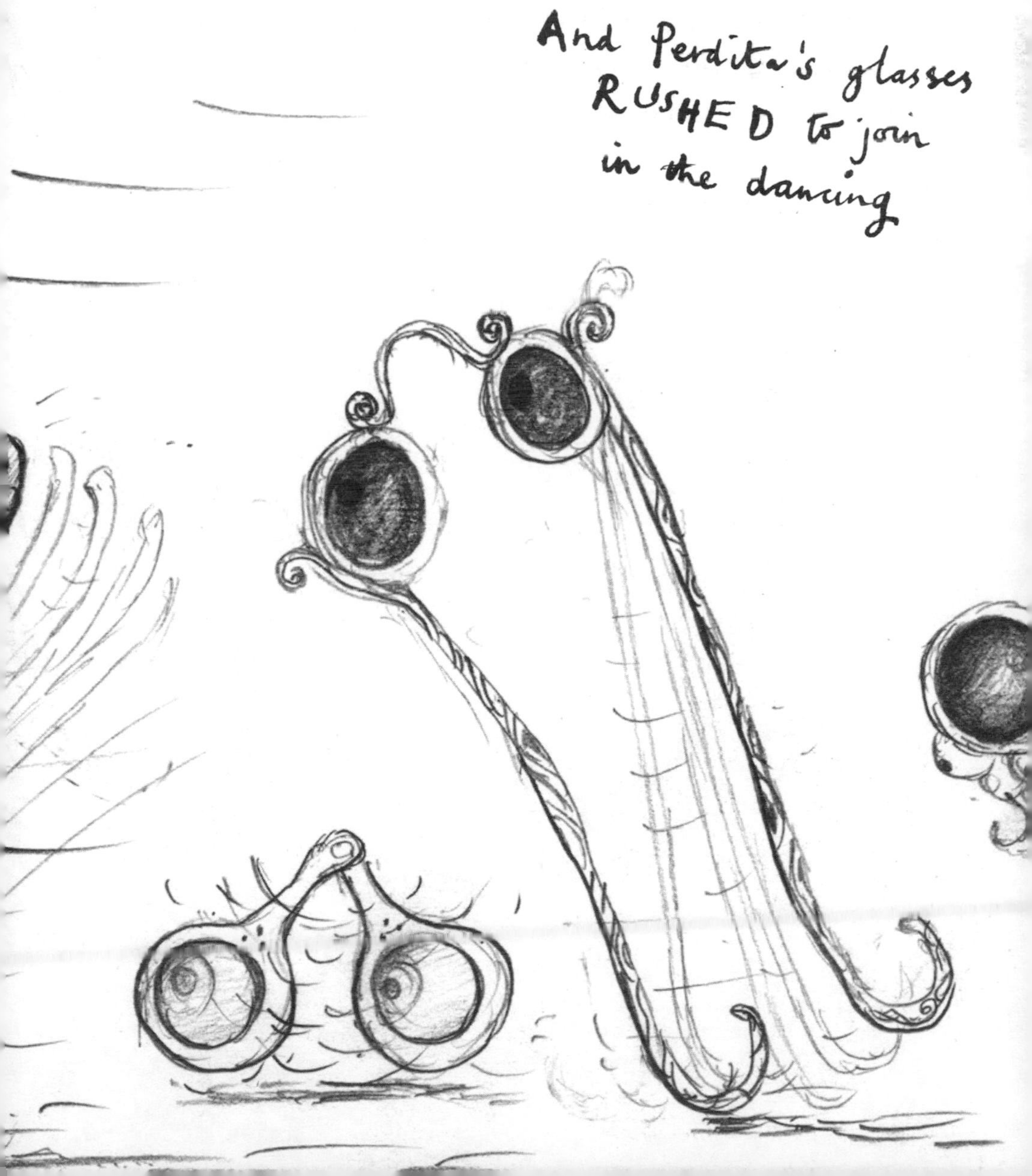

We're the best! We're the best!

We're the best! We're the best!
We're just the most marvellous magnificent best!
See how we LOVE an impossible quest…
Make butters that fly! Make sticks that can walk!
Unfeasible mirrors that see and can talk
Lift curses that shrivel and dry up the rain
Wake love that has died and will not grow again
Impossible things, nonsensical things, let me live my life
With impossible things!
I'm a bear! You're a bird! This ridiculous premise is
clearly absurd
But for ludicrous Magic we are the last word,
Because…
We're the best! We're the best!
We're just the most marvellous magnificent best!
And…

See how we LOVE
an impossible quest!

'Oh I LOVE it here!' said Wish. 'Please please *please* let me in . . .'

'You can stay!' said Perdita, excitedly opening wide her arms. 'This is the challenge I've been waiting for!'

It was so wonderful, after weeks of wandering, friendless and alone, horribly aware that they were cursed and outlaws, to have someone actually WANTING them to stay.

'Hurrah!' said Caliburn, and Wish's heart leapt, only to fall again as Hoola the little owl landed on the desk and waddled to the centre of it, her wings on her hips.

'HANG ON A SECOND,' fumed Hoola. 'Don't forget *I* have to say yes too! What if the other children in

"HANG ON A SECOND!" said Hoola

this school write home to their parents to say that we're hiding these outlaws? The Droods will shut the whole school down! Not to mention sending us all off on some deathly shadow quest . . .'

'You're right,' said Perdita. 'Thank you, Hoola! We'll have to disguise Wish's enchanted objects. Bring them out, Wish . . .'

The spoon jumped briskly from the top of Wish's head, followed by the key, fork and pins, and they trotted out on to the desk in front of Perdita. Perdita blinked, twice, three times, and slowly the little objects changed colour, from grey to gold. The enchanted things were absolutely thrilled with the transformation. They stuck out what-would-be-their-chests-if-they-were-human, and paraded around the desk, busting with pride at their new look.

'They're still made of iron,' explained Perdita. 'But now they look like they're gold.'

'And what are we doing to do about the *Warrior*?' said Hoola, pointing at Bodkin.

'Yes, he's a bit trickier,' admitted Perdita, thoughtfully. 'We could disguise him as a hob – they're not very good at Magic.'

'What's a hob?' asked Bodkin, knowing he wasn't going to like the answer.

Perdita blinked, once, twice, three times.

'Oh . . .' said Bodkin, as he looked down at the soft brown fur that had suddenly appeared all over his body. 'My father would be so ashamed if he could see me now . . . And a *tail*! Was that really necessary?'

'Yes, sorry about that,' said Perdita. 'You can't be a hob without a tail.'

'It's brilliant, Perdita, brilliant!' said Caliburn admiringly.

'It IS rather brilliant, isn't it?' said Perdita with satisfaction.

Perdita disguised Xar's green arm by turning the rest of him green as well, and did the same for all of Xar's companions, including the snowcats, the sprites, Lonesome the werewolf, and Wish herself. Even the Once-sprite's peregrine falcon and Caliburn himself were turned a very bright, unnatural green, which Caliburn thought made them look ridiculous.

'If anyone asks, say you are bog Wizards from the east,' said Perdita.

Finally, she lent Wish her pair of broken glasses to wear over her eyepatch. 'Maybe you could not mention about the Magic eye,' said Perdita thoughtfully. 'And just try and give the impression that the Magic is coming from somewhere else . . .'

'I can do that!' said Wish.

'But I haven't said yes, yet!' warned Hoola.

HA
HA
HA
HA
Bodkin as a Hob

'Oh *please* say yes,' said Caliburn, sensing weakness. 'We've answered all your questions. The disguises are wonderful. Won't you give us a chance?'

'After all, they ARE family,' said Perdita.

'Everyone is chasing us . . .' said Caliburn.

'We're wet, we're cold, we're hungry,' said Bodkin, his tummy rumbling.

Wish laid a hand on Hoola's wing. She looked into the little owl's eyes.

'And we're scared, and we have nowhere else to go,' said Wish.

There was a long silence.

Hoola looked at them all. Bedraggled, covered in scratches, the Bodkin-turned-into-a-hob was limping, the Xar-boy had a really nasty wound on his leg that looked like it was going septic.

It would take a harder owl than Hoola to turn down such a plea.

'Oh, bother,' sighed Hoola. 'Bother bother bother bother BOTHER. All right then, you're in. But that boy with the cursed hand better not start misbehaving, or you'll all be out again . . .'

'We're IN!' shouted Caliburn.

And way, way up at the entrance to Perdita's study, the piskies, who had been trying to eavesdrop but hadn't been able to hear anything, heard the loudness of this cry and reacted jubilantly, shouting, 'They're IN they're IN they're IN! Hurrah hurrah hurrah!'

'The longer you stay here the better,' said Perdita's warm, hypnotic voice. 'It will give you time to heal, and you have so much to learn. Stay here for as long as you can . . .'

'All right then,' said Xar, grumpily. 'We'll stay . . . not for TOO long though . . .'

It would take a harder owl than Hoola to turn down such a plea.

And in his head he thought: *Just until I can burgle some of those Droods' tears . . .*

Perdita nodded, and then turned to Ariel.

'You can add the piece of flame that we took from the forest fire to the fire on my hearth-stone, Sprite-whose-name-is-Ariel,' said Perdita, 'it will be happy there . . .'

So Ariel opened his fire-box, and when he added the little piece of flame to Perdita's fire, the flames there burnt bright and high as if they were welcoming it.

'But why would you want to keep a piece of fire from such an unhappy experience?' asked Wish curiously.

'You're *already* asking questions, how wonderful!' said Perdita, which was interesting, because Wish was normally told off for asking too many questions. 'Life is made up of so many things, happy, sad, indifferent and you cannot ignore the sad things, or even the indifferent. That drop of fire will only make my own fire the stronger . . .'

Now that Hoola had finally agreed to let them into the learning place, she became very practical. 'Okay, I'm going to show you all to your sleeping quarters,' said Hoola, 'and you can get warm and dry. The snowcats and Magical creatures can stay with you, but there's a special area for giants. This bear needs to go urgently to a sleeping cave – it's *way* past its bed time for the winter.'

The sleepy bear agreed with a great bear yawn.

'You're just in time for supper at the dining hall,' finished Hoola, 'so I'll take you to that, and then I'll drop the door and the boys off at the infirmary – they all need urgent medical attention.'

And then they trooped up the stairs to be greeted with rapturous delight by the piskies. Perdita turned Crusher green and then she hurried off, saying she had work to do making good the hole they had made in the Magic protecting the school by bringing iron in with them, and Hoola would look after them in the meantime.

'OnebearonegianttwodrownedhumansthreewolvesthreesnowcatsNINEuselesssprites*one*peregrinefalconandaBabyALLTHECOLOURGREEN ... *and a hob*! *WELCOME ALL*!' sang the piskies as they trooped off towards the sleeping quarters.

'Oh for goodness' sake,' said Hoola.

'You're HOME, you're HOME, welcome to your HOME!' sang everyone all together at full blast.

'Your Magical,
marv-e-llous,
magnifi-cent ...
... new HO-O-O-OME!!!!'

8. The Nuckalavee

I have to say, I am deeply relieved that for the moment Wish and Xar have found themselves a new home, a bed for the night, and many nights to come, and a nice warm meal to fill their empty tummies. They will be there for a long while, now, thank goodness, for it was not only poor old Caliburn and the sleepy bear who needed a little peaceful time to rest, and to heal. Caliburn was so ragged he had lost all of the feathers around his neck, poor bird, and you could see the pink of his skin there and on the top of his head. And they all had burns from the fire, and had lost weight from their days on the run, so Wish and Xar and Bodkin were as bony as twigs and needed to put on strength.

I wish I could describe the food that was prepared that midwinter's evening and the careless way that they enjoyed it, for it truly was delicious. Perdita made it all, and she was the most excellent cook, for until you have tasted nettle soup mixed with Magic, you really have not tasted heaven. But, sadly, I can't entirely concentrate on how scrumptious it all is.

Unfortunately I am the narrator, so I can see *beyond* Pook's Hill, the cosy dome of chalk horse and green grass that is protecting our heroes at the moment, and what I see makes me nervous.

I can see the Nuckalavee.

The Nuckalavee is a quiet presence in the ocean, but he's a bad one.

He contains more nightmares than a Quagmire's head could hold. There're sour things in the Nuckalavee . . . disappointed hopes and the end of dreams and staffs of power too longing with evil to be left in the hands of women or men. So he is not a monster to visit lightly. In fact, no one approaches the Nuckalavee but if they are on a shadow quest, and those on a shadow quest no longer care if they live or die, which is why they are known as 'shadows'.

No one that I have heard of yet has taken the scales of a Nuckalavee and lived.

So the Nuckalavee is out there, and the Nuckalavee is waiting.

I can see Queen Sychorax too.

She is nice and cosy camping out in her richly embroidered royal tent, in the smoking remains of the forest she has burnt around her, and she has just received a visitor. The visitor is a soldier wearing the colours of the emperor, and the emperor is supposed to be her leader, so unfortunately she has to meet his Warrior, midnight or no midnight, whether she wants to or not.

'Why are you here?' snaps Queen Sychorax. 'One

'My name is Thunderous Thighs HIMSELF and *I* will be your husband and king.'

OH for goodness Sake...

might almost say I was being *stalked* . . .'

'I am here,' announces the visitor, 'in the name of LOVE.'

'LOVE?' says Queen Sychorax in a voice of snow and raising one eyebrow.

'My name is Thunderous Thighs Himself,' announces this Warrior soldier, puffing out his chest. 'I have been sent here urgently by the emperor of Warriors because the emperor is concerned that these territories are being run by a defenceless female. So I am here to offer you my hand in marriage, to be your husband and king.'

Queen Sychorax's eyes narrow. '*Really*?' purrs Queen Sychorax.

'I am a giant-killer extraordinaire,' boasts Thunderous Thighs Himself. 'I have strangled many an elf with my bare hands. I am very good looking. My axe work is magnificent, but I am also a Warrior in LOVE.'

Queen Sychorax walks around Thunderous Thighs Himself. She sniffs.

Thunderous Thighs Himself feels a slight stirring of unease. He reaches into his waistcoat for his love poetry but Queen Sychorax accidentally clonks him in the midriff with one of her sceptres.

He doubles over in pain.

'Let me tell you,' says Queen Sychorax, smiling, 'what I think of LOVE.'

Gracefully she reaches out a hand to help Thunderous Thighs Himself to his feet again.

The moment he touches her ice-cold hand, however, there is a loud explosion, a great deal of nauseous smoke, and Thunderous Thighs Himself completely disappears.

His clothes are there, in a slightly singed pile. His love poetry rains softly through the room, blackened and blasted. But of Thunderous Thighs Himself, no sign at all.

However there *is* a small round bead, circling on the

BOOM!!

floor at Queen Sychorax's feet, that hadn't been there before.

Delicately, smoothly, Queen Sychorax bends down and picks up the small round bead.

Gently, tenderly, Queen Sychorax attaches the bead next to the many other beads hanging on the necklace around her throat.

The bead she attaches is, by coincidence, *exactly* the same pattern as that on the helmet of Thunderous Thighs Himself . . .

'*That*,' says Queen Sychorax, 'is what I think of LOVE.'

Oh, she's a cold one, that Queen Sychorax.

And she will not rest till she has got hold of Wish and put her back in iron Warrior fort, locked her up as tightly as if she were trapped in the bead of a necklace.

Queen Sychorax is very confident that she will find out EXACTLY where the children are, and EXACTLY how to find them. For as the narrator, I know something you do not know.

Xar was right. It was not a coincidence that Queen Sychorax had discovered them in that forest.

SOMEONE had betrayed them.

There was a traitor in their party.

Who could it be? Was Tiffinstorm right? Can you REALLY not trust a werewolf you met in a prison?

They had better WATCH OUT, for the traitor is still there with them . . .

And even if the traitor did not carry on betraying them, it was already too late.

Queen Sychorax had one of Wish's pins.

In the confusion of running away through the fire, it had stuck itself particularly firmly into a bit of Queen Sychorax's armour, and it could not work its way out in time.

Queen Sychorax had that pin, and all she had to do was set it free and follow it, and it would lead her back to Wish.

Encanzo's out there, somewhere, too, brooding on Queen Sychorax.

Further away than that, I can see through the

ball of iron where Wish has imprisoned the great bad Kingwitch himself. He is all curled up in his bed of iron, scratching, scratching, pecking his way out, like a chick from an egg. If you think that the two Witches that you have seen already are bad enough, well the Kingwitch is badder by far, and makes the pair of them look like a couple of dusty old scarecrows. The Kingwitch has the salt-ditch, rotten-egg, corpse-breath, arsenic-wicked stench of the truly evil, and he has a tiny speck of blue dust that belongs to Wish, and he will use it when he gets the chance.

The Kingwitch will take his time.

But the Kingwitch will find a way.

So Perdita and Caliburn and Hoola and Crusher are going to have to hide our heroes, teach them, guide them well, if they're going to have any sort of chance against the future that is waiting for them.

Look inside the ball of iron where Wish has imprisoned the great bad Kingwitch himself

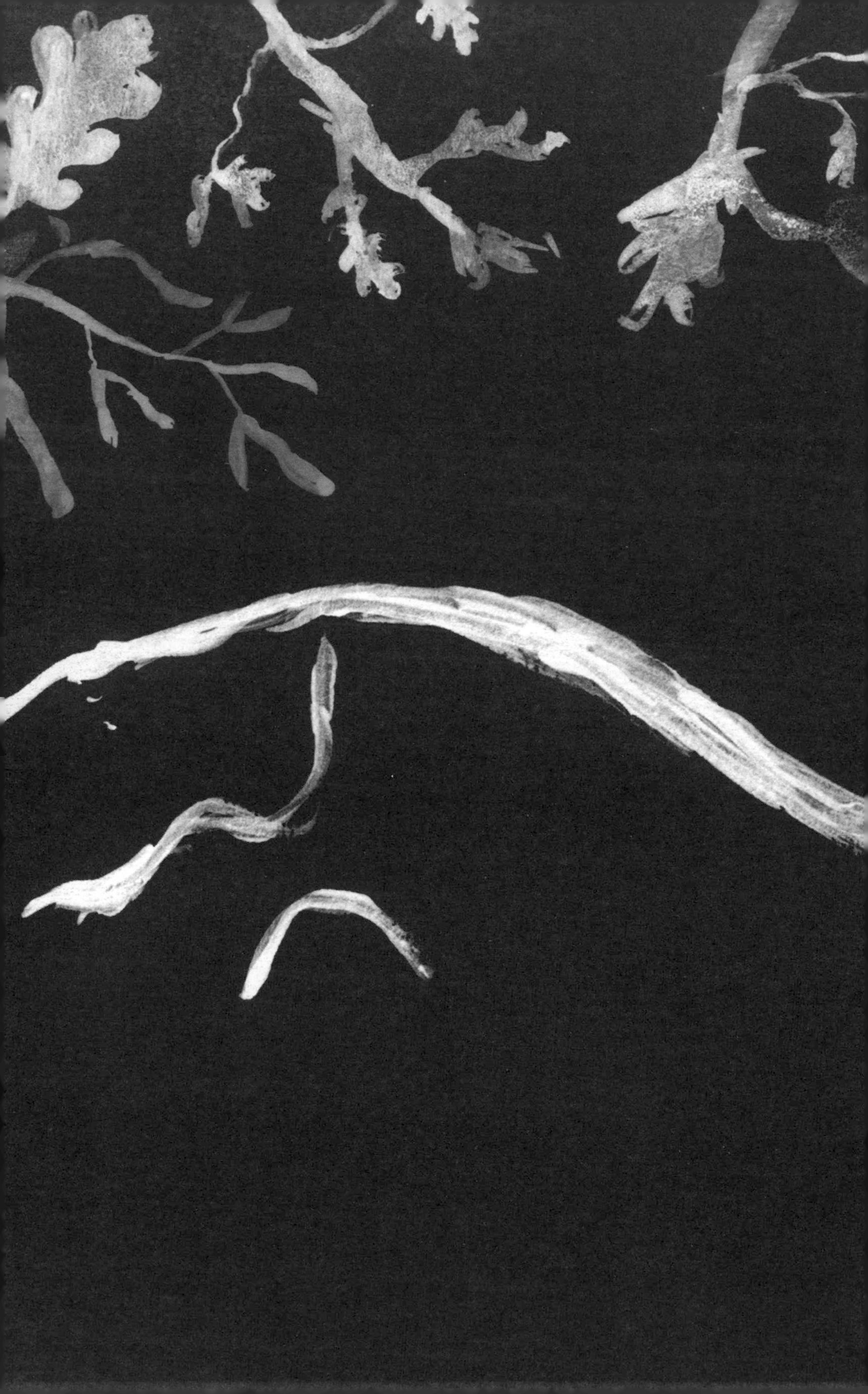

PART
Two
Refuge

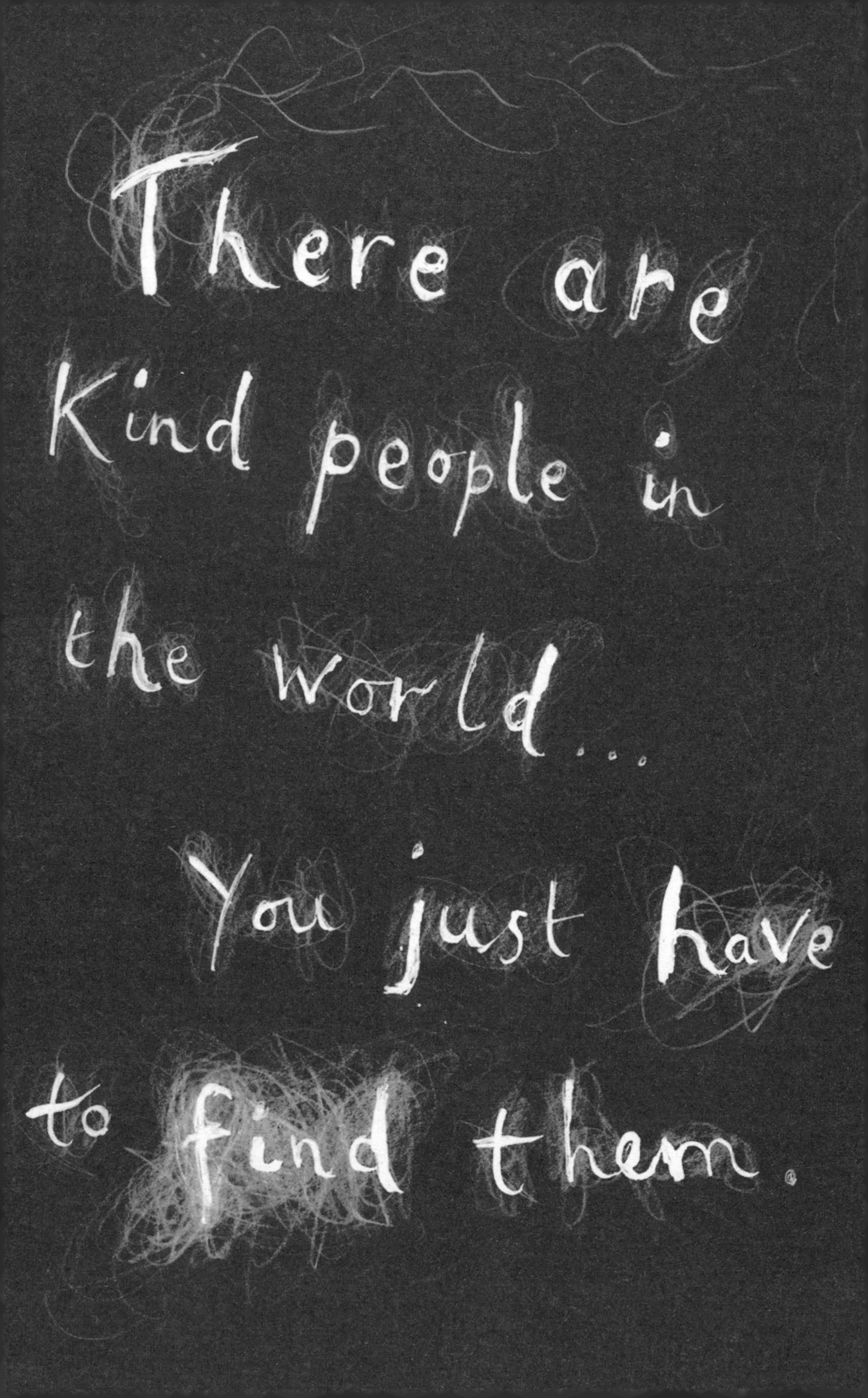
There are
kind people in
the world...
You just have
to find them.

9. The Learning Place for Spectacularly Gifted Wizards

That marked the beginning of the happiest, most peaceful time in Wish's small, short life. It wasn't anything like being taught by Madam Dreadlock. For the first time, Wish could practise all the powers that she had spent so many years covering up and smothering. She could never imagine that such a wonderful timetable could exist in the world. There were whole *terms* on trees. The different kinds, how to recognise them from their leaves, talking to them, tending them, what different woods did what different things.

And then there was starcraft, and invisibility, and transforming-into-animals, and bringing-things-to-life, not to mention flying-without-wings . . .

There was also word-learning and number-learning, of course, but they were a very small part of the timetable, and the teacher who taught them, Madam Mellows, was much more understanding than Madam Dreadlock. She had an entire set of letters and numbers that were all alive, and she kept them in boxes, a bit like Perdita's spectacle boxes.

Wish found it far easier to remember the lesson of the day when it was demonstrated by small furry or spiky or twiggy number animals and letter animals performing cartwheels and handsprings in front of her eyes.

The other Wizard and Magical creature children were very friendly and welcoming. As Perdita had said, they completely accepted that Xar and his companions were green because of coming from the east. So Wish and Bodkin found themselves, for the first time in their lives, making actual *friends*, with a Drood girl, who came from the Lake of the Lost, and had enchanted objects just like Wish (but not made out of *iron*, of course) and a boggart boy who came from under the ooze in the north.

At first, Bodkin thought that the long brown fur covering him all over in his disguise as a hob was horribly itchy and undignified, but after a while he realised how practical it was, warm and cosy, and really rather beautiful, particularly when you brushed it till it shone. He became proud of it, and the lovely important swooshing noise it made when he walked. And the tail! Don't get him started on the tail. Bodkin wondered how he'd ever lived life before without a tail. It was so *expressive*.

A tail was so expressive...

droopy when you were sad...

Perky when you were happy, droopy when you were sad, and extremely useful in the tree-climbing lessons. Bodkin could be up in the top of the tree canopy in three, four swings with that helpful addition of the tail, while the others were still climbing up the lower branches.

Bodkin had learnt to read and write from overhearing things while he swept the corners in classrooms. Now, for the first time, somebody was actually *teaching* him as though he was a real person, and not just somebody to give orders to. Bodkin was a fast learner, and he was very quickly shooting ahead in a lot of the classes – the ones that involved not actually doing Magic of course – and there were a surprising amount of them.*

He was at a disadvantage in the classes where Magic had to be performed, but Perdita had given him a do-it-yourself Magic staff that did a simple spell, which was 'sticking things to other things', in order to hide that he couldn't do any Magic at all.

* History of Magic, tree-climbing, wort-cunning, leechdom and starcraft (the three last being study of herbs and plants, medical remedies, and the art of interpreting and reading the stars, those sorts of things).

and extremely useful in the tree-climbing lessons

Everyone looked forward to Perdita's lessons. That spring, Perdita was teaching spell-making and tree studies and transformation.

'Wonderful!' she said, when somebody performed a spell correctly. 'Marvellous!'

And a strange thing happened. Whoever she said this to really did begin to think that they were quite marvellous after all. It was particularly effective with Xar. Xar had never had a mother – she died when he was born – so he was quite surprised when Perdita took out her rose-tinted spectacles and said things like, 'How fascinatingly creative!' when told the story about how he had accidentally melted one of the chairs. It made Xar behave better because he wanted to impress her.

At first, Xar was constantly in trouble.

Some of this wasn't entirely Xar's fault. His hand with the Witchstain on it seemed to have a mind of its own and often did the absolute opposite of what he wanted, in a spectacular way. So, for instance, the class would be practising shrinking spells and Xar would try and copy what everyone else was doing, and find himself *growing* instead of shrinking. On that occasion he grew even larger than Crusher, and the teacher assumed he did it on purpose to be cheeky and sent him to Perdita for insolence.

Xar was never quite sure how Perdita was going to react when he was sent to the Lair of the Bear.

Sometimes she was understanding, but other times she seemed very stern and bear-like, and punished him if he deserved it. Or it might be she was in the middle of some spell of her own, so she would be distracted and entirely uninterested in why Xar had been sent to her, and get Xar to hold the cooking pot steady while Hoola stirred it.

On the shrinking-but-accidentally-growing-instead occasion, she wasn't in the Lair of the Bear. The study was deserted, so he searched it very thoroughly, to see if he could find the Droods' tears, which he was sure she must have hidden somewhere. But Hoola came in and interrupted him, so he had to wander round the learning place until he found Perdita, eventually, in one of the side clearings. She was in the middle of a conference with a whole load of philosopher giants on the unexpected consequences and logistical possibilities of TIME TRAVEL, which was one of the very few things that the Magic people had not worked out how to do yet.

So although *terribly* sympathetic, Perdita waved him away, recommending Xar work out a way to get smaller again himself. He had to spend two days as a giant, before he got back to the right size again.

It was all a little difficult to predict.

But as time went on, Xar worked out a way of tricking the hand with the Witchstain by performing the exact opposite of whatever spell they were supposed to be doing. This didn't work *every* time, but enough so that he was in trouble a little less often.

So even Xar ended up liking the learning place more than he expected. He was very popular and had crowds of friends.

And after a while, they were all so busy that they nearly forgot that there was a world outside the charmed chalk circle of Pook's Hill. Three months passed. The bear came out of his sleeping cave. Their wounds from the fights with the wyverns and the Witches healed, and it all felt like they had arrived only yesterday.

Not that everything always went well.

Wish, of course, had a very powerful Magic indeed. More powerful, Perdita thought, than the Magic of most of the other Wizards in the whole of Pook's Hill put together, and maybe even more than that. Time would tell.

But Wish had *terrible* trouble with the spellfighting.

In spellfighting you were supposed to turn yourself into different animals, and fight as those animals. Wish started off well, transforming into snowcat, lion, dreater, ghoulfeast in impressively rapid progression . . . but her default position was always a fluffbuttle.

She did not know why this happened. She just panicked, mid-fight . . .

Her Magic eye blinked, before she could stop it . . .

. . . and there she was, a fluffbuttle again.

A fluffbuttle was, as the name suggests, not a *particularly* scary creature. Slightly smaller than a bunny rabbit, the fluffbuttle had so many natural predators in the wildwoods that Perdita had had to set up a special fluffbuttle animal sanctuary, because she was genuinely worried that the fluffbuttles might be in danger of being hunted into extinction. The sanctuary was located just beside the infirmary and Bodkin spent hours leaning dreamingly over the fence watching them, for it really was a great pleasure to see the little fluffbuttles scampering about, squeaking at each other.

Once Wish had transformed into fluffbuttle form during the spellfighting, she didn't seem to be able to transform out of it. So, unless the opponent had accidentally transformed into a *carrot* – which was unlikely but not impossible because ghoulfeasts were as allergic to carrots as vampires were to garlic, so if spellfighters were trying to be clever, sometimes they did go for the vegetable option – Wish automatically forfeited the fight.

And Perdita and Hoola and Caliburn exchanged significant glances with each other. Bodkin knew what those glances meant. They meant, 'Wish is no more ready to fight the Kingwitch in single combat than a fluffbuttle.'

But on the whole, everything was moving in a positive direction.

Xar was trying his hardest and he had improved greatly, in behaviour and thoughtfulness. Wish was struggling with the spellfighting, but she was learning so many other useful skills and had never been so content in her life. Even Bodkin had settled into being a hob.

Until Madam Clairvoy came to the school.

She was a new teacher, and from the moment she arrived, things went downhill.

Madam Clairvoy taught starcraft and she was every bit as mean as Madam Dreadlock, just horrible in a different way. Madam Clairvoy never shouted, but she was sarcastic, and she provoked Xar's pride. Xar wasn't very good at starcraft, and it was one of the lessons in which Bodkin shone, so Madam Clairvoy spent a lot of time comparing Xar to Bodkin. 'Even a *hob* can do this, Xar!' said Madam Clairvoy. 'So why, then, cannot you?'

This caused trouble between Xar and Bodkin, and Xar then acted up in the lesson, showing off, and getting into trouble, and he was sent to Perdita for being disruptive, and Madam Perdita was only halfway understanding.

'Madam Clairvoy is so *mean*!' stormed Xar.

'The world is full of people who are mean, Xar,' said Perdita.

Madam Clairvoy

'You have to learn how to deal with them without losing your temper.'

The meaner Madam Clairvoy was, the worse Xar behaved, even in other lessons as well.

So Wish was increasingly worried about Xar, who was being sent to Madam Perdita so much of the time that she thought he might be expelled. And Xar was beginning to draw away from them. Now he wouldn't be seen with Bodkin, because Bodkin was a hob, and hobs were a little embarrassing.

'Sometimes I feel like the spoon in the middle of the key and the fork,' Wish confessed to Caliburn one evening.

And even the spoon, the key and the fork were quarrelling again in a way they had stopped doing for a while. The fork would ambush the spoon and pin it down on every occasion it could, and the spoon started hiding from both of them. Tiffinstorm and Hinkypunk fell out over something and weren't speaking to each other.

And worse than that . . .

Oh much worse than that . . .

WITCHES were appearing, to the north, to the south, to the west, to the east, surrounding the school. The Witches didn't dare get too close, for Pook's Hill was protected by very powerful Magic. They were just roosting, high up in the treetops, like a gathering cloud of crows. They hadn't attacked anyone yet.

But they made everyone feel nervous.

And then two much more alarming incidents happened, that meant they were not going to be able to stay in Pook's Hill forever.

10. Two Alarming Incidents

The first alarming incident concerned Squeezjoos.

They had never really got to the bottom of why Squeezjoos had gone a little crazy and attacked Queen Sychorax's army all on his own. He seemed fine again once he got to Pook's Hill, so they didn't worry too much about it.

But then one day, Squeezjoos came to them all and said, in a slightly wobbly voice:

'I iss feelings a little bit funny . . .'

'Is it my imagination,' said Caliburn, 'or is Squeezjoos looking a little more green than the rest of us?'

'And he's behaving very oddly – he keeps gobbling up my spellsss!' said Tiffinstorm.

'I doesss not!' said Squeezjoos. 'Is liess, all liess . . . ooh, is that a piskie over there?'

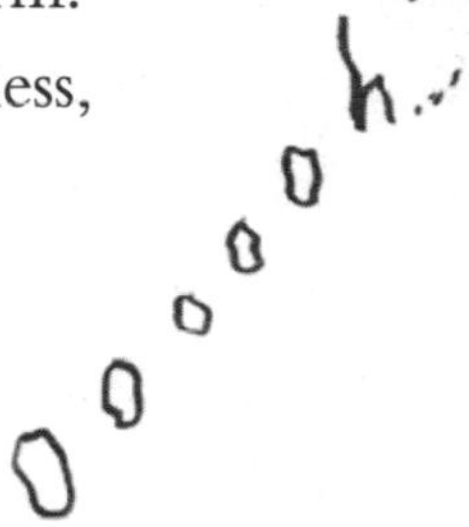

Tiffinstorm jumped and drew her wand, a sharpened thorn, and whirled around in the air to face the imaginary piskie. And while she was distracted, Squeezjoos reached out, bit one of the spells off her belt, and zipped off again.

'Don't eat that, it's a fire-spell!' hissed Tiffinstorm. But it was too late. Squeezjoos had already swallowed the spell. 'I'ss hassn't eaten anything,' said Squeezjoos, blinking with huge innocent bug eyes and shaking his little head so vigorously that smoke came out of his ears. But then – Oh! He went cross-eyed and, 'hIC!' he accidentally hiccuped, and a great spout of flame came out of his mouth and set fire to one of the leaves of Tiffinstorm's dress. She hastily put it out.

'Ooh!' said Squeezjoos putting a little hairy hand over his mouth in surprise. '*Peppery*!'

'Squeezjoos, stay still for a second, we need to have a look at you,' said Xar.

'I isss fine! I iss fine! I iss fine!' chanted Squeezjoos, nipping out of the way, but Xar eventually caught him in his cupped hands. And when Xar opened his hands a smidgeon, they got a good look at Squeezjoos, and his fur was definitely tinged with a deep hint of emerald that was darker than it ought to be, and you could even see a slight lime tint to his little spotty eyeballs.

'I isss FINE, let me go!' said Squeezjoos crossly, letting out little tongues of flame every single time he opened his mouth, and then when Xar didn't let him go immediately, his little eyeballs suddenly flashed a very bright pure green and he leant down and bit Xar.

'OW!' yelled Xar, dropping the little hairy fairy.

The green disappeared as quickly as it had flared, like sheet lightning, and Squeezjoos was mortified, for he hero-worshipped Xar. 'I isss so sorry!' whimpered Squeezjoos with huge horrified eyes. 'Forgives me Masster . . . I don't knowsss whatss came over me. It was an accident.'

He went cross-eyed. 'Hic! . . .' said Squeezjoos, in surprise, shooting out a flame, and then putting his hand over his mouth again. 'OOOh! . . . *Spicy*!' And then he shot this way and that, with a 'Hic! Ooh! *Scorchy* . . .' and a 'Hic! Ooh . . . *Sweltry*!' and 'Hic! Ooh! . . . *Zesty*!' Until finally he collapsed on his back on Wish's shoulder, moaning, 'Squeezjoos feeling *so sick* . . .'

And then he threw up, so violently, and fierily that they had to rush him to Perdita's tree office to give him urgent medical attention, wrapping him up in one of Xar's flameproof handkerchiefs to get him there.

You would never have thought that one little sprite could have eaten so many spells, but Squeezjoos threw up lovespells, invisibility spells, stink spells, curse spells, every kind of spell you could think of. When he was throwing up the invisibility spells he disappeared for a moment, but they still knew where he was from the 'Hic! Ooh! . . . *Gassy*!' noises. Eventually he got to the water spells, and that was good because they seemed to quench everything else, and by that time the little sprite was so exhausted he fell asleep, snoring loudly. Every now and then little mustard-coloured snot balloons drifted out of his nose, up into the air, where they burst, spraying the remains of stink spells all over everybody.

Wish explained to Perdita that Squeezjoos had been stained with the Witchblood trying to save Xar long ago in the forest, and how they had put him on the Stone-That-Takes-Away-Magic, but that Xar may have taken him off a little too quickly.

Perdita gave the little sleeping sprite a thorough examination, and when she finished she looked very grave. Even looking at Squeezjoos through her rose-coloured spectacles wasn't really helping.

'Is he going to die?' whispered Xar.

'No, no,' said Perdita hastily, 'he's just sleeping. Look, he's waking up!'

Squeezjoos sat up, shaking his head, and a few little mustard bubbles fell out of his ears, and a great big bubble of a stink spell burped out of his mouth.

'Yes . . .' said Perdita, 'if the little hairy fairy put his hand on the Stone-That-Takes-Away-Magic, that will have got rid of most of the bad Magic, so he won't die . . . but the Witchblood is giving him a craving for power which is why he is eating all these spells, and there is this remote possibility that he *may*—'

'Fly off to join the Witches at some point,' Caliburn finished the sentence for her.

'NO!' gasped Xar. 'Squeezjoos would never leave me and fly away, would you Squeezjoos?'

'I's bets he wouldn'ts. You isss lovely, Master, best Massster in the world. Who iss he, this Squeezjooossss? Who are we talking about?' asked Squeezjoos in an interested sort of way, hovering in front of Xar.

'What do you mean who is *he*? He is *you*! *You're* Squeezjoos!' said Xar in alarm.

'I isss not!' sang Squeezjoos happily, kissing Xar on the nose. 'I iss *SOOJZEEKS*!'

'I believe "Soojzeeks" may be Witch-speak for Squeezjoos, spelt backwards,' said Perdita, looking very worried indeed, 'which is not a good sign, but I will start administering my most potent antidotes, and we shall just have to hope for the best. On the plus side, he does seem awfully fond of you all . . .'

The remains of one of the lovespells were still fizzing around Squeezjoos's little hairy fairy bloodstream and so he was buzzing around trying to kiss everybody, squealing, 'Soojzeeks lovesssss YOU . . . and YOU . . .

and YOU . . . and *YOU!*'

'Oh dear,' sighed Perdita. 'This explains why there have been so many Witch sightings near the school recently . . .'

'*What?*' said Wish, sharply.

'They can't get into this school,' said Perdita soothingly. 'My Magic is invulnerable, but they may sense you are here and that Squeezjoos is turning towards them.'

It was all very well to say 'don't worry', but it was a horrible feeling to think that the Witches were gathering, hissing invisibly in the darkness, sharpening their talons, whether they could actually get in or not. And even worse to think that adorable little Squeezjoos might end up going over to the dark side.

So that was the FIRST incident that gave Wish and Xar an anxious feeling that they were no longer safe in the school, and that they really should be leaving and getting on with the quest to find the Nuckalavee so they could get rid of the Witches forever, and save Xar and Squeezjoos at the same time.

The next incident was, if anything, even more alarming.

One morning, Perdita was giving Xar, Wish and Bodkin a 'catch-up' lesson on trees, in her study, because they were a bit behind the other pupils in this subject.

Xar found these kinds of lessons boring. He much preferred the ones where they turned into birds, or deer, or different kinds of fish. Fidgeting wildly, his eye landed on a bottle marked 'Interesting Transformation Potion, Treat With Extreme Caution', poking out of one of Perdita's many pockets. Perdita was distracted, excited about telling them how trees secretly talked to one another by sending each other chemical messages. Xar winked at Squeezjoos, who giggled, and picked the pocket of Perdita, giving the bottle to Xar, who put it in his waistcoat. Only Bodkin saw him do it.

When they left the room, Xar showed Wish and Bodkin the bottle, and said he was going to taste it.

'Xar, don't be stupid,' said Wish.

'We should give that back to Madam Perdita,' said Bodkin.

'Oh, are you going to tell on me?' said Xar jeeringly.

'We're not going to tell on you. We're trying all the time not to get you expelled!' said Wish in exasperation. 'Didn't you learn anything from the whole Witchstain disaster?'

'But this isn't Witchblood, it's just some old transformation potion. Aren't you interested in what the

Interesting Transformation Medicine might be?' said Xar. 'I dare you, Bodkin, to taste it with me . . . Go on, don't be a stick-in-the-mud old hob for once!'

To do Xar justice, he said this quite affectionately – he just thought he was teasing Bodkin, but Bodkin was in a sensitive mood.

Underneath his green fur, Bodkin was turning very red. 'I am not a stick-in-the-mud old hob,' said Bodkin.

'Of course you're not!' said Wish. 'Don't listen to him, Bodkin, you don't have to prove anything.'

'Does anyone have a spoon they can lend me?' teased Xar, uncorking the bottle. The Enchanted Spoon buried itself very firmly in Wish's waistcoat.

'No way!' said Wish.

'Okay, I'll just swig it straight from the bottle, very cautiously of course,' said Xar. 'And then Bodkin, you can have a taste afterwards . . . or are you Warriors too *scared*?'

'I am not scared!' said Bodkin furiously, absolutely purple under the fur, if anyone could have seen it. 'And I am NOT a stick-in-the-mud old hob!'

Wish closed her eyes and held her head in her hands as Xar tipped back his head and drank very incautiously indeed from the bottle, then handed it to Bodkin, who defiantly took a good swig himself. There was a loud

BOOM!

BOOM!!!

But when Wish opened her eyes again, expecting to find two graxerturgleburkins in front of her, or worse, there was only one Bodkin and one Xar, looking entirely unchanged, if a tiny bit traumatised.

'Phew!' said Wish. 'It hasn't worked . . . you probably have to boil it up or something. But you were both still incredibly stupid to try it, and I'm getting fed up with you squabbling all the time. And have you forgotten that we're all on a quest together? I thought I could rely on you, at least, Bodkin, to be a bit sensible, and—'

But she was interrupted by Bodkin.

'Oh, it's worked all right,' said Bodkin.

'And it's certainly *interesting*,' said Xar.

'This is a disaster!' said Bodkin, who looked like he was panicking somewhat. 'This is a total, bronze-bottomed, fire-breathing, howling hairy disaster!'

'What on earth do you mean?' said Wish. 'Nothing's happened . . . you look exactly the same.'

'Except that Bodkin's turned into *me*, and *I've* turned into the stick-in-the-mud old hob!' said the boy who looked like he was Bodkin, but who was in fact Xar. '*We've switched places*!'

'Ah,' said Wish.

'Now that IS interesting,' said Caliburn.

'We have to tell Madam Perdita immediately so she can get us the antidote!' said Xar.

But Wish wouldn't hear of that, particularly once she had read the small print on the other side of the bottle that Xar hadn't bothered to read. 'No way,' said Wish. 'You've been in such trouble already, Xar. At any other school they'd have expelled you ages ago . . . And it says here that it's perfectly safe as long as you don't drink the whole bottle, and the effects will wear off after twelve hours or so.'

'A whole DAY being Bodkin!' said Xar in horror.

'A whole DAY being Xar!' echoed Bodkin, equally appalled.

Unfortunately, once Wish had established that they were perfectly safe, she wasn't a bit sympathetic. 'Maybe it'll be good for you,' she said. And the sprites thought it was hysterical.

So . . .

Bodkin and Xar had to go through the day being each other.

11. The Surprising Things You Learn When You Spend a Day as Someone Else

Xar was surprised at how lonely it was to be Bodkin. Of course the sprites and the animals couldn't hang out with him as much, because that would have attracted attention, so they just suddenly weren't there any more, and it gave him a very odd feeling to be totally . . . alone.

Did Bodkin always feel this alone?

It wasn't that anyone was positively *mean* to him. They just tended to ignore him when he said things. Their eyes passed over him as if he wasn't really there.

Apart from Wish.

Xar could see why Bodkin liked Wish so much. She was the only person who seemed interested when he said something. *When I get back to being Xar again, I'm going to be a lot nicer to old Bodkin,* thought Xar.

And Bodkin found he learnt a great deal from a day being Xar as well.

At first it was nice to have everyone laughing when he made a joke, everyone looking to him for guidance, all the attention from the other Wizards and the sprites. But then it began to feel like quite a lot of pressure to be funny, to be naughty, to amuse everyone. And being told off all the time turned out to be extremely wearing.

As for the hand with the Witchstain, Bodkin didn't

see how Xar could stand it. He couldn't remember Xar ever mentioning this (maybe Xar was too proud), but it hurt all the time, a burning, itching, yearning ache. And worse than that, he could feel it trying to control him, lead him in the wrong direction, confusing his thoughts and turning them upside-down and inside out. It was most unpleasant.

Oh dear oh dear oh dear . . . thought Bodkin. *I'm worried that time is running out for poor old Xar. I had no idea that the Witchstain was such a burden.*

Last lesson was with Madam Clairvoy.

After a whole day of being told off by teacher after teacher, Bodkin was thoroughly fed up and he found himself answering back and being nearly as cheeky as Xar would have been himself. Madam Clairvoy was in a really mean mood and she gave Bodkin two detentions for 'rudeness and insubordination', and Bodkin felt a little guilty about that until he realised that Xar wouldn't turn up for the detentions anyway.

At the end of the class, Bodkin headed with relief to the door, for there were only a couple more hours to go and then he could go back to being himself again. Xar followed, equally keen to get to the end of this stupid day as quickly as possible.

But Madam Clairvoy called Xar back.

'Stay behind, Bodkin,' said Madam Clairvoy. Xar

couldn't quite get used to being Bodkin, so he looked around him for a second, before he realised that Madam Clairvoy was talking to *him*. Why did she want Bodkin to stay behind?

Bodkin was wondering that too. And as he looked over at Madam Clairvoy, he had a sudden, shocking realisation. A memory of something that he had seen once, long ago, in the dungeons of Warrior fort . . .

He knew why Madam Clairvoy wanted to see Bodkin, and he had to prevent that at all costs.

'Bodkin can't stay behind, Madam Clairvoy,' said Bodkin with real urgency in his voice. 'Madam Perdita wants to see him and Wish and me in the Lair of the Bear right now.'

'I'm sure Madam Perdita can wait a few moments,' snapped Madam Clairvoy. 'Off with you, now, Xar! I've had quite enough of YOU for one day!'

And she shooed Bodkin out of the room.

Madam Clairvoy carefully shut the door behind him.

Bodkin knelt down so that he could hear what was going on in the room. He put his eye to the keyhole of the door.

Madam Clairvoy glided to a cupboard in the corner of the room, and opened it. There was something inside. And what she did next, Xar, and Bodkin, watching through the keyhole, could not really believe.

She took off her head, as if she was taking off a hat.

The now headless woman gave a quick, satisfied pat of Madam Clairvoy's hair, and placed the head of Madam Clairvoy on a stand inside the cupboard. And peering, goggle-eyed, into the cupboard, Xar realised there was ANOTHER head in there. The arms of Madam Clairvoy reached inside the cupboard, picked up this other head and put it on her shoulders, gently pushing it down as if to make it secure.

And then she turned round.

And it wasn't Madam Clairvoy standing in front of Xar.

It was Queen Sychorax.

Part Two: Refuge

12. The Story Takes Another Unexpected Turn

Well, well, well.

Unsurprisingly, Xar just stood there, with his mouth open. Xar was never that glad to meet Queen Sychorax, who he would have described, if asked, as very scary indeed. Super scary. Scarier than a whole load of vampires feeling a little peckish because their blood sugar was running a little low. But how much scarier than ever was she when you met her swapping heads and pretending to be someone other than she was?

You're not supposed to BE here!!! thought Xar, rather hysterically to himself. *You're a Warrior! We should at least be safe from you in a learning place for gifted Wizards!*

But he didn't say that. He was much too flabbergasted.

All he said instead, in a bewildered sort of way, was, 'Queen Sychorax! What on earth are *you* doing here? Why did Madam Perdita let YOU in?'

'Madam Perdita thinks I am Madam Clairvoy,' snapped Queen Sychorax. 'Madam Perdita may think of herself as a great leader, but she's a fool, and like so many other fools, she is not clever enough to look past appearances . . . She interviewed me a couple of weeks ago as a new teacher for the starcraft lessons, and she didn't even guess that I was a Warrior.

'Now, I know perfectly well that it is *you,* Bodkin, who is hiding underneath that really rather pathetic hob disguise, so don't waste my time trying to deny it,' said Queen Sychorax.

(For Queen Sychorax, of course, was not quite as clever as she thought she was, and she was under the impression that she was talking to Bodkin.)

'I have a task for you, Bodkin. I want you to get me the spoon and the Enchanted Sword and Wish's Spelling Book,' ordered Queen Sychorax. 'I've been trying to get hold of them, but Wish never lets them out of her sight. But Wish trusts you, Bodkin. She will give them to you if you ask to borrow them for a moment. I'm sure you can think of a reason why you need to borrow them.'

Xar kept quiet, thinking, *What is going on???*

Why is the ridiculous Bodkin boy staring at me with his mouth open? thought Queen Sychorax irritably.

She then spoke very slowly, as if she thought Bodkin was a little slow on the uptake.

'Wish will not give herself up to me unless I have the spoon and the sword and the Spelling Book,' explained Queen Sychorax. 'As soon as I have those things I can take you and Wish back to the safety of iron Warrior fort You know in your heart of hearts that the fort is the only place where she will be safe from the Kingwitch. If *I* can get in to this learning place, you can be sure that the Kingwitch can too . . . and it is your duty as her bodyguard to protect her.'

Xar said nothing.

Queen Sychorax smiled, one of her lovely golden ones, sweeter than honey. 'If you do as I want, I will reward you, Bodkin,' cooed Queen Sychorax. 'Do you want to be an Assistant Bodyguard all your life? If you bring me the spoon, the Spelling Book and the sword, I will never tell her you did it willingly. I will say that I took them off you by force . . . and finally you will be worthy of her, for I will make you a knight Warrior and a Hero of my Queendom. Think how sad your father would be to see you dressed like this, as a ridiculous hob, and how PROUD he would be if his only son was made a knight Warrior!'

No, you won't make Bodkin a knight Warrior, thought Xar. *Don't believe her, Bodkin! She's a lying, cheating queen who doesn't keep her promises!*

Queen Sychorax's honey smile faded as she revealed the sting behind the sweetness.

'But if you do not do as I want, there will be penalties,' said Queen Sychorax grimly. 'I will tell Wish that YOU are the one who betrayed her . . . YOU are the one who sent word to me about where you were in the wood . . .'

Bodkin betrayed us!!! thought Xar. *It was Bodkin's fault that Queen Sychorax ambushed us in the forest all along!*

'. . . and Wish will never trust you again, Bodkin,' said Queen Sychorax, sorrowfully. 'Never love you again . . . There was never any chance of her loving you of course, as a mere Assistant Bodyguard of no birth or consequence at all, while Wish is a royal personage, but there was still *hope* . . . You could still have held her sword, polished her armour and done all those Assistant-Bodyguardy-type things . . .' Queen Sychorax was a little vague at this point because she really hadn't a clue what an Assistant Bodyguard's duties were – they were way below her notice. 'But if you go the way you are choosing, all hope will be gone, not to mention Wish falling into the grip of the Kingwitch.'

There was a long, long silence.

Outside the room, kneeling by the keyhole of the door, Bodkin was crying. He wiped away his tears with the back of his sleeve, got up, and ran away.

Inside the room, Queen Sychorax was waiting for an answer from the boy she thought was Bodkin.

'I can see you are beginning to come back to your senses,' said Queen Sychorax with satisfaction. 'You are beginning to realise that your recent defiance has been a mistake.'

At last Xar answered.

'It is *you,* Queen Sychorax, who has made a mistake,' said Xar, almost too cross to get the words out.

It was Queen Sychorax's turn to be surprised.

'*I beg your pardon?*' said Queen Sychorax.

And then, when Xar whipped out Bodkin's do-it-yourself Magic staff, and pointed it at her, she was more surprised still.

What does this stupid staff do, again? thought Xar. *Oh yes . . . it 'sticks-things-to-other-things'. Well, I can work with that.*

PEEEOOW!!! He pointed the staff and it stuck Queen Sychorax's hands to the table.

'Have you gone completely mad?' said Queen Sychorax, staring at her hands, trying to pull them off the table and getting increasingly irritated as she realised that wasn't possible. 'Pointing a Magical weapon at a teacher? USING a Magical weapon on a teacher! I'll report you . . . You'll be expelled! Put that staff down, you disobedient Bodkin-boy!'

'You're not the only one who can look like someone

else!' raged Xar. 'I'm not Bodkin, you stupid Queen!'

'Oh, don't be ridiculous!' snapped Queen Sychorax. 'Of course you're Bodkin! I saw through your ridiculous disguises in about two seconds – a little green colouring and some fur isn't going to trick *me*. Release me, or I will tell Wish all about your betrayal.'

'Tell away!' yelled Xar. 'I don't care! Because I may be looking like Bodkin at the moment, but I'm not really Bodkin! I'm *Xar* . . .'

Now it was Queen Sychorax's turn for her jaw to drop and to stare at Xar with a goggle-eyed expression of amazement.

'No . . .' whispered Queen Sychorax, 'it's not possible . . .'

'We took the Interesting Transformation Potion and changed places,' said Xar.

'Oh dear,' whispered Queen Sychorax. 'It *is* possible . . .'

'I'M Xar, And YOU,' shouted Xar, 'are the WICKEDEST most TREACHEROUS most LYING Warrior Queen I have met in my ENTIRE LIFE!!! I have met ADDERS more straightforward than you are! YOU'RE TRICKIER THAN A TRICK LOAD OF WEREFOXES! YOU'RE MORE CROOKED THAN THE BACK OF A CROOKED-BACK SNAIL!

Only Xar could be that rude.

Queen Sychorax turned as white as a sheet.

'Okay,' said Queen Sychorax, her lips pursing sourly. 'You're definitely Xar-son-of-Encanzo.'

Xar was the rudest boy that Queen Sychorax had ever met and a real thorn in Queen Sychorax's side. Queen Sychorax was used to people being terrified of her, or at least respectful. But in this particular thirteen-year-old boy she always seemed to have met her match, and that was why she had been so mean to him when she was looking like Madam Clairvoy. But Xar was even trickier than she was. And he was a lot ruder.

'I OUGHT TO HAVE KNOWN THAT HORRIBLE MADAM CLAIRVOY WAS YOU ALL ALONG!' roared Xar. 'YOU MAY HAVE THE MOST BEAUTIFUL NOSE IN THE WILDWOODS BUT EVERY SINGLE TIME YOU TELL A LIE IT GETS JUST A LITTLE BIT POINTIER!'

Queen Sychorax sniffed thoughtfully. It was nonsense, of course, but Queen Sychorax was very proud of her nose, which was, indeed the most beautiful nose in the wildwoods, and the thought of it getting pointier, or being any other shape than the perfect shape it was, was *most* disagreeable. The beastly boy!

Queen Sychorax was nothing if not adaptable. She was thinking. Fast.

'Even if you *are* Xar-son-of-Encanzo, you're in

big trouble,' said Queen Sychorax. 'I have sent word, anonymously, to your father that you are hiding here, and my spies tell me that Encanzo is about to turn up to claim his son, and take you back to the prison of Gormincrag where you belong.'

Xar had calmed down. Now he was less angry, but very sad.

'Well, he won't find me here,' said Xar. 'We're running away again – and we were happy here,' said Xar longingly. 'Wish was happy. Bodkin was happy. I was happy, and you've made us run away . . .'

'The happiness was just an illusion, wasn't it?' said Queen Sychorax. 'This is real life, and in real life Wizards and Warriors can never be friends. Who are you going to run away *with*? The Bodkin boy who has already betrayed you? He can't come with you, surely . . . and if Wish can't even trust *Bodkin*, why would she trust you?'

'I would think about your own problems, if I were you, Queen Sychorax,' Xar advised her. 'You're stuck to that table. You can't reach the cupboard to put your Madam Clairvoy head on. So Madam Perdita and everyone are going to find you here, a queen of Warriors in a learning place for Wizards.'

'For all her roaring, Madam Perdita is soft,' said Queen Sychorax scornfully. 'She will let me go.'

Xar walked towards the door, and just as he reached

it, he turned round.

'You were never going to make Bodkin into a knight Warrior and a Hero of your Queendom, were you, Queen Sychorax?' said Xar.

'Of course not!' said Queen Sychorax. 'We Warriors have very strict rules about that sort of thing. Once a servant always a servant. I just said that because lies sometimes have to be told—'

'. . . in pursuit of the higher good,' Xar finished her own saying for her.

'And Bodkin believed me because he *wanted* to believe me,' said Queen Sychorax. 'Love is weakness, Xar-son-of-Encanzo – you need to remember that if you want to be a leader one day. But who am I talking to? You, of all people, should know that. The boy who wanted power so much that he took Magic from a Witch . . .'

'I was young, and I made a mistake, but maybe I am not what you see. You may think of yourself as a great leader, Queen Sychorax,' said Xar, 'but like so many other fools, perhaps you are not clever enough to see past appearances.'

Only Xar would have had the cheek to quote Queen Sychorax back at Queen Sychorax.

'I don't yet know what I want to become,' said Xar. 'But I do know, whatever it is, I don't want it to be what

YOU seem to have become.'

He shut the door very quietly.

And that last comment made Queen Sychorax think a good deal more than any of the insults.

13. Bodkin's Letter

Xar was expecting Bodkin to be outside the door of Queen Sychorax's room, but Bodkin was not there.

It took Xar a bit of time to find Wish, but eventually he found her running through one of the courtyards, surrounded by all the sprites and animals. *She* was looking for *him*. She was carrying a letter, folded in half, and Xar's waistcoat.

'Bodkin gave me this letter, but he said I couldn't look at it until I was with you,' said Wish. 'And then he ran off. He wouldn't let any of us go with him except Nighteye, and he looked so upset . . . What's happened? You *are* still Xar, aren't you? You haven't switched back again yet?'

'That's not the problem,' said Xar grimly. He explained about Queen Sychorax, and Bodkin betraying them both, and Wish could not believe it.

They looked at the letter together. It was written in scribbled, hasty handwriting and it said:

Dear Wish and Xar,

By the time you read this, you will know I have betrayed you.

I don't know how to say how sorry I am. I wanted to keep Wish safe, and I did not realise how bad Queen Sychorax had become until she burnt down the forest, and then it was too late.

I should have told you, but I could not bear to see the look on your faces when you found out.

I found a page in the Spelling Book that told me where to find the Nuckalaree, and I ~~—~~ am going away on a Shadow Quest, to get the scales, to prove that I have courage, and that I can be a hero too.

Please do not follow me, it is too dangerous. stay safe here with Madam Perdita, and learn how to be heroes and Wizards.

If I don't come back, I will have got what I deserved.

Very best wishes,

Bodkin

Your ~~bodyguard-and-~~ would be-bodyguard-and-betrayer

P.S. I have taken Nighteye with me. I won't let her come to any harm

'This is partly your fault, Xar!' said Wish, turning on Xar fiercely.

'Hang on a second, *Bodkin's* the traitor, not *me*!' protested Xar. 'Don't blame this on *me*!'

'You're not very TACTFUL!' said Wish in a rage because she was worried about Bodkin. 'You kept going on and on about how he was a hob and everything . . .'

Xar opened up his mouth to protest . . . and then shut it again. Maybe he hadn't been quite as tactful as he might have been.

'Poor Bodkin . . . He only did it because he was jealous,' said Wish. 'I wish he'd told me . . .'

'Poor Bodkin . . .' agreed the key in a little creaky voice, drooping on the letter. 'Jealousy makes you do stupid things, doesn't it, fork? Luckily *I've* never been the jealous type . . .'

And then suddenly, in the distance, out in the woods, there was an unforeseen, dreadful noise.

Wish turned white.

The Witches that were out there waiting had been quiet, so quiet, up until now. Eerily quiet.

But Wish knew that new, fresh sound. It was the dreadful, heart-stopping noise of attacking Witches.

'Bodkin!' gasped Wish. 'They must be ambushing him! We have to help . . . Thank goodness he's taken the sword with him.'

'Maybe *not* "thank goodness",' said Xar, even whiter than Wish. 'Because if Bodkin took the sword with him, the iron will have created a hole in the Magic protecting Pook's Hill . . . '

Xar was right.

When Bodkin took the sword out of the school, the iron had indeed tunnelled a hole in the Magic, and even now, a gigantic feathered nightmare was crawling rat-like through that hole.

For the first time in hundreds of years, the sacred space of the learning place was invaded by a WITCH.

Much nearer than those distant dreadful noises, there was a confused screeching, and a great cry of 'WITCH ATTACK!' and the sound of swarms and swarms of piskies from inside the school hissing, 'witcheswitcheswi tcheswitcheswitcheswitches . . .'

The Witch feathers in Xar's waistcoat glowed with a strange unnatural light.

And little Squeezjoos's eyes lit up with a similar, unearthly green, as he crept forward in the air, hissing, 'sehctiw . . . sehctiw . . . sehctiw . . .'

Instinctively, Xar grabbed the little sprite, and put him in one of his pockets, buttoning it tight, and sticking it fast with the do-it-yourself Magic staff.

'Lets me *out*!!!' squeaked Squeezjoos, peering through a little tear in the material.

'No, Squeezjoos,' said Xar, 'I think you're safer in there for the moment.'

Wish and Xar ran towards the noise, the animals running beside them, their huge sympathetic bodies giving them courage, and the sprites flying above in a twitter of speculation.

It is sometimes only when we sense we are about to lose something that we really see it and appreciate it. The electric shock of the attack had woken Xar into a state of bright awakeness, so that every one of his senses was highly alert, and as he ran through the beloved, friendly, messy world of Pook's Hill in his bare hob feet, vaulting over the twisting tree trunks, gaining speed with every comforting familiar piece of ground that his feet touched, he had the oddest and dreadest sensation that he was seeing it for the very first and also the very last time.

He hadn't wanted to come here. But now he didn't want to leave.

They burst into the eastern clearing to find Perdita, great streams of Magic coming out of her fingers, fighting a swooping, diving shock of a Witch.

They were too late to help her.

Wish had her eyepatch up, ready, as they ran forward.

Perdita swelled. The energy force wracking her got more and more intense, and a great heat came off her so that Xar and Wish had to throw up their arms in front of their faces to protect themselves . . . and they were blown right off their feet by some sort of combined explosion from Perdita and the Witch.

There was a terrible tearing shrieking, and the ghastly vision of the swooping Witch turned invisible again . . . and patterings of green blood fell like rain as the Witch retreated, back towards the hole in the Magic at the eastern entrance of the school.

The animals gave howls of victory all around Xar.

The Witch has gone, thought Xar.

But at what dreadful cost?

'Madam Elfrida! Mister Yewtree! Chase the creature from the school. Close up the Magic there. Don't step in the Witchblood,' screamed Hoola.

Madam Elfrida and Mister Yewtree ran after the invisible, retreating Witch, carefully avoiding the drips of green.

The terrible form of Perdita, in the shape of a great unmoving bear, lay on the ground.

Oh no . . . please let her be all right, begged Wish to herself.

Xar and Wish crawled forward to Perdita's side. She was still steaming hot, too hot to touch.

'Is she going to be all right?' whispered Wish.

'I don't know,' hooted Hoola, anxiously fluttering

above Perdita's heart.

For a few dreadful seconds the bear remained unmoving.

And then an eyelid flickered, and weakly the bear opened an eye.

'Oh, by the great green gods that protect us,' breathed Hoola, 'I think she didn't have to use a life . . . I think she will survive. No thanks to *you*,' snapped Hoola fiercely, her head swivelling round to look furiously at Wish. 'It's all very well for you young people . . . *You* may have many lives, Wish, but Madam Perdita may only have one left.'

The relief of Perdita being alive was almost as if Wish's own heart had stopped for a second, only to start beating again.

A little troop of piskies came buzzing up in a state of high excitement, for nothing as sensational as this had happened in many a long while. 'Madam Elfrida says she has made good the hole in the Magic, and she thinks it was just the one Witch who got in,' one of the piskies gabbled before they all flew off back to where the action was.

Thank goodness – so at least that was *one* problem solved.

'I'm so sorry, Perdita,' said Wish. 'But Bodkin is in trouble. We have to leave in a hurry. Thank you for everything.'

At this the bear lifted her head weakly. 'No!' growled Perdita-as-a-bear, and she staggered to her feet, shook her shaggy fur, and in front of their eyes the outline of the bear faded. She stood before them, much smaller than normal, and terribly old and weak. Her face was blasted with Witch-lightning. 'You should not leave . . . it is too dangerous . . .'

'You know they must leave, Madam!' snapped Hoola. 'It is only your weakness that has let them stay here this long. I don't like to say, "I told you so," but for the first time in centuries, a WITCH has entered this sacred learning place. And these cursed children have let it in. I TOLD you that the boy was unsaveable, and that we'd have to expel him in the end.'

Xar's face darkened, and he looked furious.

'I TOLD you that the girl's Magic could not be controlled, and that she would bring bad luck on all of us,' said Hoola. 'What am I supposed to do with all this Witchblood?'

Hoola pointed an angry wing at the steaming spots of green that the teachers were now surrounding with forcefields so that nobody accidentally stepped on them.

'It'll be years before we get those stains out. Maybe even decades! And listen to those hell creatures clamouring outside . . . Look at the calamities these children have brought on us! Burning forests . . . Witch attacks . . . And now Pook's Hill itself is in danger . . .'

'We're sorry about everything . . . but we have to go to the Nuckalavee to save Bodkin!' said Wish in a wretched state of anxiety. 'Xar and Bodkin changed places, and— It's too long to explain. Please let us out!'

'I said it myself,' said Perdita sadly, 'you were always just passing through. You can't run away forever . . . But when I said that,' she continued, bursting into tears, 'I never knew I was going to *like* you all so much . . .'

Caliburn patted her on the shoulder with one wing.

'Love is weakness,' warned Hoola, still huffy.

'Maybe it is,' said Perdita, smiling, 'but what a very nice weakness, it is indeed.'

'Can you come too, Perdita?' asked Wish, wistfully, for she knew what the answer was already.

Perdita looked affectionately into Wish's eye. 'I cannot,' said Perdita. 'Spells must be tended, suppers must be made, trees must be looked after, even when the world is burning. This is *your* quest . . . And my brother will look after you, won't you, brother?'

Caliburn sighed. 'I'll do my best. Thank you, sister, for hiding us for so long. We leave Pook's Hill a lot more prepared than we were when we arrived.'

'Until we meet again!' replied Perdita. 'And if you need me, all you have to do is . . . *Knock three times* . . .'

Right on cue, just as Perdita finished speaking,

there was a very loud knocking at the eastern entrance. KNOCK! KNOCK! KNOCK!

Hoola's head swivelled round one hundred and eighty degrees. 'Whoooo could that be?'

'Oh! Maybe it's Bodkin!' said Wish in horror. 'Trying to get back in because the Witches are attacking him! Let him in! Let him in!'

Perdita tipped her head to one side, listening. 'That's not Bodkin,' she said. 'The Nuckalavee is to the west. Summon your door, and Hoola, take them all to the *western* entrance very secretly and quietly, and then I'll go and see who's at the *eastern* entrance. Whoever they are, they may be in trouble.'

'But Madam, are you well enough?' asked Hoola.

Perdita drew herself up to her full height. She looked quite *wild*, for she had been in the middle of looking after a spell when the Witch attack happened, and she had been so distracted that as well as everything else the spell had exploded on her. So she had bits of slimy seaweed tangled in her scorched hair, and other unidentifiable but revolting-looking ingredients smeared all over her clothes, and her hands were wrist deep in some sort of goo that had a sulphurous and most appalling stink of rotten eggs.

And on top of that, she could hardly stand up because she was so bruised and battered by fighting off the Witch. She clearly wasn't well at all. But . . .

'I'm *fine*, Hoola, stop fussing!' snapped Perdita. 'I'm only four hundred and eighty-five years old, after all, the prime of middle age. I don't know why you keep treating me as if I'm on the brink of death. OFF YOU GO!'

As soon as she had said these words a great humming, bee-cloud of piskies appeared out of nowhere, several of them so wildly over-excited that they actually threw up.

'Nothing to see here, piskies . . .' said Hoola uneasily, but she might as well have been hooting at the wind.

'They're OFF! They're OFF! On a VERY SECRET QUEST! One bear one giant TWO humans three wolves three snowcats eight USELESS sprites one peregrine falcon and a Baby noneofthemgreenanymore . . . *OFF* . . . on a very, very secret . . . absolutelycrazy . . . madlysuicidal . . . absolutelySecret . . . terrifyingStupyfyingIdioticLunioticLOSEYOUR *BREFFDIOTIC*deathdefyingIMPOSSIBLE newQUEST!' sang the piskies.

Perdita transformed into a bear larger than Wish had ever seen before and ROARED at the piskies, who stopped buzzing a moment in shock.

'That's better,' said Perdita, changing back into herself again. 'Now, piskies. I have somebody arriving at the eastern entrance . . .'

'OOOOOOOOOO,' said the piskies.

'. . . and you absolutely must NOT tell anyone they are here. Not a word, piskies. I mean it . . . NOT A WORD.'

'OOOOOOOOO, wewonttellwewonttell . . .' sang the piskies, in a positive swarm of delight, and they buzzed off in vast bee-swarm numbers, a hum of creative curiosity to see what was going on in the eastern entrance.

Only one or two very tiny ones were left to squeak about what Xar and Wish were doing.

'I have faith in you, Xar,' said Perdita. 'Never forget that. And I have a parting gift for you . . .' She pressed something into Xar's hand. He shoved it in the pocket of his waistcoat, trying not to cry and pretending he did not care, and then they all hurried off after Hoola towards the west.

Perdita watched them go a moment. And then she turned

and limped to the east, where the knocking was getting more and more urgent.

'You'd better use invisibility spells now,' Hoola warned Xar and Wish as they reached the western perimeter of the learning place. 'From the moment you leave this place, the Witches will be watching. Remember, *don't stay invisible too long*, just until you get out of range of the Witches who are surrounding us. Invisibility is very bad for you.'

The sprites took out their wands, and Xar and Wish used their spelling staffs to turn everyone invisible. As she looked down at her disappearing legs, Wish felt a familiar queasy lurch of the stomach. Turning invisible was almost like parts of you were going to sleep, or as if you had become a ghost.

Hoola led them to the wall at the edge of the mound, and Wish put the door up against it and knocked three times with her now-invisible fist.

Knock!

Knock!

Knock!

The door swung open.

Outside, the cold night air was full of shrieks and the screams of Witches, so loud and eerie Wish's blood ran cold to hear them. It went against every instinct to leave the warmth and safety of the learning place.

But they had to do this.

The invisible Wish and Xar walked through, leaving Hoola and two little piskies hovering on the other side.

Wish made it bigger for a second, so Crusher the giant could walk through the door too.

And then smaller again.

And then slowly, sadly, Wish closed the door.

'HOOOOOOOOO . . . ' Hoola hooted through the keyhole.

'One giant one bear TWO humans three wolves three snowcats eight USELESS sprites one peregrine falcon and a Baby noneofthemgreenanymore... OFF . . . on a very, very secret . . . absolutely crazy . . . madlysuicidal . . . absolutelySecret . . . terrifyingstupyfyingidiotic new QUEST,' chanted the two little piskies from the other side of the door. 'Leaving their wond-er-ful . . . marv-ellous . . . magnificent new Ho-o-ome . . . probably never to see it again . . . but to die miles away from anywhere in the ravenous jaws of the Nuckalavee . . . instead of staying cosycomfyhappy . . . and I think it's galiciousstarcurlers for supper again . . .'

'We'll be back, I promise,' Wish whispered back through the keyhole.

She let her hand rest on the door a second. And then, firmly, she stepped away.

'Follow Bodkin and Nighteye,' Xar whispered into the invisible ears of the snowcats.

Then they climbed on the invisible door and Wish whispered a word to make it fly, moved the key, and they flew very low over the ground – for up above was the terrifying sight of the Witches attacking the school. Wish could see the dark outlines of their feathers, swarms of them, Magic screaming out of their mouths like lightning, and her palms began to sweat.

Love is weakness...
But what a very
nice weakness it is indeed.

KNOCK!
KNOCK!
KNOCK!

14. Encanzo and Sychorax Have a Little Explaining to Do

Wish and Xar only just left in time, for:

Knock!

Knock!

Knock!

KNOCK knock KNOCK knock KNOCK!!!!!

The person knocking frantically at the eastern door was Xar's father Encanzo.

The eastern door was the official entrance, so it was enormous and had a stone with big curly sprite writing on it saying 'Pook's Hill, the Learning Place for Spectacularly Gifted Wizards', just in case anybody had any doubt where they were.

Encanzo wasn't just knocking with both fists, he was drumming on the door with his feet, shouting, 'COME ON! COME ON! FOR MISTLETOE'S SAKE, *LET US IN!!!*' for he was in a terrible state.

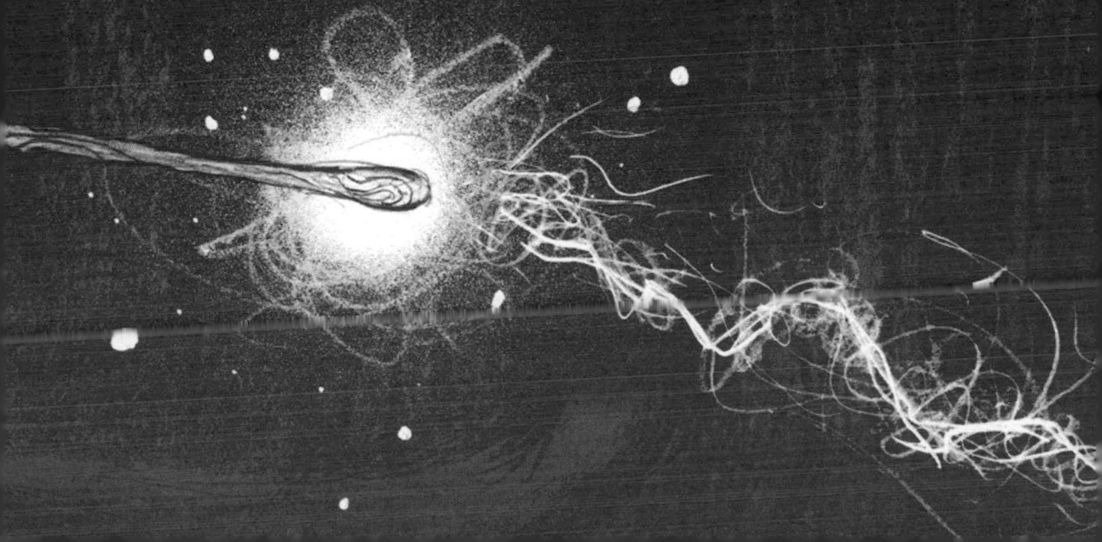

Riding through the forest on their snowcats, Encanzo and Looter, Xar's elder brother, had been ambushed by Witches. Encanzo had begun by fighting them off with Magic, but there were too many of the creatures, so in desperation Encanzo had to set up a forcefield over the two of them, and they had only just reached the learning place in time. Now they had their backs against the door and Witches were attacking the forcefield with terrible cries.

Looter was tall, handsome, good-looking and extremely pleased with himself. He had just spent three months changed into a graxerturgleburkin,* but he seemed to have recovered from the experience. In fact, it may even have improved him somewhat. He was *ever so slightly* less self-satisfied than he had been three months earlier.

But right at this very moment he was looking absolutely petrified. Looter had never come this close to a Witch before, and he was cowering at the back of the forcefield, scrabbling at the door as the terrifying creatures swooped and struck. It was so dark that you could not really see them, but you could hear the appalling noise as they dived, and see the red of their eyes.

Knock!

* Long story. You can read about it in 'Wizards of Once, Twice Magic' if you like.

Knock!

Knock!

KNOCK! KNOCK! KNOCK! KNOCK!!!!!!!!

And then, to Looter and Encanzo's intense relief . . .

'All right, all *right*!' came a rather harassed voice from a long way away. 'I'm coming! I've just forgotten the password. What is it again? Oh, I remember now . . . ARDEN!'

C-R-e-e-e-akkkkk! The door opened. The light was so dazzling that Encanzo and Looter couldn't quite see what they were stepping into, but they and their snowcats FELL in through the door, Encanzo exploding the forcefield simultaneously so that the attacking Witches fell back with terrible screams of pain.

SLAM! The door closed behind them with the sound of a rain of talons landing as it shut.

'Thank the green gods . . . ' gasped Encanzo, and Looter was so out of his mind with fear that he could only just gulp slightly. Even Encanzo's very dignified ancient snowcat had his fur standing up like the quills on a hedgehog, and his equally distinguished sprite was a mess of anxiety.

But when Encanzo and Looter's eyes adjusted, to their surprise they were not standing in the large impressive entrance hall that the appearance of the eastern entrance for the Learning Place for Spectacularly

Gifted Wizards might suggest.

No, they were standing in a small, very tidy study. There was only one person in the room and that person was Queen Sychorax, sitting down with her hands on the desk.

Looter and Encanzo could not have been more surprised than Queen Sychorax.

For from *Queen Sychorax's* point of view, the knocking had come from the other side of her cupboard door.

Imagine how alarming it must have been to have the door of a cupboard in which you have very tidily left the head of Madam Clairvoy, suddenly start knocking at you, and behind that door hear the dreadful scream of attacking Witches.

That would be truly terrifying, particularly when you can't run away, because your hands are stuck to the desk. She hadn't been behaving very well recently, but you have to feel sorry for Queen Sychorax in this situation. A lesser person than Queen Sychorax would have passed out with the shock of it.

Encanzo and Looter ought to have been less amazed, because space and time can work in a mysterious and unexpected way in the Wizarding world, particularly where doors are concerned. But the truth is, you never quite get used to it when it takes you by surprise like this.

And it is impossible to explain quite how this worked in human physical terms, but Madam Perdita was in a hurry, and she just wanted to get these two people together as quickly as possible, so the old door trick was the quickest way to do it.

Neither Encanzo nor Sychorax were even remotely pleased to see each other.

'*You* . . . ' hissed Queen Sychorax.

'You!!!' spat King Encanzo.

There was always a little hiss or a frizzle in the atmosphere when these two met, a sort of jarring in the universe more noticeable on the outside than on the in, but if it were possible for the air to suddenly darken as if internal thunderclouds were gathering, then it did, and a couple of the candles blew out, just like that. *Pffft.*

Encanzo was particularly irritated to find himself confronted by his old enemy when he was in such an undignified condition, shirt raked to ribbons by Witches' talons, one side of his face blasted by Witch lightning. He adjusted the ruins of his waistcoat, as if that was going to make any difference, and straightened up to his most majestic and magnificent height.

BAM!

To both the monarchs' surprise, the actual door to Queen Sychorax's room now opened on the other side of the room, and in ran the owner of the harassed voice Encanzo had heard a couple of minutes earlier. Perdita was looking, if anything, even more ragged and frazzled than Encanzo, with five pairs of spectacles crawling all over her, several bits of clothing on back to front, Witch burns on her face and what appeared to be bits of food in her hair.

'Yes, yes, yes, we're going to have to be quick here. This isn't a good time for visitors!' snapped Madam Perdita. 'I'm containing a Witch attack, and then I have to get back to rather a complicated recipe for the young people's supper . . .'

'Who ARE you?' demanded Encanzo. 'If you're supposed to be containing a Witch attack you're not doing a very good job of it! You are facing a sustained assault by the forces of dark Magic and I need to speak to the head of the learning place, not the cook!'

'I just told you, the Witch attack is completely under control, and I AM the head of the learning place! The head of the learning place should *always* be the cook, it's the most important job,' explained Perdita.

'Well, I am King Encanzo, King of Wizards,' said Encanzo fiercely, 'and—'

'Yes, yes,' interrupted Madam Perdita impatiently. 'I know who you are, and you are bringing your son Looter to be a pupil here, because you think he's spectacularly gifted. Run along through that door there, Looter, dear, you're admitted . . .'

Looter goggled at her.

He was used to being the most important person in his father's and everyone else's life, not swept out of the way as if he were nothing.

'Do you not realise who you are speaking to?' said Encanzo sharply. 'This is my eldest son, who will be the next King of Wizards, so you are incredibly lucky to have the honour of schooling him.'

'Quick, quick,' said Madam Perdita, not obviously impressed, 'you're a bit in the way at the moment, Looter, but I'm sure you'll make a *lovely* spectacularly gifted Wizard. Just step through the door and ask the piskies to take you to the sanitorium, to have a look at those Witch burns you have on your arm, and then to the head of Year Ivy*, she'll look after you.'

Almost as if hypnotised, Looter moved towards the door of the room, opened it, stepped through, and the door shut after him.

A little chorus of excitable piskie voices came floating through the door. The little voices sounded somewhat dubious.

'WELCOME largeverypleasedwithyourselfboy whothinkshe'ssocleverandusedtobeagraxerturgle burkinandwhoisusedtotellingeveryonewhattodo! WELCOME to your marvellous . . . magnificent . . . magical new ho-o-ome!'

'Mff,' sniffed Madam Perdita thoughtfully. 'Looter's spectacular gifts aren't *immediately* apparent, but I'm

* Year 12

sure we will find them, we always do . . . Now,' she said briskly, 'I understand, Encanzo, you are also here to collect your *other* son, the one who is spectacularly cursed?'

'You knew about that?' said Encanzo, trying to regain control of the situation.

'You're too late,' said Madam Perdita.

With a wink of Madam Perdita's eye, she released Queen Sychorax's hand from the desk. Queen Sychorax leapt to her feet.

'Do sit down,' said Madam Perdita.

'I prefer to stand,' said Queen Sychorax.

'As do I,' said King Encanzo.

'As you wish,' said Madam Perdita.

She snapped her fingers. A chair ran towards her. She sat down.

Both Encanzo and Sychorax regretted saying they would stand because suddenly it felt like Perdita was the royalty, sitting on her throne, even with bits of food in her hair, and *they* were the naughty children who had been sent to the head.

'You don't mind if I knit? It helps me to concentrate,' said Madam Perdita. One knitting needle pushed its way through the keyhole of the cupboard and flew into Madam Perdita's left hand. The other knitting needle pushed its way through the keyhole of the door, and flew into Madam Perdita's right hand.

Madam Perdita began to knit, unravelling her own scarf as she went and using it as the wool.

'*You*, Sychorax and Encanzo, have a little explaining to do,' said Madam Perdita, and now she sounded very grim indeed. 'You are too late to catch your children. They and their bodyguard have gone to see the Nuckalavee.'

Both Sychorax and Encanzo whitened in horror.

'And you let them?' gasped Sychorax.

'But that's like sending them to their deaths!' said Encanzo. 'Why did you not keep them here?'

'This is a learning place, not a prison,' said Perdita, knitting away merrily. 'Although both you and Sychorax seem very fond of locking your children up.'

Now Sychorax and Encanzo went from white to red with embarrassment.

'I had no choice!' said Encanzo. 'You said so yourself! Xar is spectacularly cursed!'

'As is Wish!' said Sychorax.

'Then *un*curse them,' said Perdita.

'There's no such thing as *un*cursing,' said Encanzo.

'The young people seem to think so,' said Perdita. 'Which is why they are off to find the ingredients of the spell to get rid of Witches.'

'Wish fulfillment,' said Sychorax.

'Child's play,' said Encanzo.

'And *dangerous* child's play, at that,' said Sychorax. 'Listen to the sound of those creatures out there! You've exposed our children to the Witches who are hunting them . . .'

'Perhaps,' said Perdita. 'But the young people are in grave danger already, and you do not seem to be helping them with that so far.'

Both Encanzo and Sychorax turned red.

'I've very much enjoyed getting to know your children over the past few months,' said Perdita, continuing to knit. 'It seems to me that the reason that Xar got the Witchstain in the first place is that he was so desperate not to let his father down by having no Magic at all, that he was prepared to go to extreme lengths to get just a little approval.'

'You can't blame ME for this!' growled Encanzo.

'Have you noticed,' said Perdita, 'that the more you tell Xar off, the more disobedient he becomes?'

Encanzo was silent.

'And as for Wish, I have never met a child with Magic as powerful as she has, but she seems to think, Queen Sychorax, that *you*, her own mother, are ashamed of her,' said Perdita.

'Am I supposed to be PROUD of a daughter with such cursed Magical skills?' stormed Queen Sychorax.

'She's an embarrassment. How dare you tell us what to do? We know best, for we are the children's parents!'

'And how do you think your parenting is going so far?' asked Perdita sweetly.

There was an uncomfortable silence inside the study.

Outside, the screaming of the Witches seemed to be underlining that the answer to that question was: *Not very WELL, actually, since you mention it.*

'We're doing our best!' protested Encanzo. 'Being a parent is not as easy as it looks!'

'That, at least, is true,' admitted Perdita. 'Very well then, if you want to stop them, you're going to have to catch them. Which is why I brought you together. That, and showing you, Sychorax, what a *real* learning place ought to be like.' Perdita seemed amused about something. 'Did you think I did not see through the Madam Clairvoy disguise? Of course I did . . . I just thought you might learn something from being in Pook's Hill.'

'This is a ridiculous place!' raged Sychorax. 'Children being taught by birds! Lessons in tree climbing! I am the only person in this entire establishment teaching anything sensible . . . '

'But the children are happy,' said Madam Perdita. 'What should they be learning, Sychorax? How to burn down a forest? However, if *you* haven't learnt anything, never mind. I could be wrong, of course, there's always that possibility.'

Madam Perdita considered that improbable possibility for one interested moment, and then rejected it.

'No,' said Perdita briskly, 'no, I'm not wrong.'

As Madam Perdita was talking, Sychorax suddenly realised that along with a bit of rug from the floor, the edges of Sychorax's *own cloak* were unravelling themselves and being knitted into Perdita's knitting, along with little pieces of Encanzo's shirt. 'What on earth are you doing?' snapped Sychorax, trying to wrench her cloak away, but it held surprisingly fast.

Encanzo looked amused, but said, 'Stop that, Madam Perdita.'

'Oh, I do apologise,' said Madam Perdita, 'this is a very bad habit of mine . . .'

A little pair of bronze scissors hopped out of her pocket, danced up to the pieces of thread and snipped them apart, snip, snip.

'Now I brought you together, for you both want the same thing, do you not? You want to catch your children, so catch them if you can. They have gone to find the Nuckalavee, so you can follow them and find them, the two of you, alone . . . For neither of you want anyone to know the secrets of your past, do you? You'd rather that the Wizards and the Warriors did not find out that you were once in love and that that is the reason that Wish has been born with Magic-mixed-with-iron?'

'It *is* best if we keep this to ourselves,' admitted Sychorax.

'Just one other reason that the predicament the young people find themselves in may be more YOUR fault than their own . . .' Perdita reminded them.

Sychorax's hands were in fists. Normally nobody tells the truth to queens, and she wasn't enjoying the experience. But what could she do? This was Madam Perdita's territory. She had to bide her time and wait for revenge.

'Encanzo knows where the Nuckalavee can be found, don't you, Encanzo?' said Madam Perdita.

'I do,' said Encanzo. 'The Nuckalavee was part of my shadow quest, after you abandoned me, Sychorax,' said Encanzo. 'I nearly never came back.'

'A quest where you gave the Nuckalavee your heart,' said Perdita, in her cosiest voice.

'You gave the Nuckalavee your heart?' said Sychorax, forgetting her fury at Perdita for a moment and raising one eyebrow at Encanzo.

'Well, what was I supposed to do with it after you had stomped all over it?' said Encanzo bitterly. 'I couldn't go on living with a broken heart. It was very inconvenient – the edges of it were all uncomfortable in my chest. I had to get on with my life, live and love again . . .'

'So the two of you can go together,' said Perdita, getting up. 'With absolutely no chance of either of you catching any of that nasty love disease again. One without a heart. The other having drunk the Spell of Love Denied. No risk whatsoever, I would say.'

'We're free to go?' said Encanzo.

'*Of course* you're free to go!' said Perdita, extremely exasperated. 'I don't know WHY everyone keeps saying that! This is a learning place, not a prison. I may not agree with your methods of child rearing, but they are, after all, your children. It sounds like the Witch attack is now under control.'

The sound of the screaming outside had indeed died down somewhat.

'But I would recommend invisibility, nonetheless,' Perdita advised, 'and suggest you leave by the cupboard door, thereby avoiding the piskies. Or better still, the trapdoor. I have Witchblood to clean up and a recipe to finish. Off you go!'

15. The Chase

Meanwhile, Bodkin had left Pook's Hill by the western entrance. It was lucky that he was still in the body of Xar, for it meant that he could use Xar's powers and make himself invisible. He had a piece of map torn from the Spelling Book, and it said the Isle of the Nuckalavee was opposite somewhere called the Beach of Shoes, and that was to the west.

Bodkin had a slight setback when he saw the huge dark outlines of the Witches roosting in the treetops above him, like gigantic crows. Even though he knew they couldn't see him, he passed out on the back of Nighteye. When he woke up again a few seconds later, he was so rigid with fear, his hands clutching Nighteye's fur hadn't even unclenched. Looking back over his shoulder as Nighteye ran on, he could see that the Witches were still unmoving.

After a while, when it seemed clear that he wasn't being followed, he stopped Nighteye and turned himself visible again, for he didn't know how long he would continue to inhabit the body of Xar, and when he was back in his own body, he wouldn't have any Magical powers at all. Even the staff that Perdita had given him was with Xar now, so he couldn't use that. Not that 'sticking things to other things' was likely to be *all* that useful when you were facing what must be the terrible nightmare of a Nuckalavee . . .

I have the sword, though! I can use the sword, thought Bodkin with excitement. As he rode on, he was still elated at leaving the school without being discovered.

I'll show Wish what a Hero I can be . . . I've betrayed her, but now I will prove myself.

But then there was a dreadful scream behind him, which was the sound of the triumphant Witches discovering the hole in the Magic that Bodkin had made when he took the iron Enchanted Sword out of Pook's Hill. In terror, Bodkin thought it might be the Witches coming after him. He urged Nighteye on, on. He had entered a bit of the forest that had been scorched to the ground by Sychorax's wildfire, so the burnt landscape was depressing. And by the time he found a place to sleep for the night, the enormity of what he had done was beginning to creep over him.

He shivered under brambles, trying to get to sleep on a cold, cold night, hugging as close as he could to Nighteye in the hope of getting some warmth. The snowcat's fur was soaked through. Her tail was in a puddle. Bodkin cried himself to sleep.

Xar and Wish left from the western entrance about an hour after Bodkin. They, too, escaped without apparently being detected by the Witches, who were now attacking Encanzo and Looter on the other side of Pook's Hill. On and away they flew on the back of the Enchanted Door, just above the level of the undergrowth, following the very faint noise of the running snowcats and wolves, who were panting with fear as they ran through the burnt forest. Wish and Xar looked over their shoulders every two or three minutes to check that they were not being pursued by Witches.

To Wish's intense relief, the snowcats following the traces of Bodkin's path were heading further and further west. *So Bodkin must have got away without the Witches seeing him*, thought Wish jubilantly.

After a while, they felt confident that they were far enough away to turn themselves visible again. And Xar let Squeezjoos out of his pocket. The little sprite was recovered from the odd attacks that seemed to beset him when he was too close to Witches, but he was terribly upset. 'Why dids you shut me up?' asked Squeezjoos.

'It was for your own good, Squeezjoos,' said Xar. 'You have to trust me, I know best.'

Squeezjoos could not stay cross with Xar for long. He looked into Xar's eyes, and licked him on the face. 'It's true!' said Squeezjoos. 'You DOESSS know best!'

Eventually they were too tired to go any further.

Squeezjoos was so exhausted that he actually crawled

back into Xar's pocket and did up the buttons himself. Lonesome had a thorn in his paw and was limping.

'We need to sleep,' said Xar. 'Daytime is a better time for travelling anyway – less chance of Witches. We'll catch up with Bodkin and Nighteye tomorrow.' Xar was in a belligerent mood, exhilarated to be back on their quest again, but still oddly cross with Perdita for letting them go. 'Nobody wants us, even *her*, but we can do this on our own.'

Talking about Perdita made him look in his pocket for the thing that she had given him just before he left. It was one of her handkerchiefs, wrapped tightly round something in a little bottle, and when he unwound it, out fell . . .

'*The Droods' tears*!' gasped Caliburn. 'The fifth ingredient in the spell to get rid of Witches!'

Sure enough, there were five shining tears of the Droods from the Lake of the Lost, gleaming like dark diamonds in the centre of the bottle.

'My sister trusts me again!' said Caliburn. 'Even though I made a mistake last time!'

'She trusts me too!' said Xar, all his ill humour disappearing. 'Even though I have the Witchstain.'

'There's a note,' said Wish, picking up a piece of paper that had been wrapped around the bottle along with the handkerchief.

The note was in Perdita's handwriting and read:

Dear All,

You have truly earned these Drood's Tears. Life is made up of sorrow as well as joy, and there is a reason why tears are such an important ingredient in so many spells. You may try as hard as you can, and yet still fail...

BUT being a Wizard is about making impossible things happen, and happy endings have to be fought for.

Good luck!

Love Perdita

15 Tears of the Dra... DANG...

'Maybe we *did* belong in Pook's Hill, after all,' said Xar. He tied Perdita's handkerchief around his arm with the Witchstain. 'If I ever wanted a mother – and I *don't*,' he added hurriedly, 'I would choose a mother like Perdita.'

Perdita's present made them all feel more cheerful. They were progressing in their quest. If they had been successful in getting four of the ingredients, surely they could win the last one, and save Bodkin at the same time?

It was raining, so Tiffinstorm set up a weather spell to protect them while they slept.

'Whyissitalwaysmewhohastodoeverything?' complained Tiffinstorm, getting out a number four wand and taking a weather spell out of her spell bag. She batted the spell up in the air with her wand, and a nice little umbrella of wind sprang out of the end of the spell, hovering some three or four feet above them, and the rain poured over the edges in a waterfall.

So Wish and Xar slept far better than poor Bodkin that night.

They slept wrapped up in the middle of the comforting heat of a tangle of animals – the shaggy fur of the snowcats, the werewolf and the wolves, and the bear, keeping them warm. And curled around them all, in a protective way, was the great sleeping form of Crusher the giant. Longstepper High-Walker giants don't need weather spells. They are waterproof. Their great bodies give off such warmth that the rain just bounces off them, turning into steam.

In the middle of the night, Xar could feel his appearance changing back from Bodkin-as-a-hob into Xar again. It was the same strange, unsettling feeling as it had been last time – very sick-making – and when he looked at his arms, he could see the fur gradually dissolving, leaving his own Xar-like skin beneath. He rolled over and went back to sleep again.

When Wish woke up every now and then, she could see that the snowcats were taking turns to keep awake. One time it was Kingcat keeping lookout, watching the skies above through the glass of the rain-washed spell. The next it was Forestheart. So she would fall asleep with the comforting drumming of the rain on the spell above, the desolation of leaving Pook's Hill alleviated by the closeness of her friends.

Bodkin, don't be afraid . . . thought Wish dreamily. *We're coming to find you.*

About half an hour after Wish and Xar left Pook's Hill, Encanzo and Sychorax set out in pursuit.

They had to share a ride on Encanzo's snowcat and there was a big argument about who should ride at the front and who should ride at the back.

They began the trip invisible, but by the time they set out, Perdita and her Wizards had made good the Magic protecting Pook's Hill and the Witch attack was over. In their invisible state, they had to weave their way past several Witch corpses, which explained why the Witches had stopped their invasion. The Witches had now retreated to the treetops where they were chanting dreadful curses, like vengeful monkeys.

Sychorax and Encanzo rode without talking to each other, both of them grimly angry. Once they reached the scorched part of the forest, Encanzo turned them visible again. The broken stumps of trees were quiet, so quiet.

As Sychorax rode through the forest that she herself

had burnt to the ground, steadily growing in her mind's eye with each leap of the snowcat were the remembered ghosts of trees that were heavy with the numberless leaves of the summer time. The memory of a much younger Encanzo riding by her side, and they were hunting deer perhaps, flocks of birds shocked up into the air as they raced past, out of control with youth, and the wind making them giddy by blowing straight into their brains, and the seemingly endless forest stretching out in front of them.

And then she blinked, and here in the present there were no trees. Which was a shame, because when she stopped to think about it, Sychorax *liked* trees. The ashy remains of the tree stumps were making her feel uncomfortable and, irritably, she stared straight ahead so she didn't have to look at them.

They rode until they were so tired they were in danger of falling off the snowcat.

And they made camp in the open air.

'Once you were a wild thing, just like me, Queen Sychorax,' said Encanzo bitterly, staring into the fire of many colours he had conjured up with his staff as they settled down for a few hours of sleep on the forest floor. 'But it will be many years since your Majesty camped out without your toothpick.'

'I am a Warrior,' said Sychorax, tossing her head. 'We camp out all the time.'

This was a lie. It had indeed been a very long time since Sychorax had camped out in the woods without a richly embroidered tent, a feather bed, a tiptoeing lady to turn down the warm, dry covers and wish her a good night's sleep.

But she was too proud to show that she minded.

'I am sorry I cannot offer you trees for shelter,' said Encanzo, pointing upwards at the empty darkness. The bleak, cold rain was coming down very heavily now.

'Once, there would have been branches above us where birds used to sing,' continued Encanzo, 'homes where the forest creatures lived . . . But they are burnt, all burnt, so that you Warriors can build your forts and your fields and all the THINGS you need to have – the nick-nacks, that golden bracelet around your wrist . . .

'But I ask you, Sychorax, is it worth the freedom you have had to give up? The moon, the stars, the wind, you sold them for?'

Sychorax did not answer.

She WAS getting awfully wet.

Her bottom was definitely soggy. She thought she may have sat on a damp patch.

'Let me tell you a story,' said Encanzo, 'of how twenty years ago my heart turned into stone.'

No! I do not want to hear it!

The Story of How Encanzo's heart turned into a Stone

you have to look inside the hut of the Wizard Who Waits

How the boy, Tor, Became the Wizard, Encanzo

'Once upon a time, long, long ago, there was a young Wizard known as Tor, who fell in love with a young Warrior princess. Wizards and Warriors should NEVER fall in love, but the young Warrior princess declared she did not care for silly rules such as this one. The young Warrior princess promised she would marry Tor. She promised on her heart that they would run away together, and find themselves a world where it did not matter where they came from, where Wizards and Warriors could love and live in peace.

TOR'S SONG Never and Forever – Part 2

They told me careful where you love
But I did not listen

My heart was born when I met you, I got my second chance
Flying side by side together in a never-ending dance
Why should I listen?

But now I'm
Waiting
For the knock on the door
When SHE will come
Forever waiting
And waiting …
And waiting.

Closing
My eyes until SHE comes back
Longing
For the knock on the door
When SHE will come …
Forever waiting
And waiting …
And waiting.

But the princess did not keep her promise.

But the princess did not keep her promise . . .'

'I had responsibilities, duties!' interrupted Sychorax. Encanzo carried on as if she had not spoken.

'She took the Spell of Love Denied and the love died in her heart . . . She wrote a letter to the Wizard boy saying she did not love him and she never had. Meanwhile, Tor waited many long weeks in the appointed waiting place. He got the letter. He read it, refused to believe it. A hut grew around him and the sprites in the forest felt so sorry for him, they brought him food and water. They called him "the Wizard-who-waits".

'I will take you inside that hut now. Look at him, the poor young Wizard-who-waits,' said Encanzo bitterly.

'Two long years he waited, said Encanzo. Until he realised . . . she was never coming back. And THAT,' said Encanzo, 'was when the young Wizard turned his heart into stone, and become the Wizard sitting before you now. The Wizard Encanzo.'

And Encanzo turned his heart into a stone.

No longer … WAITING
for the knock on the door.
No longer longing.
For there is no song …
there is no heart
there is no knock

And the true love never comes

Listen. Be careful where you love.
I will make a new start.
Without a heart.

There was a short pause as Encanzo came to the end of his story. Queen Sychorax swallowed hard . . .

and then Encanzo thrust his staff into the ground and he muttered a few words, and a weather spell rushed out of the end of the staff forming a protective canopy over where Encanzo was intending to sleep.

'I can extend the spell to cover *you* as well, if you like,' says Encanzo.

Queen Sychorax put her pretty little nose up in the air.

'Humph,' said Queen Sychorax. 'I do not need your spell. We Warriors are not afraid of a little rain. We are made of tougher material than that.'

'Suit yourself,' said Encanzo, shrugging, wrapping himself in his cloak and falling asleep under the protection of the spell.

Queen Sychorax settled underneath a little tangle of burnt and broken brambles. It took a while for her to fall asleep in the pouring rain. It was going to be a miserable night for Queen Sychorax.

And it may be uncharitable of me as a narrator, and I really shouldn't comment . . .

BUT

I think . . .

I think . . .

I feel sorry for her even though she has brought this all on herself.

Follow me, if you DARE...

NOW . . . I do not want to alarm you, dear reader, of course I do not.

But I have to tell you, it would be truly remarkable if three children, a flying door, four snowcats, various wolves, a werewolf, a bear, two adults, numerous sprites, and a humungous Longstepper High-Walker giant were able to leave Pook's Hill without even ONE Witch noticing, even if they were invisible at the time.

The fact is, although Perdita and Hoola and Elfrida and the other teachers were able to fight off the Witches and make the learning place safe by sealing up the hole in the Magic made by the Enchanted Sword, there were other Witches who had noticed the exit of these three separate parties while the fight was going on.

And they were following.

They did not want anyone to notice, so the Witches were pursuing, not in the air, but on foot, or rather using their folded-up wings as if they were legs, scuttling in between the burnt trees of the broken forest.

They had used the opportunity of the hole made by Bodkin to attack Pook's Hill, because there were things in the learning place that they wanted.

But why were they now choosing NOT to attack the various parties on the quest to find the Nuckalavee?

We are about to find out why . . .

PART Three

The Shadow Quest

16. The Beach of Shoes

When Bodkin woke up, cold, shivering, the transformation medicine that turned him into Xar had worn off, as had any residual excitement. Maybe there was some bit of Xar that was still left in there when he had briefly taken over Xar's body. But whatever mad impulse had taken him over, it was now gone.

He looked down at his arms, skinny as weeds.

He wasn't even a hob any more. He was just *Bodkin* . . . an extremely ordinary Assistant Bodyguard who had betrayed the trust of his princess.

Bodkin was used to being alone, even when he was in company.

But for the first time in his life he really was completely . . .

ALONE.

With shaking hands he took out the map that he had torn from the Spelling Book that showed him the way to the Nuckalavee. The path that led through the burnt forest was shining bright on the map, which meant that he was heading in the right direction. The path ended somewhere called the Beach of Shoes, and opposite this beach was an island called the Isle of the Nuckalavee.

There was a warning on the bottom of the map, saying in big dark letters:

DON'T FORGET TO TAKE OFF YOUR SHOES.

But there was no time to wonder what that might mean.

Bodkin drank a glug of water from his water bottle. He was sick with hunger, but the burnt forest contained no food and he couldn't return now. He had to go on, riding on Nighteye's back, all the while taking terrified glances up at the sky above, scared that at any moment he might see a Witch, even though Witches weren't all that keen on flying during the daytime. The broken trees didn't provide much camouflage.

Bodkin arrived at the Beach of Shoes very late in the evening, hungry and thirsty, and so terrified by the sight of the distant island of the Nuckalavee, crouching like a dark predatory creature on the horizon, he fell asleep on Nighteye's back and Nighteye had to carry him on, in a dead faint, to the edge of the water.

He woke up again at the brink of the ocean, waves breaking on the shore, looking out at the island. Bodkin shivered and thought, 'I have to do this, for HER . . . I have to prove that *I* can be a hero too, even if I will only be a dead hero . . . Maybe if I'm a dead hero, she'll at least forgive me.'

Nighteye swam out to the island, with Bodkin, who could not swim, holding on to her tail.

What am I doing? thought Bodkin. *Some hero I am. I can't even swim.*

Bodkin and Nighteye landed on the Isle of the Nuckalavee, and Nighteye shook off the water like a cat. Bodkin felt rising determination as he put a hand on the hilt of the Enchanted Sword and pulled down his visor.

Before him were the sands of the beach, and the waters of the ocean were running into a dark and dreadful cave, open like the jaws of a monster. The Cave of the Nuckalavee. Bodkin felt his heart shrivel within him as he looked at it.

But I got here on my own! I can do *this!* thought Bodkin. *I'm stronger than they think I am!*

He tried to pull out the Enchanted Sword, but for some reason it would not budge from its scabbard. It was stuck fast, as if it were glued there.

By the whiskers of werewolves! thought Bodkin. *I'm not even strong enough to draw the sword!*

But Bodkin made himself put one foot in front of the other, even though it felt like each foot was made out of lead.

Bodkin stopped suddenly.

Feeling he'd forgotten something.

What was it?

What on earth could it be?

He looked down.

I've forgotten to take off my shoes!!!

Bodkin's eyes closed and his head slumped gently to one side.

Snore!

He tipped forward, face down in the sand.

There was a terrible high-screeching noise from behind and above, like the sound of swooping furies. The sound of many, many scrabbling feet on the sand, panting furiously, running towards the intruders.

Nighteye gave a terrified yowl, her fur all on end. She picked up the fallen Bodkin and ran into the Cave of the Nuckalavee, the unconscious Bodkin dangling from her mouth, like a cat carrying a kitten.

And goodness knows what awaited them in there.

No, I don't think Bodkin was *quite* ready to perform a quest all on his own.

Wish and Xar and their companions arrived at the Beach of Shoes the next morning, so early that the sun was not yet up.

They had lost track of Bodkin for a bit, and it took the snowcats a while to pick up his scent again. When they finally reached the Beach of Shoes, Wish and Xar found a small log boat hidden in a reed bank which they would be able to use to cross the sea to the island of the Nuckalavee. They hid the Enchanted Door under branches and leaves.*

Many of the rocks on the beach had sprite writing that gleamed in the light of the moon scrawled all over them.

The sprite writing said, quite politely,

PLEASE TAKE OFF YOUR SHOES . . .

And then added, more ominously,

. . . OR *ELSE* . . .

'You have to take your shoes off,' explained Caliburn, 'out of respect for the sea, and the impossible quest. Then you become the shadow men and women, the shoeless ones, and only when you return are you allowed to put them back on again.'

Obediently, Wish and Crusher took off their shoes. Xar wasn't wearing any shoes anyway because he had left the Learning Place for Gifted Wizards dressed as a hob.

Crusher walked ahead a few steps and carefully laid down his shoes in the grass at the edge of the beach.

And for the first time the children noticed that all along the outer permimeter of the shore, higher than the tide could reach, was a line of shoes patiently waiting for their owners to come back. Some of them had been waiting a long, long time. Their leather was wind-battered, storm-eaten, half-broken and buried in the sand. Others

* For complicated Magical reasons, doors have difficulty flying over oceans. They get seasick, and capsize.

looked perkier and more hopeful, as if their owners had only just taken them off and were about to return.

'Not very many people come back to collect their ssshooessssss . . .' squeaked Bumbleboozle in nervous alarm.

Ariel's eyes gleamed green and then red. 'Particularly when you conssssider these are the shoes of some of the greatest Wizards in the wildwoods . . .'

They couldn't find Bodkin's shoes, so they weren't sure if he had got there before them or not.

Crusher picked up the small boat, carefully carried it across the beach and put it gently in the water. The others followed in his giant footsteps.

There were will-o'-the-wisps flying right out of the bogs and on to the beach in a glorious firework display, singing and taunting and pulling the hair of the sprites.

Will-o'-the-wisps are mean little faeries that sprites hate even more than piskies. At least piskies are only mischievous. Will-o'-the-wisps wilfully lead unwary travellers to their doom.

'Don't you DARE go after the will-o'-the-wisps, sprites!' shouted Xar, shaking his fist. 'I'm warning you all! Pay no attention!'

But it was very hard to ignore the impudent little creatures, and their eerie song sent a chill into Wish's soul and made her swallow hard. Whatever was over on that island must be very, very scary indeed.

'The Nuckalavee!' sang the will-o'-the-wisps. 'The fools on their way to the Nuckalavee . . .'

The Fools on Their Way to the Nuckalavee

Care-less, love-less, heart-worn, soul-blast?
Come this way . . .
Thought-less . . . shoe-less . . . hope-less?
Come this way . . .
Love is weakness . . .
Love is kindness . . .
Love is childish . . .
Love is thoughtless . . .
No more second chances
No more silly dances
LOVE is weakness . . . so
Come this Way . . .

'Take no notice. Don't look back until we've got in the boat,' said Caliburn, all of a fluster.

Crusher tied a rope to the front of the boat and they all jumped in. The giant waded out thigh-deep, and then he gave a great shiver of 'it's cold!' before holding his nose and launching himself into the sea in a great breaststroke, sending backward waves that nearly overturned their boat.

When the sky turned dark, the moon shone and the swimming giant pulled the boat after him along the path of the moon, heading out to the island of the Nuckalavee with the sprites singing overhead.

The wolves and the snowcats put their heads over the side of the boat, wind waggling their ears, as they looked back at the beach. They could still see the shoes.

The shoes were waiting.

They would wait forever if they had to.

And little did they know it, but there were eyes OTHER than the eyes of will-o'-the-wisps watching them leave the Beach of Shoes . . .

The eyes of *WITCHES*.

Witches were crouching like great dark spiders in the reed beds, muttering to each other, 'Sehs gnimoc . . . sehs gnimoc . . .' which means, 'She's coming . . . she's coming . . .'

But oddly, they did not yet attack. They were waiting too.

What were *they* waiting for?

Crusher swam through the quiet black water, so far out that they could no longer see the shore and the beach with the waiting shoes behind them, and then Wish began to feel not-so-brave.

As they drew closer to the island of the Nuckalavee, the shadowy outline coming nearer and nearer, bottles began to appear in the ocean – at first only a few passing the log boat every now and then, but then there were more of them, and more, and more and more.

Xar leant over the side of the log boat and picked one out of the water. It was a perfectly ordinary bottle with a blank piece of paper on it, and a bit of hair, and a fingernail, and some other things he couldn't quite identify.

'Why are all these bottles here?' asked Wish.

'They're curse bottles,' said Xar, putting the bottle back in the water. 'Somebody on that island must be putting them in the water and pushing them out to sea. Whoever it is really doesn't like someone else, but I don't know who. Normally you write the name of the person you are cursing on that piece of paper, but there's nothing written on the paper.'

Wish shivered. There were so many bottles bobbing past in the sea around them. That was an awful lot of cursing, and she didn't really want to meet whoever was behind it.

Mists suddenly descended out of nowhere, great choking sea mists, treacherous, shifting, there one minute

Curse bottles

gone the next, sometimes so thick that they could barely see the comforting head of Crusher swimming out in front of them.

But they knew they were still going the right way, for they were following the bottles.

Ariel tasted the mist. 'This fog is not natural – it is Magic, summoned by the Droods,' whispered Ariel, his eyes gleaming red for danger in the swirling, confusing fog all around them. 'The Droods are concealing something.'

The mists cleared and there it was, finally, close-up.

The Isle of the Nuckalavee.

'Oh my goodnesssss!' squeaked Bumbleboozle, turning multiple somersaults in panic. 'It's not an island, it's a MONSTER! Look at how big its JAWS are . . . Pleassse let's go back . . .'

But Wish screwed up her eyes and flicked up her eyepatch a smidgeon because her Magic eye was good at seeing through magic-made mist.

'That isn't a mouth,' she said at last. 'It's a CAVE . . .'

A dark island, shrouded in fog, with a gigantic dark sea cave like the open mouth of a monster.

17. In the Sea Cave of the Nuckalavee

The sea and the bobbing bottles went right inside the cave, but it was very dark in there and they did not dare take the log boat in, in case the cave narrowed further down and the boat got stuck. They wanted to get off the Isle of the Nuckalavee as quickly as they could once they'd completed their quest.

If they completed their quest, that is.

So Crusher the giant dragged the boat up the beach and left it there, beside forty or fifty other log boats hauled up high above the sands. A bit like the shoes, these boats were a melancholy presence, because whoever had crossed the sea in them had made a one-way trip and never returned.

They made themselves slo-o-o-o-owly enter the sea cave, trying to ignore every nerve in their bodies screaming 'DON'T GO IN! DON'T GO IN!', not to mention Bumbleboozle buzzing around in such a state of anxiety that she had blown up like a pufferfish.

Poor little Squeezjoos had not left Xar's pocket since they had travelled further and further away from Perdita's healing influence. He was trembling and going rigid again, the Witchblood poison affecting him as it had done once before. Now he put one green eye to a hole in Xar's pocket and peered out fearfully.

It was not surprising that they needed COURAGE to go into that cave. For there were extraordinary rock formations that looked uncannily like TEETH, and gave the impression that you might indeed be entering the mouth of a monster, as Bumbleboozle had suggested. And this cave contained some of the Droods' greatest secrets, so all around them in the cavern's hush there came a wicked whisper of '*Beware . . .* ' that sent the hairs at the back of everyone's necks quivering electrically upward, along with strange scuttling noises, that might have been the pattering feet of rats or mice, or were they just the fearful scurry of Wish's frantically beating heart?

'Beware . . . Beware . . . beware . . .' sang the unknown voices, and they could be ghosts or they might be will-o'-the-wisps that were appearing out of nowhere, laughing and cackling, and then adding more eerily, '*Come here only if you dare . . .*' as they dived and swooped and vanished back into the darkness, leaving haunting echo whispers of 'Beware . . .' in sound and in sprite writing fading into the dark air in front of them. And then they heard louder scraping noises, this time made by larger and more malevolent creatures with paws that had talons.

'I bet those are nixes,' said Caliburn, shivering. 'I HATE nixes . . . horrible animals. Everyone, watch out, for they'll strangle you if they catch you.'

'Isss ssppooky down here,' whispered poor little Squeezjoos from Xar's pocket. 'I'sss really don't like it . . . can't we go home to Pook's Hill? Pleeeeeasssee??'

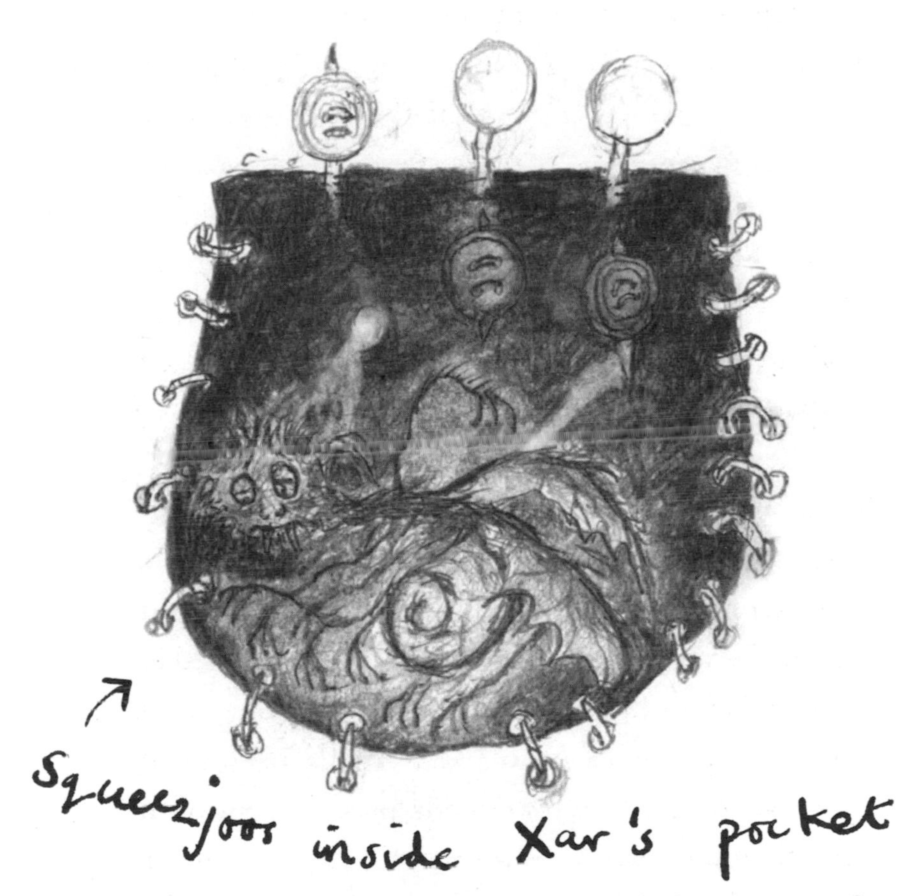

But Squeezjoos's plight only reminded everyone of the urgency of their quest.

'We have to go on,' said Wish. 'We must find Bodkin and get the scales of the Nuckalavee so we can make that spell as quickly as possible.'

Now this was where Xar was extremely helpful as a companion. When things were really dangerous Xar's eyes would light up, and he would stick out his chest and whistle, out of tune, as if he didn't care about any of it. 'Bit damp and smelly in here,' sniffed Xar, and even if he was more scared than he looked, his cheerful defiance was useful in fooling them all that this was a lot less dangerous than it seemed.

So on, on, they went. Sometimes the cave narrowed and the beach disappeared entirely, and Crusher had to carry them across the water to the next bit of shore. Xar had explored many a sea cave in his short life, but this was the largest he had ever seen, and it was a long time before they reached what surely must have been the heart of the island, where the cave opened up to reveal a great underwater lake.

All around was darkness and a smell of secrets that made them all shiver with the coldness of it, the air so chokingly foul it was hard to breathe. The sprites lit up as high and bright as they could so that they could see, and the weird green light of little cave slugs gave off a gentle, queasy glow.

On the edge of the lake was a great heaped-up mound of treasure in the form of

Magical objects the Droods deemed too powerful to be in the world. Harps that played themselves, arrows made of moon, hats with wings and seven-league boots and talking heads and speaking stones and singing swords, all bewitched items of such threatening strength that the air around the heap of treasure gave off a sickly shimmering stench of muffled, ghastly power.

The sprites hissed like hornets.

'That treasure is *cursed*,' hissed Ariel uneasily. 'Lettsss go back . . .'

In front of them, the lake was smooth and serene as a sheet of black glass.

And deathly still, sitting upright in the lake like rows and rows of soldiers, were thousands and thousands and *thousands* of bottles.

'Uh-oh,' gulped Caliburn. 'I think we may have found what we are looking for . . .'

They certainly had.

For high up on a ledge on those very cavern walls, Bodkin was lying, having cried himself to sleep. He was beyond hope, poor Bodkin. He knew he was going to die here in the darkness.

A little higher up still perched Nighteye the snowcat, clinging to the walls, his head drooping, poor cat, for he too was in despair.

But now Nighteye lifted his head eagerly, his

Bodkin knew he was going to die there, alone in that darkness.

whiskers twitched, he swivelled his black-tipped ears. He let out a happy yowly miaow of excitement as he caught the sound of approaching sprites and humans and a giant that he recognised.

'Don't worry, Nighteye, we'll be fine,' lied Bodkin, waking and trying to give the snowcat the reassurance that he did not believe himself, and he closed his weary eyes again.

And then Bodkin heard the voices of Wish and Xar.

For a second he thought he was hallucinating, for he hadn't eaten anything for a while now, and all he had had to drink was the drops of water that he could lick from the cavern walls.

He lifted up his poor exhausted head . . .

And to his total delight, *there they were*!

Wonderful Wish, her hair all a mess with electric anxiety, and staunch, proud Xar, cheek to the backbone, whistling to pretend he wasn't scared as he looked around at the terrifying cavern.

His friends.

He thought he'd never see them again.

'I'm up here, Wish and Xar!' he whispered in a shaky voice from way, way up in the heights of the cavern. They looked up.

'Bodkin!' cried Xar.

'You're alive!' shouted Wish, waving madly back.

But the moment of delight passed in an instant, as Bodkin remembered why they were all there. They mustn't risk their lives to save him, he wasn't worth it.

'You shouldn't have come!' cried Bodkin in a terrified whisper. 'Go back!

Leave me here! I betrayed you to Queen Sychorax . . .' said Bodkin.

'We forgive you, Bodkin. You thought it was for the best and you made a mistake,' said Wish. 'We all make mistakes. We all need second chances.'

'And I'm useless . . .' said Bodkin.

'You're not useless. Xar should never have said that!' Wish shouted. 'Should you, Xar?'

'No, no, I shouldn't!' Xar cried. 'You're not useless! Why are you up there?'

'I kept my shoes on,' said Bodkin.

There was a silence.

'Well you have to admit, that is a BIT useless,' muttered Xar.

'Shut up, Xar,' hissed Wish,

'Oh!' Xar hurriedly remembered that he was supposed to be being tactful and boosting Bodkin's confidence. 'I'm sure you had a very good reason, Bodkin, but why did you keep your shoes on? There were all those signs up and everything . . .'

'I fainted on the beach . . . and then when I came to, I forgot to take my shoes off . . . The only thing I'm supposed to be good at is following rules and I can't even do *that*!' said Bodkin. 'Go away! I'm not worth it!'

'You ARE worth it, Bodkin!' Xar shouted up in response to agonised tugs on his jacket, reminders from Wish that he was supposed to be Being Nice. Xar tried to think of something nice to say. 'You've got a . . . you've got a . . . you've got a . . . very nice smile!'

Oh, for mistletoe's sake, thought Xar to himself. *Can't I think of anything better than that?*

But there was a short silence from above.

Bodkin appeared to quite like that.

'Have I?' said Bodkin in a quavery, quite-pleased voice.

A glimmer of light was returning to Bodkin's dark world. Whatever happened next, at least they both forgave him.

'Don't worry, Bodkin,' said Wish. 'We're going to save you. Come down from there!'

'You don't understand,' said Bodkin, 'I kept my shoes on, and I was so scared that I didn't even realise until I was standing right in front of that ruddy great THING . . . It gave me the shock of my life I can tell you . . . and that THING really didn't like it . . . It was going to kill me, if I hadn't climbed up here . . . It didn't even let me get to the bit where you bargain with it, but I suggest you don't even try that. I really don't think that THING is going to be reasoned with. Go back to Perdita! There has to be a better way than this— OH!'

Bodkin broke off, and pointed down towards the lake.

'*IT'S COMING BACK!* RUN AWAY, GUYS, RUN AWAY!!!'

What was that, surfacing in the distant waters of the lake, like the back of a humpback whale, sending the curse bottles dancing and bobbing in the water?

It was not a whale.

It was an eyelid that slowly opened to reveal a gigantic yellow eye. And then slowly two, three, four, five . . . countless more giant eyes opened in the lake. And the dripping head of the most enormous monster they had ever seen, rose, slowly, slowly, out of the lake, like the rearing of a mountain, and fixed them with its many yellow eyes.

'I don't seem to be able to draw the Enchanted Sword, it's stuck in the scabbard and the scabbard is stuck in my belt!' cried Bodkin.

'Don't worry, Bodkin! We have our staffs and I brought your own staff too!' yelled Xar, throwing Bodkin the do-it-yourself Magic staff. Bodkin caught it in one shaking hand.

'GET READY TO DEFEND US, SPRITES!' cried Xar, as Wish and he pointed their own shaking staffs at the emerging monster.

'How?????' squeaked Bumbleboozle, looking up as the creature coming out of the water revealed itself to be

larger and larger and larger.

The monster opened its mouth and its breath was cold as corpses.

'WHO,' said the monster, 'are you?'

'Who,' said the monster, 'are you?'

18. Dead Boys Can't Make Bargains

The Nuckalavee was in darkness so they could not really see him properly. But whatever he was, he was BIG. He loomed over them like a great gloomy precipice, only his thirteen yellow eyes visible, staring down at them. His voice bellowed and echoed most eerily round that cavern. Every now and then he gulped, as if there was something stuck in his throat and it was bothering him. It was most disconcerting.

'WHOOOOOO ARE YOUOUUUUUUUU?' repeated the Nuckalavee. '*Gulp.*'

Both Wish and Xar knew better than to answer that question correctly. You start telling your real name to a beast that ghastly in a cave that eerie, and you're deader than doornails before you've even started.

They tried to keep their Magic staffs steady, pointing them straight at the gigantic horror in front of them, but my goodness, even the staff in Xar's hand was slipping and sliding in his panicky sweating palm.

'We are humans,' said Wish.

'Very, very powerful humans,' said Xar, hoping to impress the mammoth opponent in front of him. 'We may look unimpressive but we have Magic swords, and Magic eyes, and the girl here has more than one life and everything . . . and we're here on a very important shadow quest.'

'Your Magic will not work in here,' said the Nuckalavee.

Oh dear.

Xar tried to cast a spell with his staff, and sure enough, nothing happened.

Wish put her eyepatch up a smidgeon, and her Magic wasn't working either.

Oh dear oh dear oh DEAR. This already wasn't going well.

'Why were you talking to the dead Wizard?' said the Nuckalavee.

'Dead Wizard? What dead Wizard?' said Xar.

All thirteen of the Nuckalavee's eyes turned towards Bodkin, crouched, shaking, on his ledge.

'*That* dead Wizard,' said the Nuckalavee. 'The boy-who-didn't-take-his-shoes-off.'

'He's not a dead Wizard, he's a Warrior and he's alive,' said Wish.

Unbeknownst to Wish and Xar, this was good news for the Nuckalavee. The Nuckalavee had an aura about him that dampened and digested the Magic of Wizards, but it worked better when they had their shoes off. The Nuckalavee's Magic-quenching properties travelled up through their bare feet and smothered the Magic inside them most effectively.

When they kept their shoes on, the Nuckalavee had to fight them before he killed them, which took a lot of energy. Even though Wizard *Magic* didn't work well against him, Wizards were very clever and tricksy at using Magical objects.

However if the boy-who-didn't-take-his-shoes-off wasn't a Wizard after all, he wasn't going to be a problem.

The Nuckalavee relaxed.

'He won't be alive for long,' said the Nuckalavee. 'He can't stay up there forever. He will starve and if he comes down, I will kill him. Normally I offer visitors to my island the chance to make a bargain with me. But they have to take their shoes off before they come here. This boy was dead the moment he stepped on my island . . . *in shoes*,' said the Nuckalavee. 'Dead boys can't make bargains.'

It wasn't a great start to a conversation, on the whole.

'*You*, however, are both shoeless,' said the Nuckalavee. 'And therefore you are welcome to try to make a bargain with me . . . *if you wish*. What are you bringing me?' asked the Nuckalavee.

'We're not bringing you anything,' said Xar. 'We didn't know we were supposed to bring you something.'

'Don't you know the rules of this particular shadow quest?' asked the Nuckalavee.

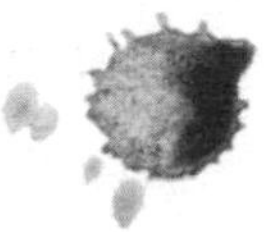

The eyes, from their various different perches on the Nuckalavee's great barnacled head, swivelled in to look down. Six of them looked at Xar. And seven of them at Wish.

The eyes were old, and it was very difficult to see their expression.

'Foolish,' said the Nuckalavee, 'to come on a quest without knowing the rules yet.'

'But the rules are a secret!' Wish pointed out. 'Apart from the bit about taking off your shoes!'

'Taking off your shoes is polite,' said the Nuckalavee, 'and shows me that you can follow the rules.'

'Now let me tell you the rules of this particular shadow quest,' continued the Nuckalavee. 'You don't have to accept the bargain I offer, because at least you have taken your shoes off. You can walk away from this cavern free and alive. But if you take the bargain, then you must keep to the rules and pay the price I ask. Is that understood?'

'Yes,' said Wish.

'I am a sin-collector . . .' said the Nuckalavee, 'a secret-keeper . . . a guardian of power . . . I am a prisoner of the Droods, and the shadow men and women come to me and I look after objects for them that are too dangerous to be in the world.'

That would explain the extraordinary amount of treasure in that cavern.

This was the secret of the Nuckalavee. It was all treasure that the Droods and the Wizards considered needed guarding.

'And in return . . .' said the Nuckalavee.

'Yes,' said Xar. 'In return?'

'You answer a riddle that I ask you,' said the Nuckalavee. 'If you win, you walk out of here, free and alive.'

'And if we lose?' asked Xar.

'The shadow men and women who lose stay here on this island to look after me,' said the Nuckalavee. 'I turn them into nixes and they become my slaves forever . . .'

Oh dear.

A nasty clammy cold feeling stole over Wish and Xar.

'The clever and the lucky know the answer to my riddle,' said the Nuckalavee. 'They are the ones who escape. Accepting my bargain takes courage.

'Now, what is the treasure that you have brought me?' said the Nuckalavee. 'Is it that staff you are carrying? It looks a very powerful one . . .'

'We already said, we have nothing to bring you,' said

Wish, her voice trembling with fear. 'And in fact, we are wanting to change the rules slightly . . .'

The Nuckalavee's eyes narrowed. His yellow eyes blazed orange for a second. 'I hate it when people want to change the rules,' said the Nuckalavee. 'It's like people who come here without removing their shoes. Very rude.'

'It's just a *small* change . . .' said Wish. 'We don't want to BRING you something, we want to TAKE something from you. Two things, actually. If we lose, we will stay here as your slaves. But if we win, you must give back the life of my bodyguard, and . . . you must also give us four of your scales,' stammered Wish. Suddenly the request did seem a little, well, *cheeky*. 'I hope you won't miss them. You have an awful lot of scales, after all.'

All thirteen of the Nuckalavee's eyes swivelled to look at Wish.

'Really?' said the Nuckalavee. 'You want me to give you four of my scales?' said the Nuckalavee, repeating Wish's request thoughtfully. 'Now, that IS an interesting suggestion. My scales are very precious, of course . . . they're powerful, powerful Magic, and they make the bearer a mighty Wizard indeed. But Magic as potent as this must be handled very carefully.'

'It's for a good cause,' said Wish. 'The

scales are ingredients in a spell to get rid of Witches.'

The Nuckalavee thought for a very long time, all of his yellow eyes looking this way and that over Wish and Xar and their companions. Wish could feel her stomach going liquid with fear.

'If you want to change the rules,' said the Nuckalavee, at last, 'in all fairness, *I* must be allowed to change the rules too. You have asked for two things, so if you guess the answer to my riddle, I will want two things back. You must not only answer my riddle correctly, you must also perform a task for me. If you do both of those things, you can walk out of this cavern free as birds, and take the boy-who-didn't-take-his-shoes-off with you. Otherwise, you stay here as my slaves just like the others.'

'What is this task we have to perform?' said Xar.

'I have something in my throat that has been bothering me for twenty years,' said the Nuckalavee, and he gulped again. They could hear from his voice that there was indeed something that had lodged in there. 'You must walk into my mouth, and remove it for me.'

'But if we walk into your mouth, you might just swallow us!' said Xar.

'I promise not to swallow you,' said the Nuckalavee. 'That is part of the bargain. I want this thing removed, and you can remove it. And I think that you are both lucky and clever, and that you will know the answer to my riddle. Do you take my offer?'

'You swear that if we walk into your mouth, you will not shut your mouth and swallow us?' said Wish suspiciously.

'You drive a hard bargain, small girl. But I swear by mistletoe and all things Magic, I will not shut my mouth and swallow you,' said the Nuckalavee. 'My life shall be the forfeit, if I break this promise. That is our contract, if you care to take it. But if you do *not* take it . . . the boy-who-did-not-take-his-shoes-off is dead indeed.'

How could they turn this deal down when Bodkin's life would be the forfeit?

The idea of climbing into the Nuckalavee's mouth and removing something from it, trusting that he would not close it, was very unpleasant indeed. But what do you expect from a shadow quest? Of course it was going to be gruesome, and challenging, and terrifying. If the ingredient you are searching for represents courage, well, it seems logical that your bravery should be properly tested in order to find it.

Wish and Xar had a short, whispered conversation.

'I think the Nuckalavee wants us to win the bargain. His voice sounds terrible. I know how I feel if I even have a sore throat for a week. Imagine having one for *twenty years*!' said Wish. 'The Nuckalavee will feel better if we take whatever it is out, and a promise made on mistletoe and all things Magic is an unbreakable promise.'

'We've come all this way,' said Xar. 'And we need those scales. The Nuckalavee says we are lucky and clever, and we are . . . He thinks we might know the answer to his question. We need to have courage . . .'

'Don't take the bargain, Wish and Xar!' Bodkin shouted down. 'Seriously, Wish, as your bodyguard I have to urge you not to do this!'

But Xar and Wish took the Nuckalavee's bargain.

They swore the oath of the shadow quest.

And the Nuckalavee asked his riddle.

19. The Riddle of the Nuckalavee

'Before I ask my riddle I need to tell you a story,' said the Nuckalavee. 'Listen well . . .

'By extraordinary coincidence,' said the Nuckalavee, 'you are not the first people to have asked to change the rules. Twenty years ago, someone *else* asked to change the rules, and by very strange coincidence, that person asked for the very same thing you have asked . . .'

'Oh dear,' groaned Caliburn. 'I HATE coincidences, I really, really do . . .'

'About twenty years ago,' said the Nuckalavee, 'I was visited in this very cavern by a young man. The young man was carrying many wonderful Magical objects. I hoped he wanted to leave them for me to guard, but instead he offered me a different bargain. I would give him four of my scales, and then if I asked him a riddle to which he knew the answer, he would walk out of the cavern, free and alive. If, on the other hand, I asked him a riddle he could not answer, he would give me his heart. For the young man was heart sick – ever so heart sick. He did not care, this boy, if he was risking his heart, apparently, for he was in love with a young lady who was not in love with him.

'Well, I thought, what a stupid boy! Even if I gave

him some of my beautiful shining scales, he would not be able to take them anywhere because if I had his heart, I would have ALL of him, and the wonderful Magical objects into the bargain. Doesn't that make logical sense?'

'It's a bit gruesome,' said Wish, grimacing. 'But I guess it makes sense.'

'So, even though it was a little unorthodox, and a breaking of the rules, because it looked like such an easy win for me, I took the boy's bargain.

'The boy thought he was lucky, and he knew he was clever. But *I* was cleverer, and I asked him a riddle, and I made it a hard one, so he would not know the answer . . .

'So far, so good.

'The boy lost. So the boy was supposed to give me his heart, and therefore all of him. He was supposed to walk into my mouth, with his heart safe inside of him. But the boy' – now the Nuckalavee gnashed his teeth at the memory of it – 'but the boy was tricksy, ever so *tricksy* . . .

'*He had made his heart into a stone!*' said the indignant Nuckalavee.

'He threw the stone into my mouth, it lodged in my throat . . . and he ran out of this very cavern with my scales still warm in his hand. He took with him the Magical Cup of Second Chances that ought to have been mine, and he escaped out of here, quite lickety-split! That thieving MAGPIE of a trickery spick of a boy! And oh . . .' groaned the Nuckalavee, 'that stone that was his heart got lodged in my throat, and it has *ached* me ever since . . .' (That must be the strange gulping noise the Nuckalavee made every now and then.)

'I think a nix did bite him, at least, on the finger,' said the Nuckalavee. 'And so he carries a little memory of us with him, for the bite of a nix has a sting. But if I ever get my hands on that trickster of a boy I will swallow the rest of him whole, no questions asked!

'And every day I get the nixes to send out curse-bottles, with curses in them, and I have been waiting to know the Boy-who-Tricked-Me's name, so that it can be written on that curse . . . One day the curse will reach him,' said the Nuckalavee, 'and then he'll be sorry.

'So my question is . . .' said the Nuckalavee, eyes narrowing.

'*What is the name of the wicked licketty-split of a trickery spick of a boy?*

'That's the question. Tell me the answer and, if the answer is true, it will Magically appear in every one of the curse bottles floating in this lake around me, and that's how you'll know you've won the first part of our bargain,' said the Nuckalavee.

'You trickster!' fumed Wish. 'You said it was a

question we might know the answer to! If it was twenty years ago it could have been ANYBODY!'

How could they possibly guess the name of this unknown boy?

It could be any name at all. There were as many names in the world as there were trees in the wildwoods, or curse bottles in a lake.

The children began discussing random names: Tinker, Jack-in-irons, Torremalay, Rumbelsomething, and so on, any name at all that popped into their heads.

'Think,' said the Nuckalavee, bringing his great head with those glowing yellow eyes on it, closer and closer to the children standing on the beach. '*Think*, as hard as you can . . .'

'Hang on a second, it wasn't just anybody,' said Xar, slowly, remembering another story. 'That's why it's not a coincidence!'

The bite on the finger . . . Wasn't *his father* once long ago meant to have gone on a shadow quest, after Sychorax had abandoned him? Didn't *his father* have one finger that had a melancholy mark on it like a dark purple bruise? Was that the bite of a nix?

'I know who it was!' shouted Xar.

'Oh I know, too,' moaned Caliburn. 'Don't say, Xar, don't say!'

But it was too late.

'The boy's name was Tor,' said Xar excitedly. 'But he's now called . . . *ENCANZO!!!*'

ENCANZO! ENCANZO! ENCANZO! called the echoes in the cavern. ENCANZO! ENCANZO! ENCANZO!

20. Did you think a Quest for Courage was going to be easy?

'Oh dear oh dear oh dear oh dear,' said Caliburn.

As Xar spoke the name, the Nuckalavee sighed, a sigh of satisfaction.

Blink! Blink! Blink!

With a flash of Magic, every single curse bottle bobbing in the lake lit up with light. And in every single curse bottle there blazed the word:

Encanzo!

with a bright, vengeful orange light.

'You're right!' whispered the Nuckalavee, eyes agleam with hatred of the boy called Tor. 'I feel it in my heart that you are RIGHT. The treasure-hunting, staff-stealing, trickery spick of a burglar of a boy WAS called Tor . . . and he used MY treasures, MY staff, MY cup, MY scales, MY adderstone, MY treasures to become the greatest Wizard in the wildwoods. So the boy called Tor has become the noble *Encanzo*, the great *Encanzo*, the oh-so-clever *Encanzo* . . . I've heard that name, even down here in my dark and terrible dungeon, and I should have guessed it was him.'

The Nuckalavee spat out every 'Encanzo' with as much disgust as if the word had been made out of burnt-and-bitter mustardseed mixed with the pus-like ooze of putrid-green-bad-eggs.

'I've been cursing him ever since,' spat the Nuckalavee. 'Every night I get the nixes to build a little bonfire down here in my dungeon and scramble the wrong way around it, wishing ill on the boy who stole my treasures and all of his descendants.'

'Oh dear . . .' said Caliburn. 'Oh dear oh dear oh dear . . .'

It was clearly going to be quite important for the Nuckalavee NEVER to find out that one of Encanzo's descendants was standing right in front of him.

Unless he already knew . . .

'I thought that you might know the answer,' said the Nuckalavee, all thirteen yellow eyes now burning orange in fury, 'because in *another* extraordinary coincidence, YOU, boy, are carrying the very staff that Encanzo was carrying when he tricked me twenty years ago. Where did you get that staff, boy?'

'I stole it,' said Xar, looking the Nuckalavee straight in all his eyes, one by one. 'We have answered your question correctly. Now give us those scales!'

'Oh, I've been tricked before, so I don't make the same mistake twice,' said the Nuckalavee. 'You will climb into my throat and remove the stone that is lodged there. Bring the stone out of my throat, where it has been burning, itching, torturing me – take it out of here and up to me and THEN I'll give you four of my scales. And then you and your companions can leave this cavern with your hearts intact, and with your bodyguard and your selves free and alive.'

Suddenly the second part of the bargain they had made with the Nuckalavee seemed very, very foolish indeed.

'But you might close your mouth and swallow us,' said Wish, in a very small voice indeed.

'I've already promised not to,' said the Nuckalavee. 'By Magic and mistletoe, and giving my life as forfeit. Complete the bargain and remove the stone, on your honour.'

The monster put his head down and they saw him clearly for the first time.

Ah, it was a scary one, that Nuckalavee, now that they saw him right up close.

Great dark tentacles swung from his ancient, barnacled chin, and these tentacles were slimy with secrets, besmeared with curses, encrusted with hates and petty spites and mean little thoughts, and every kind of thing you might want to dispose of, and they were clinging like glue to the hairs on those tentacles.

The monster rested his chin on the ground before them, and opened his great mouth like a gigantic cavern.

A smell in that mouth of disappointed hopes, and deep despair, and power bad and power strong, secrets that the Droods wanted to get rid of, Magical objects too wild for the hearts of men, lies so bitter they would turn your lips green to speak them. There right in front of them were the giant daggers of his great green teeth, and even more spookily, and horribly, down right at the bottom of his throat, you could see *another* mouth, further down, *another* set of jaws, closed tight shut, so that nothing that went down there would ever get out.

'We do have to keep our promise,' said Wish, shivering, trying to concentrate, even though the stink of the monster's breath was confusing her, as she peered inside the great grim depths. 'Just as the Nuckalavee must keep his. We said that this was a test of our courage, didn't we?'

They *had* said that, but they hadn't quite realised *exactly* how courageous they were going to have to be.

The sprites and Caliburn offered to fly in first and see where the stone was lodged. Which was brave of them, not only for the obvious reasons, but because sprites have a very strong sense of smell, and so for them this stink was even worse than it was for the humans. They buzzed into the mouth of the great beast, wands drawn, prickling with anxiety, and quivering with revulsion, and they were gone for so long that Wish and Xar began to get nervous.

When they eventually emerged, they all looked

green with nausea, and Bumbleboozle actually threw up. 'Isss YUCKY in there,' said Bumbleboozle. 'But we found the ssstone,' said Ariel. 'A small grey stone, stuck tight as anything. We couldn't budge it . . .'

'It looksss very ssssorre in there, very sore,' said Bumbleboozle.

There was no point in trying to transform into birds, or fish, or anything Perdita had been teaching them at school, because when they got down there, they wouldn't have hands to remove the stone with.

'Didn't I TELL you that education wasn't important?' fumed Xar. 'Perdita said we were learning all that stuff for a reason, that we might need it in the fight against the Nuckalavee.'

They did a quick mental review of the things they had learnt at Pook's Hill over the last six months:

Transformation, telepathy, speaking to animals, illusions, wort-cunning, starcraft, leechdom.

And it did seem that none of these skills would come in handy right now.

'But that doesn't mean they're useless on EVERY occasion, Xar,' said Wish. 'There are some quests where speaking to animals might be terribly important.'

'Well, not right now it isn't,' grumbled Xar.

Sometimes there are problems that even *Magic* can't help you with. You have to do it the good old-fashioned way.

'You're going to have to let me down on a rope, and I'll try and dislodge it,' said Xar. 'I should have spent the last three months practising my rope work – that would have been a lot more helpful.'

Crusher had a long rope twisted round his waist and he tied one end round a stalactite, and the other end round Xar. The giant braced himself against one of the Nuckalavee's gigantic green teeth. And then slowly, slowly he let Xar down the throat of the Nuckalavee, the sprites buzzing in with him, to give out some light from their glowing bodies and offer helpful advice.

'Stop!' yelled Xar, when he spotted the stone, half way down the creature's gullet. It was much smaller than Xar expected, so Encanzo must have shrunk down his broken heart to fit into the confines of the pebble. Crusher held the rope steady and with a shiver of revulsion, Xar reached out to try and work the stone free.

You, dear reader, I hope will never have been in the position of being lowered down the throat of a Nuckalavee, trying to remove a stone that has been stuck in it for twenty years, while being dripped on by the disgusting goo that is sludging down the sides of the monster's throat walls.

However, it is likely that you have been in the situation of trying to do something tricky, like take the top off a bottle, or mend something that is stuck, or turn a handle that WILL NOT BUDGE, so you will probably sympathise with Xar, who was trying to do something rather like this under very trying, frightening (and disgusting) circumstances, while being given useful suggestions by the sprites, such as:

'What happensss if you wigglesss it the other way?'

'Try pulling it . . .'

'Try squiggling it . . .'

'Have you tried wiggling it?'

But absolutely nothing worked.

'Okay, Wish!' Xar

shouted up. 'I'm going to need your help! Even if I get this beastly thing out, I don't want to drop it, so we need two pairs of hands!'

So Wish attached herself to another rope, and Crusher lowered her down to help Xar.

Together they squiggled, and they wiggled, and their two pairs of hands worked the stone out of the sore burning spot where it had been bothering the Nuckalavee for the past twenty years.

'We've got it!' cried Wish in relief. 'Haul us up, Crusher!'

Up where he was balancing on the rim of the Nuckalavee's mouth, Crusher began to haul in both of them at once with all the strength that a Longstepper High-Walker giant can gather.

Meanwhile, all the

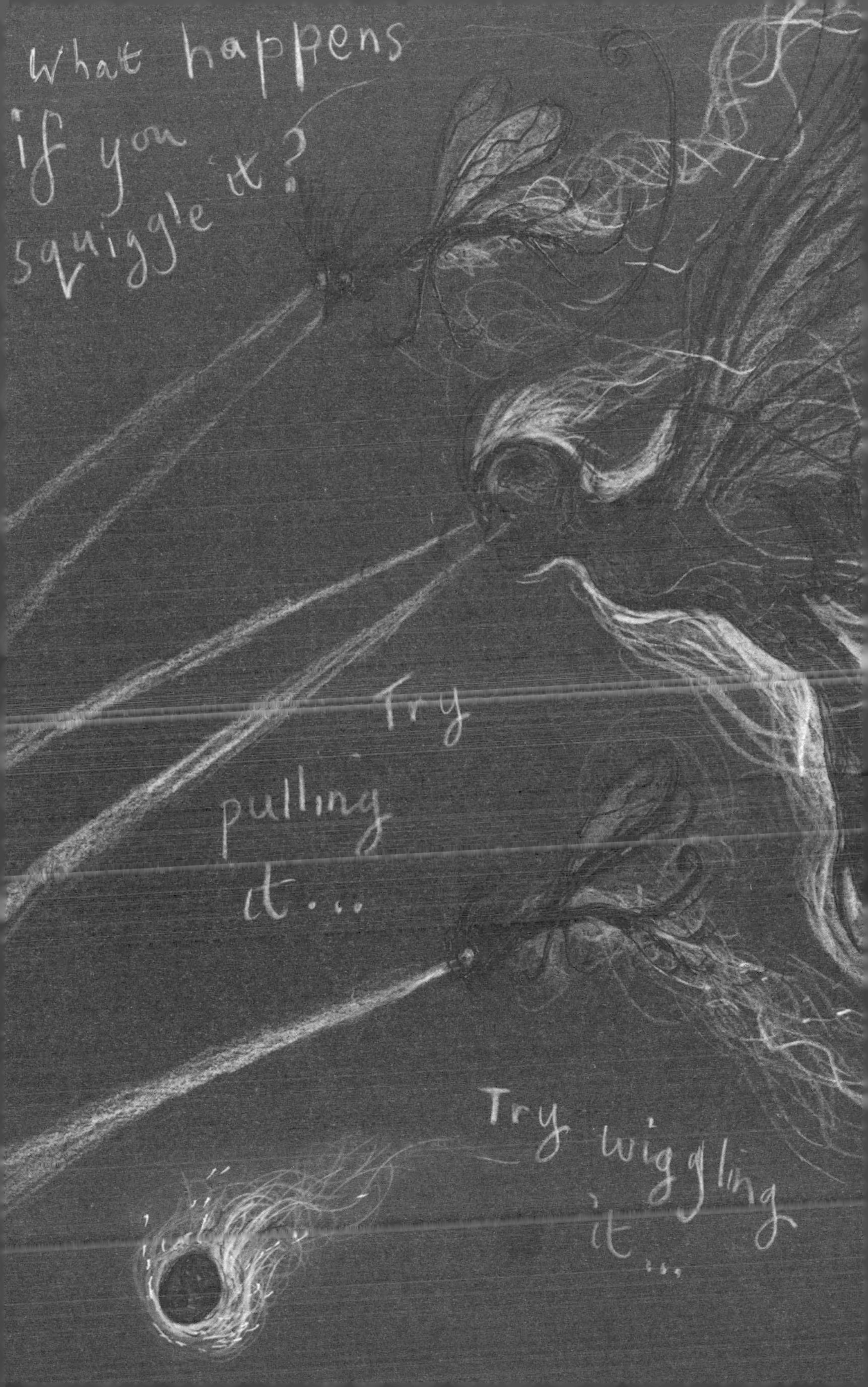
What happens if you squiggle it?
Try pulling it...
Try wiggling it...

time that they had been so intent on getting the stone out of the throat, Bodkin had been perching high on the ridge in the cavern walls, watching the Nuckalavee.

And what Bodkin had seen made his heart beat ever so quick.

Slowly,

Slowly,

Ever so slowly,

As Crusher and Wish and Xar and the sprites and Caliburn were all concentrating on getting the stone out of the Nuckalavee's throat . . . the Nuckalavee was very gently lowering his top jaw.

Slowly,

Slowly,

Ever so slowly,

The Nuckalavee was shutting his mouth.

Bodkin opened his own mouth to shout out a warning but he was so scared, no sound came out.

What on earth could he do?

Wait a second . . . The Nuckalavee had said that the Magic of *Wizards* did not work in here. The Enchanted Sword was stuck in the scabbard. But how about the do-it-yourself Magic staff? That wasn't the Magic of Wizards, that worked on its own.

Do something, Bodkin!

Maybe the staff would work in here . . .

He pointed the do-it-yourself staff at his forehead.

Squelch! The staff stuck firmly to his right temple.

Great.

Now he had a staff stuck to his head.

This sort of thing never seemed to happen to proper heroes in stories.

It took a few moments for Bodkin to remember the right words to get the staff to un-stick. Which it did, with another protesting squelch!

Okay, so he had a weapon that at least *worked*, although it was a little difficult to see how sticking things to other things was going to be helpful in this kind of emergency. He gathered all his courage together. Wish and Xar were dangling down inside the throat of that monster. They were his friends. And even though Bodkin was ABSOLUTELY PETRIFIED of the Nuckalavee,

Slowly,

Slowly,

Ever so slowly,

Bodkin climbed down from his hiding place.

It was like a very sinister game of grandmother's footsteps, with no grandmothers involved.

When one of the Nuckalavee's eyes flicked in his direction, Bodkin froze. But he kept on moving, slowly, slowly. Because he had a very bad feeling about what the Nuckalavee was going to do next.

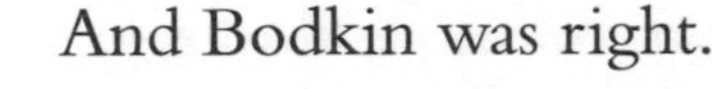

And Bodkin was right.

The moment that Wish shouted, 'We've got it!' and Crusher began to haul on the ropes to bring Wish and Xar up, the Nuckalavee's eyes blazed

orange and he shut his mouth very, very quickly indeed.

WHIRRRAMMMMM!

The Nuckalavee's jaws slammed shut, with Wish and Xar and the sprites and Caliburn and Crusher all inside.

Crusher's rope was still tied to the rock on the beach. The Nuckalavee jerked his head to work the rope free. The rope held, because the rope of a Longstepper High-Walker giant is made of strong stuff.

And Bodkin ran, as fast as he could towards the rock and the rope.

He didn't have a plan.

He just ran towards the rock and the rope.

The Nuckalavee's cyes blazed orange at him.

You're putting your filthy shoes on my beach!!! is what the Nuckalavee would have said if he didn't have his mouth full at the time.

The Nuckalavee jerked his head a second time, and this time

SNAP!

Bodkin only just got hold of the rope before it snapped from the rock and he was hauled high up into the air, dangling from one end of it.

GO, Bodkin, go!

21. Will the Parents Be Too Late?

Meanwhile, Encanzo and Sychorax had reached the beach opposite the Isle of the Nuckalavee and were following on a boat, in a sea of curse bottles, and every curse bottle now had a name in it. Encanzo reached down and picked out a curse bottle. He smeared away the seawater, and there, gleaming bright in the sunlight, was a name picked out in sprite writing, and the name was 'Encanzo'.

Sychorax looked out at the sea of bobbing bottles, the name 'Encanzo' trapped in the heart of them, gleaming, an o here, a z there, as the sunlight caught the letters. 'Someone out there *really* doesn't like you,' said Sychorax.

Encanzo turned white as snow when he saw his name in the bottles.

'What did you do to deserve this hatred?' said Sychorax.

'I came here to get rid of my heart,' said Encanzo bitterly. 'What use did I have of it? You betrayed me, and I was in a state of despair. This was my shadow man quest . . .'

Sychorax was now seeing with her own eyes the consequences of her actions on another heart, another soul, and that is always a difficult moment. It is one thing to know something vaguely. It is quite another to plant your feet in the exact footsteps of where another has gone. Sychorax was planting her pretty little feet in the hopeless footprints of the young Wizard she had once loved, the boy named Tor whose heart she had broken twenty weary years ago, and it was a most uncomfortable feeling, for with each step she could feel the lost boy's despair.

'But you endured, as I did,' said Sychorax, making herself feel better. 'There are very few who come away from a shadow man quest and live, and those who do are stronger than ever.'

'I have endured without a heart,' said Encanzo. 'And in the course of stealing myself a second chance I tricked the Nuckalavee most royally.'

'Ah . . .' said Sychorax. That explained all the curse bottles. The Nuckalavee was looking for revenge.

'Now that the Nuckalavee knows my name, Wish and Xar are in terrible trouble,' said Encanzo grimly. 'We must be quick now, Sychorax. If you want to come with me, you'll have to transform. Don't pretend you don't remember how to do it . . . it was I who taught you, long ago, don't you remember?'

Sychorax did remember.

'I only use Magic for a purpose,' said Queen Sychorax.

'Ah . . .' taunted Encanzo, 'so you never enjoy it?'

Sychorax blushed.

'What better purpose are you waiting for?' said Encanzo. 'We will have to transform into swifts, for they are the fastest—'

'Oh not *swifts* . . .' said Sychorax, for swifts were symbolic of an uncomfortable memory for her. 'What's this obsession with *swifts*, with you? Why not eagles? Peregrine falcons? Sparrowhawks? They're all fast flyers, particularly when they're hunting . . . And eagles are royal birds, Encanzo – don't forget our pedigree, we need to maintain our dignity, we should at least be birds of prey.'

'Oh for goodness' sake,' snapped Encanzo. 'There isn't a snowflake in a bonfire's chance of me ever falling in love with a she-wolf like you again, Sychorax! I have no heart. I'M going as a swift, because swifts are the fastest and most agile flyers, but *you* can be whatever you like! TRANSFORM!'

Encanzo thrust his arm with his staff up into the air, shouting out the word, and, sighing, Sychorax closed her own fist around the staff as well. Sychorax was highly competitive, so if swifts were the most agile flyers, Sychorax was going to have to be one too. She wasn't going to have Encanzo shooting off into the distance leaving her behind, however royal the wings of an eagle might be.

There was a great chemical explosion, and there, where there had been Sychorax and Encanzo, were two small brown swifts, wings beating the air.

Sychorax had forgotten how wonderful it was to live life as a bird. All the weary gold that weighed her down, the thick furs, the heavy flesh, lightened to paper-thinness before vanishing. She could feel her heart, so dull, so leaden, lightening with it, feel the air rushing into the quick of her bones with such a heady haste that she launched herself into the air the instant her flagging arms turned into joyous wings.

Encanzo hovered before her, crying with a bright pure call.

They ought to have been eagles. With eagle wings she might have remembered she was hunting. With eagle eyes she might have only focussed on the prey.

But swifts can stay in the air for six, ten months at a time. In a single lifetime a swift spends such a time flying that they could have flown seven times to the moon and back.

It was impossible not to be distracted by the pure joy of flying when you had wings so reactive to the breeze that it was almost like they were part of the wind itself, the sky above calling her to stay up there forever and never to go down.

With every beat of those curved bright wings she

was going back in time to when the young Wizard Tor first taught her to transform, a time when she was a careless young princess, as wild and fast and free as the swift itself.

The will-o'-the-wisps called after them their haunting cry:

Love is weakness . . .
Love is kindness . . .
Love is childish . . .
Love is thoughtless . . .

Care-not, love-less, heart-worn, soul-blast?
Come this way . . .
Thought-less . . . care-less . . . hope-less?
Come this way . . .
No more second chances
No more silly dances
LOVE is weakness . . . so
Come this way. . .

Will the parents-transformed-into-swifts be able

to reach their children in time to be able to save the situation?

Swifts fly swiftly, as their name suggests.

But unfortunately, even the wings of swifts will be too slow for this task. Even Magic has to obey logic and the laws of physics. I am the narrator, and even MY Magic will not get them there in time.

The children are on their own, and the situation is dire.

Love is weakness . . .

Come this way . . .

22. Inside the Mouth of the Nuckalavee

There was chaos inside the mouth of the Nuckalavee.

Darkness and a terrible rushing noise, like a roaring, churning, bellowing tide.

'THE NUCKALAVEE IS TRYING TO SWALLOW US! HANG ON AS TIGHT AS YOU CAN!' shouted Wish. She and Xar were using all their energy to cling on as hard as they could to Crusher's rope while they swung wildly this way, that way, this way, that way, turning somersaults, doing back flips, losing all sense of what was up and what was down. The sprites had lost their lights in the confusion as they rattled all around.

Down below them, the Nuckalavee's *second* set of jaws had opened, the ones hidden down at the bottom of his throat, and if they dropped through those, they would never get out again.

Crusher, the great Longstepper High-Walker giant, hung on grimly, one great arm clasping the ropes Wish and Xar were holding, the other one gripping the inside of the Nuckalavee's mouth. He was desperately trying to keep a hold on both as the Nuckalavee shook his head this way and that, and the gigantic muscles of his great gullet tried again and again to swallow them.

I . . . can't . . . hold . . . on . . . any more . . . thought Xar as the rope shuddered and swung chaotically.

And just as Wish began losing her grip, and was about to be jolted off the rope entirely . . .

. . . the Nuckalavee stopped shaking his head.

Because while Xar and Wish and Crusher were being jangled about like stones in a bucket, on the OUTSIDE of the Nuckalavee's mouth, Bodkin was being thrown about this way and that just as violently as they were on the other end of Crusher's rope. He had a brief moment of panic as he looked down and remembered, *Oh yes, I'm dangling a hundred feet up, from the jaws of a Nuckalavee, and my friends are actually INSIDE the Nuckalavee, and it's my job to save them . . .*

The rope had stopped shaking, and was now swaying gently from side to side in a way that was really quite drowsy making . . . Oh no! It was happening again!

'Don't fall asleep, Bodkin!' cried Caliburn, flapping

around in frantic circles because there wasn't a lot he could do himself while he was in bird form. 'The one thing you mustn't do is fall asleep!'

Caliburn was right.

Bodkin was *never* going to be a hero if he kept falling asleep in a crisis situation.

He *had* to stay awake.

So even though the familiar woozy feeling was coming over Bodkin, *this time* he fought it with EVERY FIBRE OF HIS HEART AND SOUL.

Wake up! Bodkin said to himself sharply, as his eyelids drooped. *Wake up now!* THIS IS YOUR CHANCE TO BE A HERO!

THINK!

The reason that the rope had suddenly stopped shaking was because the Nuckalavee had lost sight of Bodkin.

The last the monster had seen of the-boy-who-didn't-take-his-shoes-off was down on the beach, running towards him. But the boy had disappeared. Was he really a Wizard and not a Warrior, as the girl had claimed? Had he used some Magical object to turn himself invisible? Maybe he was a scarier opponent than he had looked.

The Nuckalavee's thirteen eyes swivelled in all directions, looking for the boy. No sign.

The Nuckalavee hated getting out of the water, his bulk was too much for that. But this was an emergency. He dragged the front half of his enormous body out on to the beach to get a closer look at the crevices high up in the cavern. No boy. Where had he gone?

Bodkin, meanwhile, had thought of a plan.

Bodkin swung the rope back, forth, back, forth, as though he was on a rope swing, until he hit the side of the cavern wall. He hung there a second, before kicking off with such force that he and the rope swung all the way round the Nuckalavee's chin, past the creature's ears on the other side, and he landed on the Nuckalavee's snout.

The Nuckalavee suddenly remembered the rope

dangling from the outside of his mouth. He tried to look down, but his thirteen eyes were perched right on top of his head, and he couldn't see under his own chin. Which is why he missed seeing Bodkin, who was now standing on top of the Nuckalavee's nose.

The staff that Bodkin was holding only did one thing. It was a staff-that-stuck-things-to-other-things.

You might have thought that this was quite a limited spell. It certainly wasn't one of the flashier, more spectacular ones, like mind control or invisibility or transformation or shapeshifting.

But sometimes it isn't the spells *themselves* that are important.

It is the clever ways you use them.

Bodkin used that spell intelligently now. He touched the staff on one of the Nuckalavee's nostrils and, SQUERRRRCHHHHHH!

The nostril closed in on itself, as one side of the nostril stuck itself to the other side.

The Nuckalavee tried to snort through it, and SQUERRRRCHHHHHH! Bodkin touched the staff on the other nostril, and it closed up too.

Still holding the rope, Bodkin launched himself off the Nuckalavee's nose with as much careless recklessness as if he had been Xar himself.

Round the other side of the Nuckalavee, Bodkin fell

so that the rope had wound itself in a circle all the way round the Nuckalavee's head. And when Bodkin swung back down to the bottom of the circle, he touched the staff to the rope and it stuck tight.

The Nuckalavee tried to breathe through his nostrils, but they would not unblock.

The Nuckalavee tried to open his mouth that he had been keeping closed so firmly.

But his mouth would not open.

The Nuckalavee was part of a crocodilian family of monsters that have great strength in the muscles that grasp prey, so they exert extraordinary force when they are keeping their jaws shut. But the muscles that OPEN the jaws are far

SQUERCH!

weaker, so weak, even, that they cannot break through the rope of a Longstepper High-Walker giant.

And then there was chaos in the cavern of the Nuckalavee.

The Nuckalavee's thirteen eyes bulged and blazed with absolute incandescent fury.

He thrashed about in the underground lake, with Bodkin desperately hanging on to the madly jerking rope.

Lightning bolts shot off the Nuckalavee's tentacles as his enormous body swung this way and that in the jangling mass of curse bottles . . .

But however hard he thrashed, the Nuckalavee could not catch his breath.

The Nuckalavee knew when he was beaten.

The jerking of the great monster's body became weaker and weaker.

And now that he knew he was vanquished, the Nuckalavee was dignified in defeat. He lay his head down quietly on the beach, and closed all thirteen of his eyes, and resigned himself to death.

After all, he had broken a promise to Xar and Wish that he would not close his jaws while they were taking out the stone, and he had promised by mistletoe and Magic, may his own life be forfeit. That is a very solemn promise, and you break it at your peril, so the Nuckalavee must have known he was risking the wrath of Fate.

Bodkin dropped on to the beach when the Nuckalavee laid down his head. He unstuck the rope that was tied under the monster's chin, and the Nuckalavee's jaws relaxed and his mouth opened.

Inside the throat of the Nuckalavee, the world

stopped rocking for Wish and Xar. Crusher pulled them up and they slipped and slid out of the open mouth of the Nuckalavee, the stone held tight in the palm of Xar's hand.

'You were brilliant, Bodkin!' said Caliburn admiringly. 'You're a hero! You should have seen him, Xar and Wish!'

'You saved our lives! I KNEW you'd be a hero when the time came!' said Wish. 'Didn't I say it?'

Xar shook Bodkin's hand. 'Yes, Wish was right all along, you *are* a hero, Bodkin.'

It was a magnificent moment for Bodkin.

Xar bowed to Bodkin and then clapped him on the back. 'Here, you take the stone and complete the bargain, because if it wasn't for you we would never have got it.'

Bodkin thought he was going to burst with pride.

Wish, proud of him, Bodkin!

Xar, bowing to him, Bodkin!

He had overcome his fear. He hadn't fainted or fallen asleep. He had acted like a hero. And most importantly of all, he hadn't been an idiot for coming here, the jealousy of the betrayal was forgotten and forgiven, the quest had been a success in the end, all because of *him*.

It was a magnificent moment for Bodkin

He stepped forward importantly towards their fallen opponent.

He bowed, because that is the polite and gracious thing to do to a defeated adversary

Bodkin held up the stone. 'Nuckalavee, I am so sorry that I offended you by forgetting to remove my shoes when I landed on your island. We have answered your question. We have completed the task you set us. Here is the stone that has been worrying you for the last twenty years. Now you must complete the bargain and give us four of your scales.'

The Nuckalavee opened his thirteen eyes, wearily, slowly.

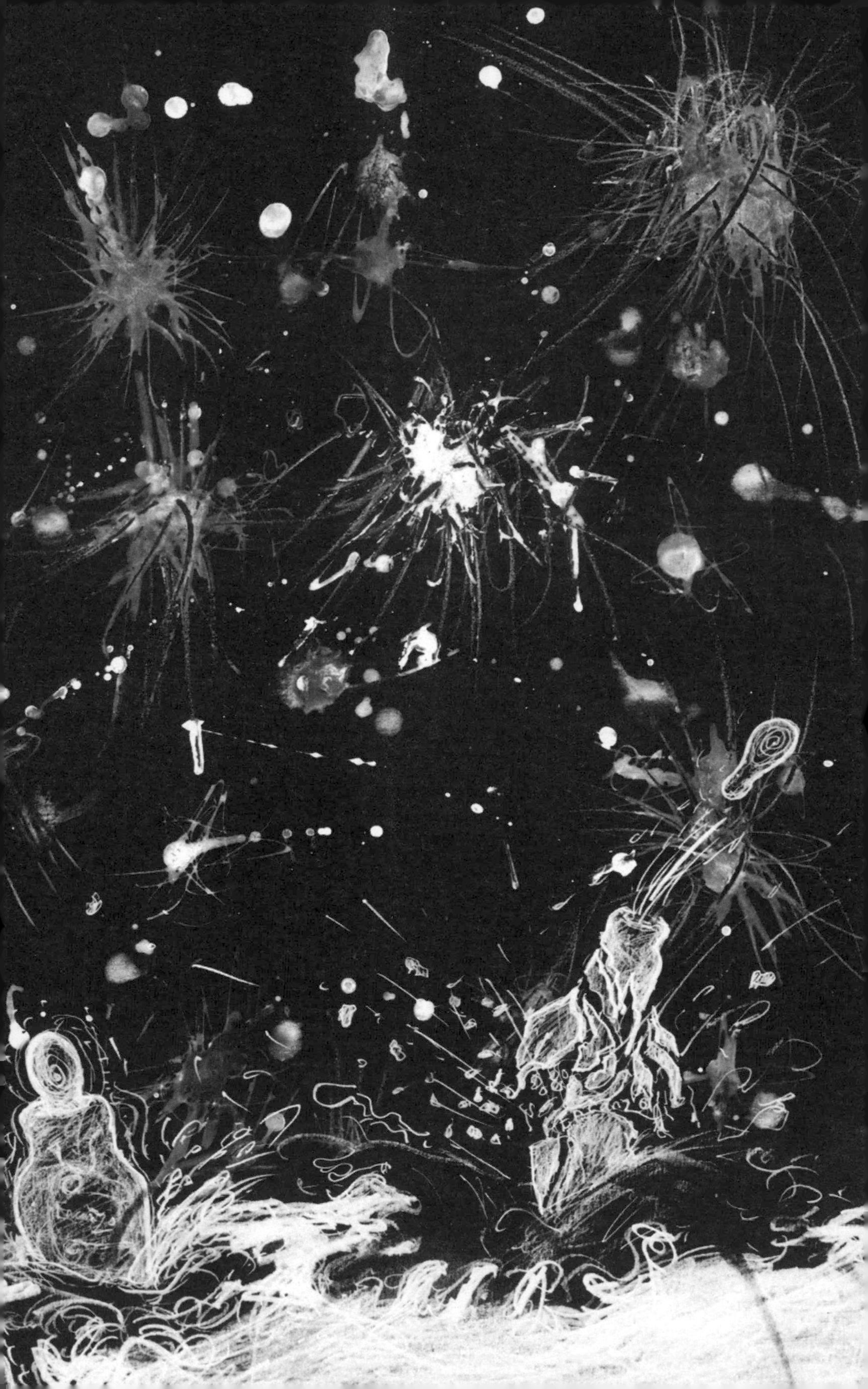

'You have the scales already,' said the Nuckalavee.

'What do you mean, we have the scales already?' said Xar, bewildered. 'No we don't! You can't try and trick us AGAIN!'

Xar reached out to take four of the Nuckalavee's shining scales—

But all at once, the curse bottles with the name 'Encanzo' exploded into little pieces. They ducked so as not to be hit by the flying glass.

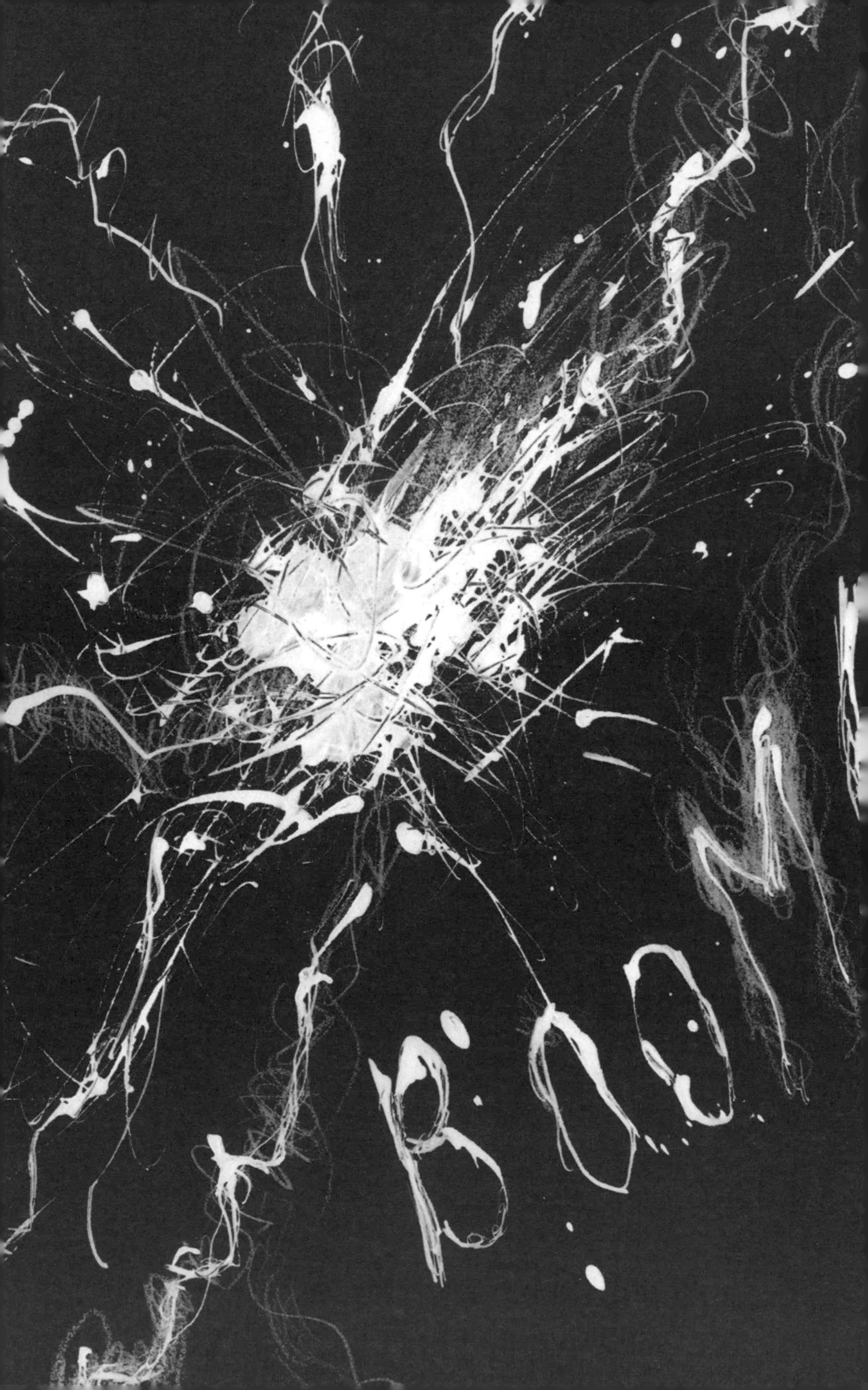

And the scales exploded off the outline of the Nuckalavee. They tried to catch the scales raining all around them, but the scales slipped through their fingers, burning bright silver for a moment, before they faded and seemed to melt into the beach.

But the Nuckalavee seemed somehow . . . *happier* without his scales.

Younger, even. He shone like a star in the cavern, glowing white as coral.

It was as if a spell had been lifted, and the beast had awoken from a trance that bound him.

A moment earlier he had seemed like he was on the edge of death, barely breathing. Now he seemed re-born.

'Thank you for breaking the Riddle and the Curse of the Nuckalavee,' said the scale-less creature before them, still weak, but gathering strength in front of their eyes.

A great sweep of the Nuckalavee's tail toppled the treasure heap, as if he no longer cared about the treasure any more.

Magic boots and caps with wings and singing swords went bouncing around the cavern in lunatic directions. Xar and Wish and Bodkin had to throw themselves on the ground to get out of the way as arrows made of moon, and horns of plenty spewing out food, and harps playing themselves in a cacophony of noise, flew around the cavern in mad eccentric circles.

'Oh dear . . .' moaned Caliburn, 'oh dear oh dear oh dear . . . all the Magical objects are escaping . . .'

Sure enough, the seven league boots were marching up the cavern walls and then right out of the cave itself, running away as fast as they could, followed by Magic staffs of indescribable power, and golden shields of destiny, and all manner of other dangerous objects that ought to be kept safe and guarded, and out of human reach.

But worse than this, much worse than this . . .

The Nuckalavee turned, and dived into the darkness of the water.

And then the Nuckalavee swam away, and out into the open sea.

Shielding their faces with their arms, Xar and Wish and Bodkin watched him go with open mouths.

'Um . . . what just happened?' said Xar.

'He's GONE! The Nuckalavee has gone! But more importantly, where are the scales?' panicked Wish.

They dropped to their knees on the beach, but the last remains of the Nuckalavee's scales slipped through their fingers like mist.

The Nuckalavee had vanished as completely as if he had never existed.

Scales of the Nuckalavee melting into the beach

And after all that work, after Xar and Wish rescuing Bodkin, and Bodkin rescuing Wish and Xar, they had failed nonetheless.

NO SCALES.

The last ingredient in the spell to get rid of Witches had gone forever.

And, believe it or not, there was worse to come.

With a magnificent, sweeping flourish, the Enchanted Sword *finally* drew itself out of its own scabbard, and placed itself into Bodkin's trembling hand.

Behind them, in a dark corner of the cavern, there came a horrible creaking hiss of a whisper.

'Foolish,' croaked the voice, 'to go on a quest without knowing the rules yet.'

They whirled around.

Out of the darkness, out of the heap of dark treasure the Nuckalavee had been guarding, there rolled, trapped in a ball of iron . . .

The Kingwitch.

Once

UH-OH . . .

23. We Are All on a Quest Without Knowing the Rules Yet

Yes, it is so, so tricky to know the rules of the quest you are going on until you reach the end of it.

This was why the Witches had wanted them to get to the Isle of the Nuckalavee.

The Kingwitch was there.

The Kingwitch was trapped inside a great ball of iron.

And only Wish could get him out.

The Kingwitch was encased in a ball of iron that Wish's Magic had melted all around him in a huge misshapen mass of spears and arrows and shields. He was clutching a tiny piece of blue dust in one claw, and he had been rubbing that piece of dust against the walls of his iron prison with such ferocity that he had turned a small patch of it invisible. Wish could just see one dreadful Witch eye glaring out at her from inside the iron ball.

The Kingwitch had been captured by the Droods and their giants with terrible difficulty, and was rolled painstakingly carefully by giant hands out of the sea and hidden in this cavern. The Droods and the giants had wedged the ball of iron tight under a crevice and heaped it up with treasure, but the newly freed Nuckalavee had accidentally knocked it free with one swipe of his joyful tail.

So, like the rest of the treasure in that cavern, the ball of iron with the Kingwitch inside it was no longer guarded but free to move of its own accord, and it rolled slowly but steadily towards them like a dark and dreadful fate.

'Wissssshhhhhh . . .' whispered the Kingwitch inside the ball of iron. 'Wissssshhhhh . . . *I* have a bargain to offer you too . . . Come closer . . .'

'Don't listen, Wish!' shrieked Caliburn, putting his wings over Wish's ears, as they all backed away from the iron ball. 'Don't listen!'

'Bring me the sprite and Xar and I will take away the Witch-Magic that is poisoning them once and for all . . .' said the Kingwitch.

'And in return,' continued the Kingwitch, 'you will releasssse me from this iron prison . . . And then you and I, Wish, will settle this once and for all in a single spellfight . . .'

It was always going to come down to this. The Kingwitch led the Witches, and while he was safe inside the ball of iron, he couldn't lead them to victory. But if he could persuade Wish to release him, and challenge Wish to a spellfight, why, then he might get his talons on the Magic-that-works-on-iron . . .

Because they had all seen, back in Pook's Hill, how bad Wish was at spellfights.

But it was almost as if Wish and Xar were hypnotised by the voice of the Kingwitch as he rolled towards them . . . *And then Xar began to walk towards the Kingwitch of his own accord.*

Little Squeezjoos, who had been tucked, worryingly rigid and still in Xar's pocket since they had left the healing comfort of Perdita, now lifted his head and began to move. He bit off the buttons that secured the pocket and he flew out towards the Kingwitch.

'I iss feelings a little funny again . . .' said poor little Squeezjoos uncertainly, flying towards the Kingwitch upside down. 'Oh! It's the Chiwgink! Hello Chiwgink!'

'Come back, Xar!' cried Bodkin, grabbing hold of the edge of Xar's waistcoat, and dragging him back. 'Xar! What are you doing?'

But Xar was half eaten by the Witch-Magic already, and he did not seem to hear what Bodkin was saying.

'Xar, come to me . . . and Wissssh . . .' whispered the Kingwitch. *'Wisssssshhhhhhhhhhhhhhhhh* . . . Give me your Magic . . . Give me your Magic . . . GIVE ME YOUR MAGIC . . .'

Louder still chanted the Kingwitch in the ball of iron, louder and louder, until the chant became an unbearable screech and the ball of iron was moving faster, faster.

'GIVE ME YOUR MAGIC!!!!'

'DON'T LISTEN!' bellowed Bodkin, leaping in front of Xar and Wish, and he held up the Enchanted Sword, which blazed for one moment with a light so blindingly bright that Xar's hypnotised eyes refocussed, and he came to his senses.

'RUUUUUUUNNNNNNNN!' shouted Bodkin.

OUT of the cavern the children ran, terrified, as the ball of iron rolled after them.

UP the tunnels of the Nuckalavee's cave.

ON TO the beach, where the log boat was waiting for them.

But above their heads, as they ran across the sand,

there was a whirr of soft wings, and two swifts flew round and round.

'My father!' yelled Xar.

The swifts circled once more and then hovered in front of the children for a second before their wings turned into the long trails of sleeves, and Sychorax and Encanzo landed lightly on the beach in front of them.

They looked absolutely hopping mad.

Great thunderclouds were rolling off the top of Encanzo's head. Sychorax was white with fury.

'Oh dear, my mother as well . . .' sighed Wish.

24. Two Angry Parents

Hurriedly, Bodkin hid the stone-that-was-Encanzo's-heart in his pocket.

'QUICK! The Witches are coming!' cried Sychorax. 'Encanzo can take all of you in the boat to safety! And— Oh, by mistletoe and all things dark, *THE KINGWITCH!* . . . As I thought, the Droods must have captured him!'

Sure enough, the ball of iron containing the Kingwitch came rolling out of the mouth of the cavern, and halted as if waiting for something.

Hovering over the ball of iron was Squeezjoos.

In the terror of the moment of running away, they had forgotten about the little sprite, and this time he was too far away for Xar to grab him and put him in his pocket.

'Come here, Squeezjoos!' shouted Xar. But Squeezjoos did not seem to hear

And worst of all . . .
What was happening to Squeezjoos?

his old friend Xar. He had turned a very bright green indeed, and his eyes were a little feverish. 'I iss with the *Chiwgink* . . .' chanted Squeezjoos. 'I iss with the *Chiwgink*!'

'Squeezjoos is saying he's with the Kingwitch,' said Caliburn, sadly. 'Chiwgink is 'Kingwitch' spelt backwards . . . *sort of* . . .'

'Come with us, Squeezjooos!' cried Xar. '*Please* come with us!'

But Squeezjoos slipped between Xar's fingers.

'I'sss can't . . .' said Squeezjoos sadly, a desperate look in his eye, before he started shaking again, and flying back and forth like a poor little upside-down trapped bumblebee.

'We can't leave without Squeezjoos!' said Xar.

'Don't be ridiculous! You can't fight the Kingwitch,' shouted Encanzo. 'LOOK UP THERE!'

Wish and Xar and Bodkin looked up, and in the distance the sky was dark with Witches. They were flying in from all directions, screaming wildly, heading towards the island of the Nuckalavee.

'Quick! Wish! Make a forcefield!' yelled Xar.

Wish took off her eyepatch. She thought of fires, and fires leapt up, forming a protective circle around the children and turning into a great humming forcefield.

We can still fight him. The Kingwitch can't get out of the ball of iron . . . thought Wish. *Don't think of what he's like* . . .

Horrible images of the times she had met the Kingwitch before had leapt into her brain and were making her sweat with fear. The Kingwitch, curled up like a great dark grasshopper inside the stone she had released him from in the first place . . . The Kingwitch springing in the air, great dark feathers spread wide, talons like swords, terrifying Magic blasting out of his mouth . . .

Don't be scared or that will make the forcefield weaken . . . He's trapped and he can't do any harm to us from in there . . . Wish's thoughts chased around inside her skull like panicking rabbits.

Only I can let him out, and until then we are perfectly safe . . .

WHAM!

The first Witch lunged down from above and rammed into Wish's forcefield with such violence that Wish fell over, gasping, as if someone had punched her in the stomach, and—

WHAM!

Another Witch punched into the forcefield again.

Sychorax drew her bow and arrows and shot at the departing Witch, and the creature let out a dreadful screech as it escaped upwards into the air.

But the sky was full of Witches, flying closer, closer.

'We'll go back for Squeezjoos later when we've got all the ingredients of the spell!' shouted Xar, trying to keep his balance inside the rocking, shaking forcefield.

'It won't do Squeezjoos any good if we stay here to get killed by Witches . . .'

WHAM! Another great ram of the Kingwitch in the ball of iron and the entire side of Wish's forcefield caved in.

'We need to go NOW!' shouted Sychorax. 'And get to the safety of the Beach of Shoes . . . THE WITCHES WON'T DARE ATTACK WITH MY IRON WARRIORS THERE!'

Sychorax had sent word to her Warriors to make haste to the Beach of Shoes. She did not know whether they had got there yet . . . but crafty war leader that she was, she wanted the Witches to *think* they were there.

'INTO THE BOAT!' roared Encanzo. Scrambling, tumbling across the beach inside Wish's dented forcefield, Wish, Xar and Bodkin ran after Sychorax and Encanzo towards the sea. The Kingwitch in the ball of iron followed them, gaining momentum as it went

downhill on
the gentle slope
of the beach.

'Only a little
further . . .' panted
Xar.

They got to
the log boat in the
absolute nick of
time. For as they
scrambled in, and
Encanzo pushed
the boat off the
shore, another great
Witch swooped to get
them.

'DUUUUCCKKKK!'
screamed Bodkin, and they
had a nightmare vision of the
talons of the Witch.

But Encanzo's staff sent
the boat shooting off the
sand with such Magical
speed that they all fell flat
on their backs –

SPPPLLLASSSHHHHHHHHHHH!

The great ball of iron slammed into the shallow water of the beach with such ferocity that a huge spray of water still reached them as they sped away.

Trembling, shaking, water in her hair and in her eyes, some of it sea and some of it tears, Wish looked back. The ball of iron with the Kingwitch inside it was stopped dead for the moment, half buried in the sludge and sand, surrounded by great whirlpool ripples. Wish half-expected it to be following after them, but even the Kingwitch seemed to have accepted that a ball of iron cannot roll on water.

Crusher came panting up and tried to catch Squeezjoos, but the little sprite dodged out of the way, screeching 'I iss with the Chiwgink!' Crusher tried again, but Squeezjoos was too quick for him and Crusher had to leave too, diving after them all.

Squeezjoos watched them go, buzzing upside down forlornly. Sometimes he seemed to get up a manic energy, fizzing with bright green sparks, and then he calmed down and

Wish could not bear to look at him, so alone and so desolate. She thought she heard him shout something . . . she wasn't sure whether it was, 'Don't leave me!'

or 'Please save me!'

Whatever it was, it was unbearable.

'We *will* save you, Squeezjoos, I promise!' shouted Wish, tears running down her face, and then she turned to Caliburn. 'They won't hurt him, will they, Caliburn?'

'No, they won't hurt him,' said Caliburn sadly. 'He is the Witches' creature now, so they won't hurt him . . .'

'TRUST ME, SQUEEZJOOS, WE'LL BE BACK TO RESCUE YOU!' hollered Xar, who was also crying. 'I ALWAYS LOOK AFTER MY SPRITES!'

Squeezjoos shouted something back, but again he was too far away to be sure of what he said, but I think it was something like: 'Don't worry, Masster! I trusts you! And I iss FINE! I iss upside-down and with the Chiwgink . . . but I iss FINE!'

And then he was too far away for them to see him any more.

They had only just got away in time.

Most of the Witches had reached the island now and although the ball of iron could not follow them on water, the Witches had wings and they were after that boat like eagles pursuing a mouse.

Encanzo shot back at them with great blasts of Magic from his spelling staff.

Sychorax took down a few with her iron arrows. But there were too many of them.

And Wish set up another forcefield, this time over the entire boat, as the screaming, screeching, yelling nightmares of Witches dived again and again, talons out, trying to rip open the forcefield and get at them.

My goodness, that boat went fast when Encanzo was spelling it. The boat skimmed across the open water of the sea. Encanzo muttered a few words and the front end of the boat reared up, and then they fairly *flew* across the water, humming on the top of the waves, sending three horrible Witches who had landed on top of the forcefield spiralling away.

The onslaught of the Witches was relentless. Again and again they attacked. The boat was in imminent danger of being capsized, and Wish was struggling to maintain the forcefield. Just when she was thinking once again, *I can't hold on much longer . . .* the attacks abruptly ceased.

They were getting near the Beach of Shoes, and from the sky the Witches could see something that Encanzo and Sychorax could not yet see.

The approach of Sychorax's army.

Sychorax had sent word for them to follow her, and the Witches could see the torches of many, many Warriors moving through the trees in the distance. The Witches were scared of the iron-tipped arrows, the spears, the swords. They let out snarls and screams of disappointment. But they would get another chance, they knew that. Screeching like banshees, the Witches whirled around, back towards the Isle of the Nuckalavee.

'Oh, thank goodness,' sighed Wish in trembling relief. 'But what are they doing now?'

'They're going to collect the treasures that the Nuckalavee has been guarding for all these years,' said Encanzo grimly. 'The Witches will now get hold of staffs of power so old and so evil that they were put there out of harm's way centuries ago. This has been the Droods' hiding place for hundreds and hundreds of years, and you have just allowed all these terrible weapons to fall into the hands of the Witches!'

Oh, those parents were so, so cross.

'Why can't you be more like Drama, or Unforgiving? Why is my own daughter so much less obedient than my stepdaughters!' stormed Sychorax.

'When will you children learn that *we* know best, and *you* shouldn't break the rules?' raged Encanzo.

'But *you* broke the rules!' Xar pointed out. 'All those years ago, you came to the Nuckalavee on a shadow quest! You stole some of his treasure yourself . . .'

'I tricked the Nuckalavee,' said Encanzo. 'I stole *a few little bits of treasure* . . . I didn't blow up the ENTIRE WHOLE SPELL that bound him!'

The force of Encanzo's anger carried that boat with such alarming speed that when it finally landed on the Beach of Shoes it just carried right up on the sand for a good thirty feet or so, before coming to a sludgy halt.

Encanzo helped Sychorax out of the boat, and guiltily, the children climbed out after them.

The two royal parents stood in front of their children, hands on their hips.

'Every single thing that you two do makes things WORSE!' roared Encanzo. 'We are TRYING to help you, but you just get deeper and deeper into more and more serious trouble . . . What if the Droods find out that *you* were the ones who released the Kingwitch, on top of everything else?'

'And what if the Kingwitch were to break out of that iron prison that holds him?' cried Sychorax. 'You have just armed his Witch army with forces that will be impossible to contain!'

'What's more, on top of everything else, because of *your* wilful disobedience, *your* selfishness, that silly woman Perdita has lost Pook's Hill! The Droods removed her when they found out she had been harbouring you two outlaws . . .' said Encanzo.

Oh no!

That made Caliburn cry too. 'My poor sister! How she loved that learning place. I should never have taken you there . . .'

Wish and Xar bowed their heads in front of their furious parents.

'You two just have to face facts. Wizards and Warriors are enemies and they should never be together,' said Sychorax. 'Encanzo and I learnt that years ago . . .'

'But you're working together *now*,' Wish pointed out miserably.

'Only to try and contain the DISASTERS that you are bringing on the wildwoods by persisting in this catastrophic friendship of yours!' said Sychorax.

'Xar will come back with me to the prison of Gormincrag, and we will do what we can to try and find a cure for that Witchstain,' said Encanzo.

'And Wish will come back with *me*, to my iron fort, and I will keep you safe from the Witches forever,' said Sychorax. 'You must never see each other again, and we will remove all these unsuitable companions from you because they are clearly unable to control you or offer you good advice . . .'

'But Ariel and I are bound to look after Xar until he grows into a wise and thoughtful adult!' protested Caliburn.

'I release you from that duty!' said Encanzo from between gritted teeth. 'From this moment you are FREE!'

'But we do not wish to be free,' said Caliburn. 'It is not yet time . . .'

The quest had failed.

What had Perdita said in her note, wrapped around the bottle with the Droods' tears in it?

There's a reason that tears are such an important ingredient in so many spells. Life is made up of sorrow as well as joy, and so you may fight as hard as you can, and yet still fail . . .

They had indeed fought as hard as they could . . . but they had still failed. There was no way they could get hold of the scales of a Nuckalavee *now*, for the Nuckalavee could be anywhere in the vast and lonely wastes of the great green ocean.

So they had no scales, Perdita had lost her learning place, they had released the Kingwitch from the Nuckalavee's safekeeping, and lost Squeezjoos.

Surely Fate was trying to tell them something. They were on the wrong track, Wish's idea about the spell was nonsense. Every single thing they had done really *had* made things worse.

Xar could feel his arm with the Witchstain on it burning him like fire. He could feel the desire to grow black wings, and join the Witches now raiding the undefended island of the Nuckalavee. There was no hope for him.

Wish and Xar were feeling so deflated and confused and depressed by the outcome of the adventure that they nearly forgot to fight back.

Until . . .

'Excuse me,' said a quiet voice behind all of them.

'Who is this?' snapped Encanzo.

Everyone had forgotten Bodkin.

'Oh, it is just Wish's bodyguard . . .' said Queen Sychorax, waving a contemptuous hand. 'A person of no importance. He betrayed Wish to me, but he should never have let her go astray in the first place. Assistant Bodyguard, you are dismissed from your position.'

'I am *Wish's* bodyguard, not *yours*, Majesty,' said Bodkin. 'And I wanted to talk to you about Encanzo's heart.'

There was a short pause while everyone tried to think what this might mean.

'My heart?' said Encanzo. 'What about my heart?'

'We took your heart out of the Nuckalavee,' said Bodkin.

'On top of everything else you took my heart out of the Nuckalavee?' gasped Encanzo. 'But it was safe there . . . *What have you done with it?'*

'I've hidden it,' said Bodkin.

"I've hidden it." Said Bodkin.

25. 'X' Marks the Spot

Sychorax sniffed. 'Very foolish of you to hide it in the Nuckalavee in the first place, Encanzo.'

'How was I to know that anyone would be totally idiotic enough to go in there and remove it!' stormed Encanzo. 'How could I have predicted the absolute madness of these ridiculous children? It's absolutely nonsensical of them.'

'Well, if you will be so careless with your heart, accidents are going to happen,' said Queen Sychorax.

'There's a bit of YOUR heart in there, too, Sychorax,' snapped Encanzo.

Ah, yes. When you have exchanged a true love kiss, a little mixing up of hearts is unfortunately inevitable, even if the kiss is later regretted.

Sychorax blushed. She tapped her pretty little foot on the beach.

'Yes, all right, all right,' admitted Sychorax irritably. 'I, too, may have been a little careless with my heart in the past . . . But it's all under control now. Where have you hidden this heart, you beastly bodyguard?'

'I'm afraid I can't say,' said Bodkin. 'I'll tell you where I've hidden it after King Encanzo gives me the four scales that he stole from the Nuckalavee twenty years ago. I expect you keep them in one of those handy pockets you have hanging from your belt, sir.'

There was a stunned silence.

Wish and Xar's heads lifted. Wish could feel her spirits lifting as well.

'Oh, very clever, Bodkin!' said Wish. '*Of course*! That's why the Nuckalavee said we had the scales already . . . *We WERE meant to find the last ingredient in the spell to get rid of Witches after all!*'

'WHAAAAT!' cried Queen Sychorax. 'I keep on telling you! There is no such thing as a spell to get rid of Witches!!!'

But Xar and Wish were not listening.

For them, this changed everything. Fate meant them to get the ingredients, and *that* meant they had a chance.

'Hand the scales over, Father,' said Xar.

What could Encanzo do? You can't leave your heart lying around for just *anyone* to find it.

Absolutely and completely and totally raging, Encanzo reached into his pocket, pulled out the four scales of the Nuckalavee and gave them to Bodkin.

'Okay, we'll be off now,' said Bodkin briskly.

'Where have you hidden my heart?' yelled Encanzo.

'I'll tell you once we're on our way,' said Bodkin.

'Where are you going, you foolish children?' asked Sychorax.

'Well, we have all of the ingredients now, don't we,

guys?' said Bodkin. 'So I expect we'll go off and put them together and make that spell . . .'

Wish put up her eyepatch a smidgeon and conjured up an image of the Enchanted Door of the Punishment Cupboard in her mind, and the door that they had hidden under some old bits of wood on the edge of the beach shook off the undergrowth covering it and flew over the sand, hovering helpfully in front of them.

And then Wish thought of shoes, and Wish and Crusher's shoes walked out from the line of shoes on the edge of the beach, and Wish and Crusher put them on. Xar and Wish and Bodkin climbed on the back of the hovering door.

Wish moved the key to UP, and as the door moved up and into the air, Bodkin shouted down to the parents while they were still in earshot:

'I buried your heart under the sand about fifty feet behind you. X marks the spot . . .'

Sure enough, while Encanzo and Sychorax were busy telling Wish and Xar off, Bodkin had crept away and buried the stone, putting two crossed twigs on top of it because it's surprisingly difficult to remember where you've put something when you bury it on a beach.

Encanzo and Sychorax ran across the sand and dug underneath the crossed twigs, and to their great relief, Encanzo's heart-that-had-turned-into-a-stone was just where Bodkin said it was.

'They've done well, really, haven't they? All on their own and everything,' said the voice of Madam Perdita. 'X marks the spot was a clever touch of Bodkin's . . .'

Queen Sychorax jumped. Standing at her elbow was Madam Perdita, laughing quietly to herself, with Hoola on her head. 'I wish you wouldn't do that,' snapped Queen Sychorax. 'It's very rude to materialise out of nothing without first announcing your presence . . .'

'Oh, hello, Madam Perdita! Hello, Hoola,' Wish shouted down, so guilty that she nearly fell off the door. 'We're so sorry about you losing your job at Pook's Hill . . .'

'Don't worry, it wasn't your fault!' Madam Perdita called up to Wish. 'And we needed a break from that learning place anyway, didn't we, Hoola? You just carry on with what you're doing, you're doing really well . . .

we're very proud of you.'

'What on earth are you talking about?' said Queen Sychorax.

Queen Sychorax shook her fist up at the door hovering just above the adults.

'Come back, Wish!' said Queen Sychorax. 'There is no hope! Life is complicated! Here in the real world, your bodyguard has already betrayed you!'

'I know that,' said Wish. 'But he's sorry, aren't you, Bodkin?'

'I'm very sorry,' said Bodkin. 'Couldn't be sorrier, but Xar and Wish have forgiven me, and I won't do it again.'

'Is that IT?' raged Queen Sychorax. 'He just says he's sorry, and you FORGIVE him? How can you ever trust him again, you fool?'

'I don't know,' explained Wish. 'I just can . . .'

Isn't it strange that the only conversations that mother and daughter seemed to have were shouted ones from the backs of doors?

'The thing is, Queen Sychorax,' Bodkin shouted down over the edge of the door, 'in *your* Warrior world, there's these immoveable class distinctions and everything – once a servant, always a servant . . . Whereas in *Wish's* world, a bodyguard can still be a hero.'

'Wish's world has never existed and it never will!' Queen Sychorax yelled.

'Come back down here, or I will arrest your snowcats and your giant! I'M GOING TO LOCK UP THAT GIANT AS AN ENEMY OF THE PEOPLE!'

Crusher was lumbering out of the sea. He looked mildly surprised and anxious to find that Queen Sychorax had drawn her bow and arrow and was pointing it at him.

'UH-OH . . .' said Crusher.

In front of Queen Sychorax and Encanzo's eyes, the mountain of a giant disappeared, faded into the wind as if there were no giant there at all.

The snowcats and wolves were also there one minute, and gone the next.

And when an extremely frustrated Sychorax pointed her arrow upwards at the door, it, too, had vanished, melted into air.

'It is incredibly ill-considered of you to teach them invisibility, Madam Perdita,' said Encanzo. 'They are way too young to be able to deal with such a dangerous power.'

'I told them how risky it was,' said Perdita. 'I warned them not to stay invisible too long. I trust them to cope.'

'You have taught Wish too much,' said Encanzo, grimly, looking up at where the door once was. 'Beware, Madam Perdita, for you may have signed her death warrant. Once Wish is too powerful to be contained, she can only be destroyed.'

'Tut, tut, tut,' tutted Perdita. 'Such violent talk is unnecessary. You and Sychorax still have so much to learn.'

'Children have a way of growing, even if you try and stop them,' said Perdita. 'Catch them if you can . . .'

'Well, real life has caught up with *you*, hasn't it, Madam Perdita?' snapped Queen Sychorax. 'You've lost your precious learning place. See what happens if you meddle? You should never have taken the child in.'

'I know,' said Perdita sadly, eyes already welling with tears, for Perdita cried easily. 'But they are worth it, the young people. And they are more grateful than they sometimes look.'

'HOO!' hooted Hoola rudely, as if she did not agree with Perdita. 'Twenty-five years! Twenty-five years of building that Pook's Hill up from nothing!' she mourned. 'In the face of all those dreadful Droods saying a woman could never be the head.'

'Did they say that?' said Sychorax, outraged. 'How dare they?'

'I'm sorry, Madam Perdita, I know you will miss the teaching and all your experiments, not to mention your beautiful garden,' said Encanzo, with genuine concern.

'I'm even missing those pesky piskies,' admitted Perdita, tears running down her face with such regularity that her rose-coloured glasses were misting up. She clicked her fingers, and one of Sychorax's handkerchiefs wormed its way out of one of Sychorax's pockets and danced up to Perdita's nose, and Perdita blew her nose on it with a great trumpeting blast.

'I'm sorry too, even if it *was* all your own fault,' said Sychorax, sympathetic despite herself. She could appreciate the struggles of fellow women trying to run things. 'Keep the handkerchief,' (for Perdita was offering it back to her).

'Oh! Thank you, how kind,' Perdita said, smiling and recovering her composure. 'Never mind. If you ever need any help with your children in the future, all you need to do is . . . knock three times.'

'If we need any help??' said Sychorax, recovering from her moment of sympathy and remembering what a danger Perdita was to the future of the wildwoods. 'We're never going to need any assistance from *you*! You're a total liability! You're completely irresponsible!'

'And in the meantime, well, you're never too old to start again.' The sparkle had come back into Perdita's eyes. 'I've always wanted to see what went on in the northern territories . . . to find out what happens if you follow the Giants' Footsteps to the utter bitter end. So I've got out my favourite walking staff, and the old trusty walking books.'

She looked down at her feet. The boots really were *old*, decaying at the edges and falling to bits, and, frankly, even a bit smelly. Perdita stamped them a bit and one of the heels fell off, with, yes, a definite stinky whiff. 'A little brisk walking will work off the pong,' said Perdita enthusiastically. 'You *could* see this as a bit of a godsend . . . Wandering free, once again, with the wind in our hair and a song in our hearts, just as a Wizard ought to do. Isn't it wonderful to be given a chance to go a-wandering once again, eh, Hoola?'

Hoola ruffled her feathers indignantly. 'We're way too old to wander, Madam. Personally, I prefer a roof over my head.'

'That can be arranged,' said Sychorax, with grim promptness. 'I'm going to put out a warrant for the arrest of you and your owl, Madam Perdita, throughout my Warrior kingdom. You'd better get used to being invisible . . .'

Sychorax had drawn her bow and arrow once more.

But Perdita hadn't worked with teenagers for twenty-five years without learning to be prepared for unexpected changes of emotion. One minute she stood in front of them as a human in very old walking boots. The next she was a bear – a great roaring bear. And then she vanished. And all about the beach around them, bear prints appeared, one line going this way, another that way, wandering round in scatterbrained circles, myriad illusions of multiple bear prints appearing, disappearing, here one second, gone the next, lost and found all at the same time, in a way that thoroughly confused Sychorax, for she didn't know where to shoot.

Hoola hovered before them for a moment longer, hooting: 'HOOO! HOOO!' (which meant, 'How ruuuuuude! How ruuuuuude!') before disappearing like mist into the sea.

And King Encanzo and Queen Sychorax were left alone upon the beach.

The Witches up in the sky had disappeared. It was just the two of them, and Encanzo's very ancient sprite, his old snowcat, and the wind.

'Being a parent is very, very hard,' said Encanzo after a while.

'It most certainly is,' agreed Sychorax.

'They are extraordinarily annoying, those children,' said Encanzo. 'But I have to admit, I miss Xar when he is not there. And at heart, I know the silly little boy does mean well. I wish I could help him . . .'

Sychorax said nothing.

'You don't think,' said Encanzo, slowly, 'we might possibly be wrong about the choices that we made in the past?'

'Of course not!' snapped Queen Sychorax. 'We had

responsibilities! Duties to our people! Not to mention TRADITION.'

'Ah yes,' said Encanzo. 'Tradition . . . of course . . .'

There was another long silence.

'So . . . what do we do now then?' said Encanzo meditatively, as he watched Queen Sychorax's little irritated foot going tap, tap, tap in annoyance on a rock on the beach, and her pretty little nostrils flaring in and out with temper.

She really does have an extremely pretty nose, thought Encanzo.

I wish . . .

But then he stopped himself. For the world cannot be lost for the sake of pretty noses.

'We will have a temporary truce,' said Queen Sychorax. 'Not just for one night, but for however long it will take to catch those children. This is a state of emergency, and in a state of emergency, normal rules do not apply.'

'So, you will stop setting fire to the wildwoods?' said King Encanzo. 'And stop capturing my giants, and my elves, and generally making a menace of yourself?'

'*Temporarily*,' said Queen Sychorax. 'And in the meantime, I will take care of the Kingwitch and put him where he can never get out of that iron casing. You will get your Droods and Wizards to try and retrieve all these undesirable objects released from the guardianship of the Nuckalavee. And we will both strain every nerve . . . every sinew . . . every breath in our lungs, every itch in our fingers to CATCH those children.'

(Alongside the bearprints, an invisible hand was writing something on the beach, in letters so large they could only be read from above.)

'We will both lose our thrones, Encanzo, if we do not catch them,' warned Queen Sychorax. 'The Emperor of Warriors is watching me, the Droods are watching you . . .'

'I have always admired your fighting spirit, Sychorax!' smiled Encanzo in admiration. 'You never know when you're beaten. What a magnificent woman you are, indeed! You're the only person even trickier than I am!'

'Well, I'm so glad you said that,' said Sychorax, her usual wintry smile warming up a bit, 'because most people see my strength as a bit of a downside, but when you're being a monarch you have to take difficult decisions and— *Hang on a second!*'

'Hang on a second, indeed . . .' repeated Encanzo, as both monarchs' smiles faded. 'Are you thinking what I'm thinking? Is Perdita tricking the both of us? A TRUCE . . . working together, side by side . . . is that sensible, Sychorax? Do we trust ourselves?'

'Working together, *from a distance*,' said Sychorax

firmly. 'No turning into swifts or any such nonsense. I'm going to go right back behind my Wall and make it even *bigger*. And if Perdita can trick us, why, I think we can out-trick Perdita.'

Sychorax reached into a pocket hanging from her waist. 'This is something I carry around with me always, as a sort of promise to myself.'

She drew out a small glass phial from the pocket.

'It is the last drops of the Spell of Love Denied,' said Sychorax.

'You didn't drink it all!' said Encanzo in surprise.

'I could not quite bear to at the time,' admitted Sychorax. 'I wanted to save a smidgeon of the love, a memory of it, so that it was not entirely forgotten.'

Encanzo's face, so stern, so sad, turned young and eager for a second, like clouds lifting on a darkened hillside. It was as if, after all these years, the distant ghost of a young Warrior princess had arrived at the hut of his younger self, the poor Wizard-who-waits, and he lifted up his head, and there in the doorway . . . there she was.

'You *did* love me, after all!' cried Encanzo.

'But that was my weakness,' said Sychorax. 'If I had drunk the whole spell, Wish would never have been born with this curse, and none of this would have happened. So now we have to drink the last drops of the spell together, so that we can be strong enough to make this right again.'

Encanzo's sprite, a very ancient one that age had turned so twig-like in nature it very rarely spoke, now felt an urgent need to express its opinion. 'I must urge you, Majesties, not to drink this liquid . . .' And the sprite was so exasperated that it slapped its little stick-like hand on its forehead in its incredulity at the idiocy of these humans.

It had to be said, the mixture in the bottom of the phial Queen Sychorax was holding up looked very evil indeed. As soon as she uncorked the bottle, there was a small explosion and queasy wisps of greasy green smoke curled up from the wicked liquid remains sloshing around in

Love is weakness!

the bottom of it. It was even crackling a little, as if infested by a mini volcano and little drops spat over the rim of the bottle, landing on the grass, which promptly turned black and died.

Short of a large sign saying 'DO NOT DRINK ME. I AM RATHER MORE DANGEROUS THAN A DEADLY DEATH CAP MUSHROOM SOAKED IN ARSENIC', this was a potion that couldn't be making itself any more clear that it would be thoroughly disagreeable to digest.

'Excellent idea,' said Encanzo, producing a cup from beneath his cloak.

'I cannot stress more strongly that YOU SHOULD NOT DRINK this spell!' said Encanzo's sprite, panicking on Encanzo's shoulder.

'Nonsense!' snapped Queen Sychorax. 'I've drunk this before! It's a little spicy but perfectly safe . . . Cheers! *Love is weakness!*'

And Queen Sychorax threw back her head and took a good swig of the spell. 'It *has* got a little spicier over the last twenty years,' Queen Sychorax admitted, as her lips turned yellow-black and parched as lemons, and she handed the cup to Encanzo. King Encanzo took the cup, drained the last drops, and then he threw the empty cup at a nearby stone so that it smashed.

Every piece of grass around the stone promptly burst into wicked yellow-green flames.

King Encanzo turned to Queen Sychorax. He swept her a magnificent bow.

Encanzo had been wondering what he should do with his heart now that it was turned into stone. Where could he keep it so it stayed as safely lost as it had been in the throat of the Nuckalavee?

And now he knew.

The safest place for this stone was around the neck of Queen Sychorax, the coldest woman in the wildwoods.

'Sychorax, Queen of the Warriors,' said King Encanzo. 'Will you do me the honour of keeping this stone on your necklace for me? For safekeeping? I know it will never turn back into a heart when it is around your cold neck.'

Queen Sychorax looked at

King Encanzo. Without speaking, she put the small grey pebble around her neck, next to the other, much more splendid beads.

Queen Sychorax nodded. And then she turned away.

If she hadn't been such a magnificent queen . . . if she hadn't just drunk the last drops of the Spell of Love Denied . . . you might have thought she was thinking about crying.

But . . .

'LOVE IS WEAKNESS!' cried Queen Sychorax.

'LOVE IS WEAKNESS!' replied King Encanzo.

And then they both climbed on the back of Encanzo's snowcat.

'I will escort you to your troops,' said Encanzo.

'I will allow you to escort me,' said Queen Sychorax.

They had a short swift exchange about who was going to be driving the snowcat. (Queen Sychorax won.)

And then they had a conversation that I am at a loss to understand, given the terrible nature of the spell they had just drunk.

These human beings make the same mistakes again and again and AGAIN . . .

'Will you also allow me to lend you my cloak?' said Encanzo. 'You look a little chilly.'

'Warrior queens never get cold – we are far too tough,' said Sychorax, shivering. 'But *you* look a little warm yourself. So I will carry your coat for you as a favour just this once, to prevent you from overheating . . .'

Encanzo gave his cloak to Queen Sychorax, and Queen Sychorax kicked her heels imperiously, and Encanzo's snowcat set off in the direction of Queen Sychorax's army.

Inexplicable.

And then the beach was empty.

Looking down over the edge of the door, high up in the air, Wish and Xar and their companions could finally see what Perdita had written in enormous letters in the sand of the empty beach.

CATCH
THEM
IF YOU
CAN

26. Catch Them IF You Can

Up above, the invisible door flew much higher than Wish and Xar had ever flown before, as high as Wish dared fly it without them all passing out from lack of oxygen.

They didn't stay invisible long because Perdita had told them that it was dangerous.

Flying the door at that height was very hard work, so Wish could only take them as far as would be out of reach of Queen Sychorax's troops and Encanzo's Wizards and Droods. Xar knew a good hiding place (of course he did – Xar had good hiding places hidden all over the wildwoods). The hiding place was high on a mountaintop, in a great cave hidden behind a waterfall.

They were outlaws, on the run again.

They built the fire in the entrance to the cave, behind the waterfall so it wouldn't be seen by anyone who might be searching for them, but where they could still get a good view of the surrounding landscape. 'We'll take it in turns to keep watch through the night,' said Xar.

It was a cave that had been inhabited for many thousands of years before their own time, and they knew this because it was decorated with drawings of animals, bears and wolves and snowcats just like their own, and deeper in the cave still, with the bright red human handprints of their ancestors. This immediately made them feel at home, as if the hands of their forebears were waving them hello, helping them along in their quest with a handshake from the past.

Tiffinstorm had brought along a piece of fire from Perdita's grate in the Lair of the Bear, and somehow that made the cave feel more homely and as if Perdita was there with them. The sprites made the fire burn all different colours, and as the water of the sea steamed out of the shaggy fur of the animals and up into the night, they all felt the coldness of the Nuckalavee adventure being warmed out of them.

They were all tired, *so* tired, and happy and grateful and sad all at the same time. Happy and grateful to be back in the adventure of it all once more, sad because they were worried about Squeezjoos and were missing Perdita and Pook's Hill already. Happy and grateful because they had defeated the Nuckalavee, sad because they had temporarily lost Squeezjoos and knew that greater confrontation was still to come. Xar was unusually quiet.

'We've lost Squeezjoos,' said Xar. 'He is somewhere back there, with the Kingwitch, and it is all my fault, and the fault of this Witchstain.'

So it was Wish and Bodkin who had to cheer Xar up this time.

'Don't worry, Xar,' said Wish. 'We'll rescue Squeezjoos, I promise you we will, and we'll get rid of your Witchstain, too.'

Bodkin could feel his heart beating quick at the thought of it. *Courage!* thought Bodkin to himself. *I have fought the Nuckalavee and lived, so I am as brave as the others after all.*

'So,' said Bodkin. 'What do we do now?'

'I'm afraid you're not going to like the plan, Bodkin,' warned Wish.

Bodkin swallowed. He KNEW he wasn't going to like the plan. 'Tell me anyway,' said Bodkin. 'What IS the plan?'

'The good news is, we've got the ingredients for the spell to get rid of Witches,' said Wish.

'Here they are!' said the Once-sprite, getting them out of Xar's waistcoat and proudly displaying them. 'One giant's last breath from Castle Death (forgiveness). Two feathers from a Witch (desire). Three tears of a frozen queen (tenderness). Four scales of a Nuckalavee (courage). And five tears of the Drood from the Lake of the Lost (endurance).'

'Okay,' said Bodkin, 'we've got the ingredients . . . What's the bad news?'

'We make the spell, and then we go in search of the Kingwitch,' said Wish.

'*That's a terrible plan!*' said Bodkin.

'I said you wouldn't like it. But we promised Squeezjoos we would rescue him,' said Wish, 'and just as Perdita said, you can't run away forever. And when we find the Kingwitch, I'll make a bargain with him.'

'Bargaining with Witches isn't a good idea, Wish,' said Bodkin. 'Look how the bargaining with the Nuckalavee went! Not well, let's face it.'

'We didn't get rid of the Magic completely last time,' said Wish. 'But we have a second chance, and *this time* it's going to be different. I will say to the Kingwitch, if he takes away the last bit of Witchblood from Squeezjoos and Xar, I will use my Magic to let him out of his iron prison.'

'Brilliant plan!' said Xar admiringly. 'There's no other way for the Kingwitch to get out of that iron ball, so I bet he goes for it. And I promise I won't take my hand away too early this time.' *

'You're going to let the Kingwitch out of his iron prison?' squeaked Bodkin. *'DELIBERATELY? And THEN what are you going to do???'*

'We're going to FIGHT him,' said Wish. 'Using the spell to get rid of Witches, and the Enchanted Sword, and all our might and main . . .'

---

* In the first book of Wizards of Once, Xar puts his hand on the Stone-That-Takes-Away-Magic in order to get rid of the Witchstain, but he takes his hand off too early so some of the bad Magic remains.

'But you're absolutely *terrible* at spellfights, Wish! Remember, back at the learning place, you kept losing and turning into a fluffbuttle! And even Perdita said you weren't ready to face the Kingwitch yet!' panicked Bodkin.

'We haven't got time to be ready, Bodkin,' said Wish. 'Xar is getting worse every day, aren't you, Xar?'

'I have to admit I'm not feeling great,' admitted Xar.

'Anyway, there's a good chance we'll never be ready,' said Wish.

'But if the Kingwitch wins the spellfight, he's going to get his claws on Magic-that-works-on-iron!' said Bodkin.

'However, if we *don't* do this, Squeezjoos and Xar are going to be lost forever,' said Wish. 'Squeezjoos will be frightened and alone, and he's going to be relying on US, Bodkin. Remember how *you* felt when you were in the cavern of the Nuckalavee? What kept you going was knowing that we were going to rescue you.'

Bodkin knew this was right.

'COURAGE!' said Xar. 'COURAGE and dancing was what we do now . . .'

So as night fell, the little party of outlaws danced defiantly round their fire.

We never know what tomorrow might bring.

So tonight . . . we must dance.

First they danced wildy, recklessly, to a song they

just made up on the spur of the moment, called

One More Second Chance

ONE more second chance
ONE more silly dance
I shall grow up and my heart will turn
As cold as a stone
As hard as a rock
I'll walk stiff and talk grave and only sleep in the night-time

But till that time . . .

Dance, sprite, dance!
Dance by the light of the moon!
You've got to dance till the sun comes up
For tomorrow will come too soon

Howl, wolves, howl!
Yell to the wind in the trees
You have to make your voices heard
Above the roaring din of the breeze

We left our home a lifetime ago and we are wandering still
We don't know where we're going or what's behind that hill
But Wizards were built to wander and I never want to stop

So dance! Snowcats, dance! Make your old bones hop!

We cannot stop our dancing for this night-time is too cold
If we keep up this whirling, we never may grow old
So jiggle your antennae, sprites! Wolves move your frosty bones!
If we cease the capering, our hearts will turn to stones!

And then Xar made his flute play that old favourite, 'Once We Wizards, Wandering Free'. And Caliburn sang 'We're the best! We're the best! We're just the most marvellous, magnificent best!' but it made him cry to sing it without Perdita, so they moved on to Crusher's song.

Let me lead a GIANT'S life
NO LITTLE steps, no holding back!
A GIANT way, a GIANT'S track!

We will leave them dancing, because that is always a good place to leave people. And as they danced, putting on their biggest, loudest GIANT voices, Crusher himself was wandering down in the valley, talking to the ruins of the trees in the forest that Sychorax had burnt.

'Fear not, dear trees, you shall rise again. I see you in my mind's eye, taller than I am . . . stretching up your limbs to the watching moon…carrying the dreams of birds and the hopes of the world in your bright and spreading branches…

'You will grow again, dear trees, *that* I promise.

'For tomorrow is another day . . .'

XAR will

save me...

Epilogue

by the Unknown Narrator

Looking into the past is like looking down into a deep, deep well. Imagine that deep, deep well, where the water at the bottom of it represents the time that a person first walked on the earth. People have been on this earth for so long that if you threw a stone down that well it would be at least five minutes before you heard the splash of the stone hitting the water.

Even down at the bottom of the well, people were telling stories, whispered in the night from adult to child and handed down like jewels from generation to generation, though the well is so deep and so dark, and they are so far away, that the stories can get lost to us.

But just recently, people have begun to write down their experiences, so that their voices are trapped in the paper of the trees they are writing on. We call these things 'books', and they will be a clever way of shedding a little light in the darkness . . .

This is one of those stories.

Notice how the crucible of the story changes those who listen to it, those who are within it, and the person who is telling it, all at the same time.

This thought it was a story with two heroes. It said that, confidently, right from the beginning, and on a number of occasions.

But lo! Stories, like queens and Wizards, are tricksy, *tricksy* things. The story changed Bodkin and Bodkin changed the story.

He wouldn't stay where he was supposed to, and somehow it ended up being a story with *three* heroes, which was as much a surprise to *me* as to anyone else.

The final reckoning with the Kingwitch is very, very close now. I know it, and the Kingwitch knows it, and he is ready for the final battle, clutching his piece of blue dust within his iron prison. He has Squeezjoos, and Wish and Xar will never abandon Squeezjoos, and they need to get to him *fast*.

'They will come to me,' whispers the Kingwitch to himself, sharpening his talons like a blacksmith sharpening a sword. 'Because love is weakness . . .'

So the end approaches quick now.

And with the end, I shall tell you who I am, at last.

However I warn you, this is a true story, and *true* stories, unlike fairy stories, do not always end happily. As Perdita said, there's a reason why tears are such an important ingredient in so many spells. Hopefully all will end well, but if not, please do not blame *me*, for as we have just seen, I am not as in control of where a true story goes as I would like to be. I have to tell what really happened.

But I am wishing with all my heart that all will end well.

Wish with me . . .

WISH that Wish and Xar and Bodkin can break out of the sad circles of the history of the wildwoods.

They are young, they are hopeful.

WISH that they can write their own story . . .

WISH . . .

And in the meantime . . .

Keep hoping . . .

Keep guessing . . .

Keep dreaming . . .

And keep telling your own stories.

Stories are very helpful if you get lost in the wildwoods.

Signed: The Unknown Narrator

ACKNOWLEDGEMENTS (thankyous)

A whole team of people have
helped me write this book.

Thank you to my wonderful editor,
Anne McNeil, and my
magnificent agent, Caroline Walsh.

A special big thanks to Samuel Perrett,
Polly Lyall Grant, Lizz Skelly, and Camilla Leask.

And to everyone else at Hachette Children's Group,
Hilary Murray Hill, Andrew Sharp,
Valentina Fazio, Naomi Berwin, Katy Cattell,
Georgi Russell, Nicola Goode, Katherine Fox,
Alison Padley, Rebecca Livingstone.

Thanks to all at Little Brown,
Megan Tingley, Jackie Engel,
Lisa Yoskowitz, Kristina Pisciotta.

And most important of all,
Maisie, Clemmie, Xanny.

And SIMON for his excellent
advice on absolutely everything.

I couldn't do it without you.

Magic happens

"Once we have accepted the story, we cannot escape the story's fate."

P.L. Travers, author of Mary Poppins

Discover the Magic of Cressida Cowell
visit
www.cressidacowell.co.uk
to find out all about her books, events, and lots more!
/CressidaCowellBooks
@CressidaCowellAuthor
@CressidaCowell

Read the
amazing
HOW TO TRAIN YOUR
DRAGON
series
CRESSIDA COWELL
HOW TO TRAIN YOUR
DRAGON
How to Be a Pirate
How to Speak Dragonese
How to Cheat a Dragon's Curse
How to Twist a Dragon's Tale
A Hero's Guide to Deadly Dragons
How to Ride a Dragon's Storm
How to Break a Dragon's Heart
Dragon's Hero
How to Fight a Dragon's Fury

Love is ...
a girl and her
Enchanted Spoon.